"We can...

Adrienne blushed. "Is that what you think this is about? That I'm begging you to make love to me?"

"I think you're scared." Sam replied. "You're grabbing for all the life you can. Making love is the most life affirming act there is."

She shook her head. "No..."

"Yes." He pulled her against him, knowing she would feel his desire. "I do want you. But knowing you want me isn't enough. You have to start remembering first. I need to know you want me as the man you love." He ran his hand down her back, glorying in and dreading the telltale shiver he felt against him. "There's nothing I want more than to make love to you."

Adrienne's green eyes had darkened, indicating clearly that she wanted him, too.

"Kiss me, Sam. I really need you to kiss me."

Dear Harlequin Intrigue Reader,

This month, some of your favorite Harlequin Intrigue
authors—and a first-timer—deliver a killer selection of
books for you to enjoy.

Amanda Stevens closes the case in the final installment of
her GALLAGHER JUSTICE miniseries with Nick Gallagher's
story, *Forbidden Lover* (#557). The Gallagher brothers
were born to serve and protect, and three more sexy
lawmen you'd be hard-pressed to find. If you missed the
first two books, be sure to let us know!

In her *twentieth* 43 LIGHT STREET title, Ruth Glick
writing as Rebecca York scorches some paper with
Never Too Late (#558), the steamy story of Scott O'Donnell
and Mariana Reyes. Harlequin Intrigue is proud to bring
you this terrific ongoing series and we thank you for
making it one of our most popular features.

Also, this month, Patricia Rosemoor—Harlequin Intrigue's
most-published author—launches her very own miniseries,
SONS OF SILVER SPRINGS. Sometimes it takes a family
tragedy to bring siblings back together. But nothing is
thicker than blood. Meet the Quarrels brothers in
Heart of a Lawman (#559).

Finally, newcomer Karen Lawton Barrett contributes
her first title to Harlequin Intrigue. We know you'll love
Hers To Remember (#560) for its emotional drama and
highly charged suspense. Hang on to your seats when you
read this A MEMORY AWAY... story!

Take home all four books for an exhilarating rush of
romance.

Sincerely,

Denise O'Sullivan
Associate Senior Editor
Harlequin Intrigue

Hers To Remember
Karen Lawton Barrett

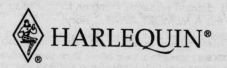

HARLEQUIN®

TORONTO • NEW YORK • LONDON
AMSTERDAM • PARIS • SYDNEY • HAMBURG
STOCKHOLM • ATHENS • TOKYO • MILAN • MADRID
PRAGUE • WARSAW • BUDAPEST • AUCKLAND

ISBN 0-373-22560-1

HERS TO REMEMBER

Copyright © 2000 by Karen Lawton Barrett

This edition published by arrangement with Harlequin Books S.A.

® and TM are trademarks of the publisher. Trademarks indicated with ® are registered in the United States Patent and Trademark Office, the Canadian Trade Marks Office and in other countries.

Visit us at www.romance.net

Printed in U.S.A.

ABOUT THE AUTHOR

Karen Lawton Barrett was raised in a small town in central California, where one of her elementary school teachers once wrote on a report card, "Karen daydreams too much." These days she uses her active imagination to create romantic suspense stories. This is her first book for Harlequin Intrigue. It is set on the Monterey Peninsula, the Barrett family's favorite destination for Sunday drives, kite flying and picnics on the beach.

Books by Karen Lawton Barrett

HARLEQUIN INTRIGUE
560—HERS TO REMEMBER

Don't miss any of our special offers. Write to us at the following address for information on our newest releases.

Harlequin Reader Service
U.S.: 3010 Walden Ave., P.O. Box 1325, Buffalo, NY 14269
Canadian: P.O. Box 609, Fort Erie, Ont. L2A 5X3

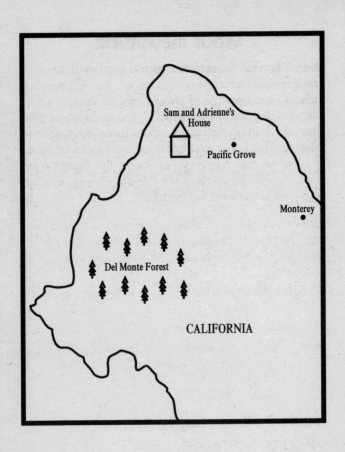

Sam and Adrienne's
House

● Pacific Grove

● Monterey

Del Monte Forest

CALIFORNIA

CAST OF CHARACTERS

Amy Donnelly —For three years, she had everything but a past.

Adrienne Winston —She has a husband she doesn't remember marrying, carries a child she can't remember conceiving and may lose them both unless she can unlock the secret to her past.

Sam Donnelly —He knew one day his wife might remember her past, but he never expected her to forget *him*.

Casey Donnelly —A devoted brother, a dedicated cop, but even his years of training might not be enough to save his brother's family from a monster.

Vaughn Winston —He'll stop at nothing to get what he wants.

Ginger Zane —Amy's friend—or is she?

Barry Owen —He knew too much and had to die.

To my friends, Courtney and Gail,
my best reader and my best fan,

And to my husband, Phillip,
always and forever.

Chapter One

She fought wakefulness as long as she could, fearing what she might face. But the pain in her head forced her from her sleep. It pounded against her skull, an unrelenting hammer.

She kept her eyes closed and tried to will it away. A useless endeavor, the effort only made it worse.

Exhausted, she lay absolutely still and tried to relax. Even the act of breathing in and out made her feel as if she'd been strapped to some medieval torture device. She knew she needed to do something, but what, when even the tiniest movement sent pain screaming through her head?

Aspirin might help, though it seemed a pitiful answer. If only she could reach her purse. Gathering what strength she could find, she willed herself to move.

Voices dashed her effort. Fear warred with pain. As hard as she'd tried to move, she now concentrated on remaining motionless.

The hushed whispers faded in and out and came from different directions, as if the people who spoke moved around her.

"How is she? Will she be all right?" a new voice demanded. It sounded deep and male and edged with panic. "She's got to be all right!"

"She's still unconscious," another man answered. "Now that you're here, I'm sure she'll respond. But you have to be calm."

Their voices sounded distorted to her ears, as if the men who spoke stood at one end of a tunnel and she at the other. *Who were they?* she thought frantically. Not *him*. She would have known his voice anywhere. Wouldn't she?

Someone took her hand. Her stomach dropped. *I can't move. I can't let him know.* Then she realized that the hand engulfing hers was big and roughened by work. Relief made her dizzy. Not *his* hand. Manual labor was beneath *him*.

"Open your eyes, sunshine. It's time to wake up," a deep, gentle voice urged. "Come on, honey, open your eyes and look at me."

The underlying note of desperation made her try all the harder to respond. She had to wake up. To get up, and run. She wasn't dead. Once he found out… She tried to lift her eyelids, but they felt weighted. She sobbed. How would she lift her legs if she couldn't even do that much?

"Everything will be all right, darling. I promise. Now, open those beautiful green eyes for me."

Since opening her eyes seemed futile, she tried to squeeze the hand that still held hers. Her fingers felt boneless. *What's wrong with me?* she cried, but the words sounded only in her mind.

"What about the baby?" the man asked.

Baby? What baby?

"They did an ultrasound. The baby's fine," the other man answered, his tone calm and somehow professional-sounding. "But the doctor says she probably has a concussion."

Panic seized her. *There can't be a baby. I've been so careful. It's impossible.*

"I should never have gone to that trade show."

"You can't seriously be blaming yourself for her accident. She slipped on a cord and hit her head on the vacuum."

"I should have hired a housekeeper, then she wouldn't have been vacuuming."

The words swirled around her. None of them made sense. Vacuuming? She hadn't been vacuuming. She'd been running, afraid he'd found her in spite of all she'd done to get away.

"You have to calm down, Sam. This isn't going to help any of you."

Sam? Who was Sam?

"Don't you understand? I could lose her and the baby, because of my own stupidity!"

Oh, God, a baby! He'd never let her go now. "Please, no baby, no baby." She'd finally found her voice, though she spoke in a mere whisper.

A hand cupped her face. "Shh, honey, the baby will be fine, and so will you. I'm going to take care of you both."

I won't be fine. Not if I'm pregnant. A dream, that's it! This has to be a dream. Or a nightmare. My worst nightmare. Oh, God, I tried so hard. Please, God, please let me wake up.

"Come on, sunshine, that's it. I'm right here."

The voice drew her. Slowly, she opened her eyes. A man's face hovered above her. At first creased with concern, it soon brightened with a relieved smile. And she knew God had answered her prayers. For this was truly the face of an angel.

Golden hair fell across his tanned forehead. Deep blue eyes the color of twilight sparkled with tears of joy. "Hi, sunshine." He touched her face with gentle fingers. Then he turned his head. "Get the doctor."

"Am I dead?" she asked the golden angel who touched her so tenderly.

He smiled down at her. "No, thank God, you're alive. And now that you're awake, you're going to feel better every minute."

She believed him. He sounded so sure, so confident. She wished she felt the same.

She licked her dry lips. "What happened? Where am I?"

"In the hospital. You had an accident. Can you remember?"

"An accident?"

The door opened and a man walked into the room. Tall, with reddish-blond hair, and nearly as handsome as the man sitting at her side, he grinned. "Well, it's about time you woke up, little sister. The doc will be here in a minute."

Little sister? Why would he call her that? She didn't have a brother. She looked from one man to the other and felt only confusion. She didn't know these men. They looked as though they could be brothers. But not hers. She was an only child.

"Casey's the one who found you," explained the man who'd called her sunshine. She guessed that made him Sam. "Can you remember what happened?"

She took in the concern on both men's faces and wanted to cry. Who were they? Why were they here? What did these strangers care what had happened to her? She didn't want to be so suspicious, but thanks to Vaughn, she didn't know who to trust anymore. She searched her memory, trying to remember what had put her in the hospital.

"Don't strain yourself, sweetie. We have plenty of time," Sam said gently.

"I'm okay," she assured him. "But I'd like to sit up a little." The sooner she got back to normal, the better. She couldn't fight Vaughn if she didn't know what had happened.

He pushed a button on the side of the bed that raised the mattress behind her back. The movement caused the pain to intensify. She closed her eyes until the dizziness went away.

The memory came suddenly. "I was running."

"Running? Was the phone ringing?"

"No, I was outside. It was dark, so dark. There was no moon. I could barely see. I must have stumbled over something. There were lights, bright lights, blinding me. Then I fell... That's all I remember." She reached up to touch her forehead and felt a bandage instead of skin. "I guess I must have hit my head."

She recalled one of the men saying something about a concussion. No wonder her head hurt so much. She closed her eyes, trying to remember what had happened next.

A voice, a man's voice. "Someone leaned over me and asked me if I was all right." She opened her eyes to gaze at the man who held her hand. "The voice, it sounded like yours," she said, not sure whether to be relieved or frightened. She still didn't know who this beautiful man was or what connection he had to her. "Were you the one who found me?"

"Yes, I found you," he said.

The strange look on his face caused her suspicion to heighten. Could this man be one of *his?* "Why are you looking at me like that?"

The snap in her voice seemed to startle him. "Amy, I..."

The name confused her. Her name wasn't Amy. "Why did you call me that?"

He looked just as confused as she felt. If he'd been one of the people who'd been following her, wouldn't he know her name? "My name's not Amy. It's Adrienne... Adrienne Winston."

"Adrienne Winston?" He said it as if he'd never heard it before. "Are you sure?"

"Of course I'm sure." She might have been confused by these strangers who'd shown up in her room, but she did know her own name.

"Sam, can I talk to you outside?" Casey asked, his voice still calm and professional-sounding.

A silent message seemed to pass between the two men. "Sure," Sam said. "Why don't you wait for me in the corridor."

Casey nodded, then turned and left the room.

The strange exchange brought her confusion back full force. "What's going on?"

The door opened again before he could reply to her demand. A petite woman walked in. Her tightly braided coal-black hair hung over one shoulder to her waist. She wore a white lab coat over a red sweater, slacks and a stethoscope around her neck. She walked over to the side of the bed, smiled and held out her hand. "I'm Dr. Ya-mana. It's nice to see you awake, Mrs. Delaney. Your husband has been very worried about you."

Adrienne stared at the doctor, confusion warring with fear. She'd called her Mrs. Delaney. Why? Hadn't Vaughn told them who she was? The doctor had said her husband was worried. How could they think he was her husband and not know her name?

She looked over at the door. Where *was* Vaughn? Why hadn't he come in when the doctor had been called? Her heart began to race. Maybe he wasn't here. She turned to the doctor. "I have to get out of here."

"All in good time," the doctor said, ignoring her rudeness. She took a small black instrument out of her pocket. "I need to look in your eyes. The light might bother you, but it will only take a second."

"Dr. Yamana, there's something I need to tell you," Sam said.

"Why don't you wait for me outside? This won't take long."

"Please, Doctor, it's important."

The doctor smiled at him. "Five minutes, tops. I promise."

When he moved toward the door, Adrienne felt a flash of panic. "Please, don't go." He'd taken care of her after the accident. His presence had made her feel safe somehow. If he left, the feeling of safety would leave, too. It had been so long since she'd felt even a modicum of security, she wasn't willing to give it up. "Please."

He smiled reassuringly. "I need to talk to Casey. You heard what the doctor said, five minutes, tops."

"All right." She didn't like it. Vaughn could arrive at any minute. Vulnerability overwhelmed her. Cooperate, she told herself. It's the only thing that's going to get you out of this place.

Finishing her examination a few moments later, Dr. Yamana stood back and smiled. "I think you're going to be just fine. But you do show signs of a slight concussion. I'd like to keep you overnight for observation."

"I can't stay!" The words burst out of her. In this hospital bed, she'd be a sitting duck.

"You were a very lucky woman, Mrs. Delaney," Dr. Yamana said, her tone grave. "You and your baby are just fine. But an injury like this is a shock to the system. It will be safer for both of you if you get some extra rest." A gentle smile lightened her serious expression. "Now, I need to ask you some questions."

"Questions?" She had a few of her own. Like why did this woman keep calling her Mrs. Delaney? And where was Vaughn? Did he know about the baby? What had he told the doctor? Could she be trusted?

"Don't look so worried." The doctor's calm voice cut through her thoughts. "It's a routine part of the examination when there's been a blow to the head. First, tell me your full name."

In spite of the doctor's professional manner, Adrienne hesitated. Should she tell her the truth? If she didn't, and Vaughn had already gotten to her, she would know if Adrienne lied. Still, Sam had called her Amy. The doctor kept calling her Mrs. Delaney. Maybe...

The doctor's beeper sounded. "I'm sorry," she said. "I'll have to take care of this."

Adrienne nodded, relieved to have more time to decide what to tell the doctor.

"I'll send your husband in to keep you company until I get back."

Adrienne's relief vanished. "No! Don't do that."

The mild shock in Dr. Yamana's expression told Adrienne she had to come up with a reasonable explanation for her outburst. She closed her eyes against the very real pain in her head. "My head aches. I'd really like to rest a little, if that's all right."

Dr. Yamana patted her hand. "Of course, it's probably the best thing for you right now. I'm sorry I can't give you anything for the pain. Just try to relax. I'll be back to finish my examination as soon as possible."

After the door closed behind the doctor, Adrienne allowed herself a sigh of relief. That was close. Thank God, the doctor had accepted her explanation.

She sat up slowly, then turned so she could dangle her feet over the side. She rested for a moment while the dizziness subsided. She had to get out of here. Everyone she'd dealt with seemed to think she was someone else. She might be able to keep that up for a while, even though she'd already told Sam her real name. She could fake amnesia, tell him she didn't know where the name had come from. But what if he was in on it? Was that the reason Vaughn hadn't show up yet?

No, she had to leave. She stood on the floor, holding on to the bed while she tested her balance. She looked around for a closet and found it. If the closet contained her clothes, it would make it much easier to escape. She didn't see them letting her out of the hospital dressed in this flimsy excuse for a nightshirt.

She moved step by step across the room. Her head hurt so much she was afraid any abrupt movement would make her pass out. She opened the door to reveal a pair of light blue jeans, a purple sweater, and a pair of white sneakers. None of the clothing looked familiar, but that couldn't matter to her now. She had to leave as soon as possible.

She dressed as quickly as her aching head would allow. Every time she heard voices outside the door, she'd stop and listen, sure that any moment someone would catch her before she could make her escape.

Finally ready, she tiptoed to the door, opened it an inch and looked out. Once she ascertained that no one waited just outside, she opened the door wider and stepped from the room.

A candy striper came out of the room next door, making Adrienne's heart pound in her chest. But the girl only smiled and continued on her way.

Seeing a sign that read Stairs, Adrienne headed for it. The pain in her head demanded an elevator, but she knew the stairway offered a safer exit.

Before she pushed open the heavy door, she looked around to make sure no one saw her. The deserted hallway eased her mind. She went through, making sure the door made no noise when it closed behind her.

Pain shot through her skull. She grabbed the railing to steady herself. She stood with eyes closed, waiting for the pain to pass. It could have been a moment or an hour. Time had lost its meaning.

When she could finally lift her lids, she saw the number two printed on the wall above her head. Grateful she had to walk down only one flight, she moved slowly down the steps.

Her luck held. She reached the bottom without seeing another soul and without losing consciousness. Although it had been touch-and-go there for a moment about half-way down.

She pushed the exit door open to find it led directly to the outside of the hospital.

She looked around. To her right was a parking lot, to her left a sidewalk lined with the cypress trees she'd thought so impressive when she'd arrived in Monterey. The light fog drifting around the trees made her shiver.

California had symbolized escape for her, being a whole country away from Boston. But once she'd arrived, she had fallen in love at first sight with the Central Coast. Now, Vaughn had ruined even that for her.

She breathed in the cool air in an attempt to clear her mind. It helped somewhat, but her head still ached.

For want of a better plan, she decided to start walking. She set off down the sidewalk in the direction she hoped would take her downtown. She could get a cab there. With each step she tried to remember the name of the hotel she'd checked into. Telling the taxi driver that it was near the beach wouldn't do much good.

Fatigue set in almost immediately. Each foot she walked felt like a yard, each yard like a block. The hammering inside her head became intense. Her mouth felt dry, her body numb. She wanted a drink and a bed, not necessarily in that order. She glanced up, trying to get her bearings, and spotted a diner about a half block up the street.

Well, they wouldn't have a bed, but they would have

something to drink. She searched the pockets of her jeans and came up with three dollar bills. Hallelujah! A nice, cold soft drink would set her back on her feet.

Jubilant, she covered the half block as quickly as her tired legs would take her. Inside, she asked the waitress for a booth at the back and ordered a large cola. The drink served, she took a long sip, then laid her head against the back of the seat and closed her eyes. She had to remember the name of the motel.

SAM RETURNED to Amy's room a half hour after he'd left it. Dr. Yamana had told him to let her rest, but he couldn't stand the waiting any longer. After what had happened to her when he'd left her alone last time, he didn't want her out of his sight. Especially since she thought she was someone called Adrienne Winston. Where in heaven's name had she picked up that?

He pushed the door open quietly and moved into the room, being careful not to wake her. A curtain shielded the bed from his sight. He tiptoed around it, then stopped abruptly. She wasn't there.

Sam didn't know how long he stared at the empty bed. Probably only seconds. Long enough for the panic that had dissipated when Amy had opened her eyes to return full force. "Where the hell is she?"

Silence was his only answer as he searched the floor on each side of the bed, then the bathroom. "I knew I shouldn't have left her alone." He exited the room and strode to the nurse's station. Two women sat going over a patient's chart. "Where is Amy Delaney?" he demanded, causing them to jump.

The older woman stood. "Please keep your voice down, sir." Her stern tone reminded him of his fourth-grade teacher, Mrs. Storm. But he was no longer a timid ten year old.

"I will not keep my voice down, Nurse...?" He looked at her name tag. "Lopez. Amy is missing."

The nurse regarded him with forced patience. "I'm sure you're mistaken, Mr. Delaney. Did you check the bathroom?"

"Of course I checked the bathroom." Did the woman think he was an idiot? "She obviously wasn't there, or I wouldn't be looking for her."

"I don't understand..." Looking puzzled, she turned to the younger woman. "Kathy, did Dr. Yamana order more tests for Mrs. Delaney while I was gone?"

"No, ma'am. She said that Mrs. Delaney was resting and to check on her in half an hour." She looked at her watch. "That was twenty-five minutes ago."

"Are you telling me no one has seen her for almost thirty minutes?" he bellowed.

"Please calm down, Mr. Delaney. I'm sure there's just been a mistake," Nurse Lopez said.

"There's been a mistake all right. Your patient has a concussion. She doesn't even know her own name, and you're letting her wander around the hospital by herself."

"Sam! I could hear you yelling three corridors away. What the hell is going on?"

Sam turned to his brother. "Amy's missing. We have to find her."

"What do you mean 'missing'?"

Sam grimaced. Casey was using his cool-cop voice. The one he usually saved for panicky mothers who'd temporarily misplaced their children in department stores.

"I mean, Officer Delaney," he returned, as composed as he could manage under the circumstances, "that Amy is not in her room, and no one seems to know where she's gone."

Casey moved off down the hall to her room, Sam and

the two nurses following quickly behind. "Have you checked the closet?"

"The closet? Why would she be in the closet?" Sam didn't need the look on Casey's face to realize the stupidity of his question. "Her clothes!"

Inside the closet, they found the gown she'd had on and nothing else.

Stunned, Sam stared at the nearly empty closet. "She ran." He looked at his brother. "Why? Why would she run away?"

Casey put a comforting hand on his shoulder. "I don't know, but we'll find her. She can't have gone far. I didn't bring her purse to the hospital with me, so she had no money."

Sam only half listened. His poor Amy. For the last three years they'd been so close. It had only been the last year that she'd had the confidence to be on her own for more than a few hours. She must have been terribly frightened and confused to have left like this. Why? It hurt to think she might be afraid of *him*.

Had he done something to scare her? Or had something else caused her to run?

"Sam, are you all right?"

He nodded to his brother, a lie. "I have to find her. If she fainted…" He couldn't complete the thought. "I'll check the stairs."

"Good," Casey said. "I'll talk to the staff, maybe some of the patients, see if they saw anything."

Sam ran down the hall to the nearest stairwell, thoughts of how frightened she must have been racing through his mind. She'd woken to a place she didn't recognize, to people she didn't recognize. All she could remember was running before the accident. Running from what? he asked himself as he went down the stairs two at a time.

The relief of not finding her lying at the bottom lasted

seconds. He still hadn't found her. She was in no shape to be traipsing around the city. He went through the exit door.

Outside, he stopped long enough to breathe in the fog-cooled air. He had to calm down. He had to think. She didn't remember him. She didn't remember her own name. Did that mean she wouldn't remember the city either?

If it did, how would she get around? Where would she go? Deciding she might try to get a ride from someone, Sam headed for the parking lot. He talked to several of the visitors who were coming and going, but no one had seen her.

"There you are, Sam." Casey strode up to him. "Any sign?"

Sam shook his head. "You find out anything?"

"A candy striper remembered seeing a blond woman dressed in jeans and a purple sweater with a bandage on her forehead, but she didn't see where she went."

"Damn it! She's too confused to be on her own." He looked into the distance, up the road and down. "I'm going this way." He moved off at a quick pace.

"Wait, Sam…"

He turned back to his brother. "What?"

"When I called the precinct for help looking for Amy, I asked one of the guys to check on Adrienne Winston."

Sam scowled. "What are you saying?"

Casey looked at Sam, compassion in his eyes. "I think it's possible she might be the link to Amy's past that's been missing the past three years."

Chapter Two

Once she'd had a chance to rest for a while, Adrienne found she didn't have the energy to get up again. The soda had helped some, her head didn't ache so much, but the rest of her felt more exhausted than she could ever remember feeling.

She looked out the window. If someone had followed her, they'd probably be here soon. She really should go. A quarter lay on the table in front of her. Enough for a phone call. But who would she call? The buck she'd have left after she made the call wouldn't be enough for a taxi. And she still didn't remember the name of the hotel she'd checked into.

Why was that? She rubbed her forehead between her eyebrows, where the pain had decided to settle. She couldn't remember talking to a clerk or being in a hotel room. Had she checked in at all? It hurt so much to think, she leaned her arms on the table, and laid her head down and closed her eyes.

"Amy?"

Startled, Adrienne lifted her head to see the big blond man from the hospital slide onto the seat across from her. She started to slide out the other way, but he caught her wrist. "Don't run, please."

She glared at his hand on her wrist, trying to work up

some righteous anger, but he really wasn't hurting her. She looked up at his face, expecting anger or menace or some other sign that would show this man wasn't as caring as he pretended. All she saw was hurt.

His expression didn't convince her. Vaughn could conjure up any emotional expression he needed on a moment's notice. This man could be no different. "Let go of me, please." She kept her tone even, not wanting to let on just how frightened she was.

His gaze searched her face. For what, she hadn't a clue. "Will you promise not to run?" he asked.

She looked him straight in the eye. "I promise nothing."

He winced, as if she'd dealt him a blow. Then he let her go.

Her wrist tingled where he'd held it. The sensation puzzled her. It felt almost pleasant. She leaned back against the bench, not sure she could have run if she wanted to. "What do you want from me?"

"Right now, I just want to take you back to the hospital. You took a pretty good knock."

The jackhammers going off in her head agreed with him. "What do you care?" She hurt too much to be polite.

"Amy..."

"Why do you keep calling me that?"

He didn't react to the snap in her voice. He smiled gently instead, as if trying to allay her fears. "Because it's your name, sunshine."

"No, it's not," she said firmly. "My name is Adrienne Winston. You know it, and I know it. And if Vaughn thinks he's going to get away with making me look crazy, he'd better think again."

"Vaughn? Who's Vaughn?"

Adrienne almost laughed. The look on his face shone innocent as a child's. If she didn't know better, she'd think he had nothing to do with Vaughn. A sudden pain shot through her head. She groaned.

Sam moved around the table to kneel by her side. "Amy! Please let me take you back to the hospital."

"No!" She put her hands against his shoulders and tried to shove him away. He didn't move. A wave of dizziness went through her. She looked into eyes that mirrored her fear.

"Please, honey," he begged. "We have to take care of you. We have to take care of the baby."

The baby, she thought. I have to take care of the baby. If Vaughn finds out… She looked at Sam. For a moment he didn't seem like a stranger. He seemed like someone she'd known for a long time. An instant later, the feeling was gone. But not the fear.

For now, he was all she had.

She reached out to him. "Please, please help me." Then she felt herself falling forward into his arms.

ADRIENNE WOKE to find herself once again in bed. She still wore the purple sweater, but the jeans had been removed and her bare legs covered with a pink thermal blanket. The blond man sat by her side. Sam.

Who was he? Why was he always there?

She looked down at her hand, held gently by his. The big, tan hand warmed hers, made her feel connected to him. Why, when he was a stranger? How could she feel so close to someone she'd seen for the first time mere hours before?

"Amy, are you all right?"

Adrienne didn't even bother to correct his use of that name. Nor did she bother to answer his question. Confusion, pain and exhaustion assailed her from all sides. She didn't want to be here. Knowing she lay hurt in a hospital bed wouldn't stop Vaughn from coming after her. That he hadn't appeared already left her more confused.

"Why did you bring me back?" she asked, unable to raise her voice above a whisper. Her little side trip had sapped whatever energy she had.

"You had a bad fall. The doctor needs to examine you before she releases you."

"I'm fine."

He grimaced. "You're not fine. You fainted."

She could feel a blush come to her cheeks. "I guess it was foolish to try to walk so far so soon."

"Maybe," he said. "Acts of survival often are. Maybe after the doctor examines you you'll tell me what you're running from."

She looked away from him, still not ready to trust.

"You rest, sweetheart," he said, a strange catch in his voice. "I'll go get the doctor."

The sound of his voice, the way he said sweetheart almost made her feel safe. "Wait," she called as he reached the door.

He stopped and looked back at her.

"What's your name?"

He looked at her searchingly. "It's Sam, remember?"

"Yes, but Sam what?"

"Sam Delaney."

The doctor had called her Mrs. Delaney earlier. Suddenly she didn't feel so safe anymore. Something very strange was going on. Something her confused mind couldn't begin to comprehend. Why would the doctor call her by the name of a man she'd never met? Why would he allow it? "What do you want with me? Why are you here?"

His blue eyes became intense with an unspoken emotion. "To make sure you get well. Now, get some rest, okay?"

Unable to help herself, she closed her eyes. She was so tired. Tired of the pain. Tired of the incessant questions in her head. She tried to focus on a once-favorite place, to let her mind drift away from the fear, away from the pain. But all she could see was Sam's face.

CLOSING THE DOOR softly behind him, Sam stood for a moment, listening. For what, he didn't know. Maybe just the sound of his name. Spoken by a woman who knew him and shouldn't have to ask why he was there.

Impatient with himself, he crossed to the nurse's station. Kathy, the young, red-haired nurse he'd yelled at earlier, looked up from a chart as he approached. Taking in her wary expression, he spoke quietly. "Is Dr. Yamana back yet?" Once he'd calmed down, he'd realized it hadn't been the nurses' fault Amy had escaped.

"No, she's not, Mr. Delaney." She smiled tentatively. "Why don't you go get yourself something to drink? We'll let you know as soon as she returns."

Sam appreciated the suggestion, but he wasn't leaving the floor. "It's very important that I speak to her. I'll be in the waiting room."

He walked to the small room at the end of the hall. Glad to see it empty, he slumped onto a barely comfortable cranberry-colored couch. The relief he'd felt at finding Amy safe and sound had worn off. Now he just felt tired. He rubbed a hand across his dry eyes. What was he going to do? He had to think.

"The nurse said I'd find you here."

Sam looked up at his brother. "Where else would I be?"

Casey sat on the couch opposite him. "Where did you find her?"

"At the diner down the block. You were right. She didn't get far." Sam sat up, leaning his elbows on his knees. "What about you? What did you find?"

"Nothing yet. Damian's still looking into this Adrienne Winston. But that doesn't mean she exists. She could have gotten the name from a book she'd been reading before she fell."

Sam rubbed his eyes. "I don't understand it. It's as if she's made up some secret life. She keeps talking about some guy named Vaughn."

Casey sat forward. "Did she give you a last name?"

Sam shook his head.

"How is she?"

"Exhausted. I managed to convince her to get some rest. It wasn't easy. She's scared, Casey. The fear's eating at her."

"Does she know who you are?"

He shook his head. "There's not one bit of recognition in her eyes. Why, Casey? Why is she calling herself this strange name? Why is she afraid of this Vaughn person? Why is she afraid of me?"

"There's something you have to consider, Sam."

The seriousness of his brother's voice spurred him from his seat. "She's not crazy!"

Casey stood up. "I wasn't going to suggest she was. In fact, I have a hunch it's the opposite."

"What are you talking about?" Sam demanded.

"Maybe she really is Adrienne Winston. Maybe she has been all along."

Sam couldn't believe his ears. "You said it was a long shot."

"That was before I knew she'd been talking about this Vaughn guy. I can see someone with a head injury picking up a name from a book. But to be afraid the way you say…"

"Stop!" Sam wouldn't hear another word.

Casey put a hand on his shoulder. "I wish I could have spared you this."

"Me? I don't give a damn about myself. It's Amy I care about. If all this stuff she's been coming up with is true, it's possible she's in very real danger. I need to see her." He strode out of the room.

Halfway down the corridor, Casey caught up with him, grabbing his arm.

Sam glared at him. "Let me go."

"You're too worked up. You think going in there like this is going to help her?"

His brother was right. He had to be strong now. And calm. He had no idea what he was dealing with. "It's been three years, Casey."

"I know, Sam."

Sam winced at the compassion in his brother's voice. Hearing it scared him. Casey was a cop. A cop whose hunches were always on target. "Learning about the baby, we were so happy. How are we supposed to deal with this?"

Casey put an arm around him. "I don't know, Sam. But you will. You're the strongest man I know. Besides, if Amy really is Adrienne Winston, the fear she's experiencing comes from three years ago."

Sam shot him a grateful look. "I hadn't thought of that. Maybe I should go tell her."

Casey half laughed. "Tell her what? We still don't know anything yet. Why don't we go get some food instead?"

Sam shook his head. "I'm not hungry."

"My treat," Casey said.

That surprised him. "Your treat?"

"You're looking at me as if I'm some kind of tightwad or something."

Sam managed a smile. "Or something."

Casey laughed. "Then you'd better take me up on it.

It's a one-time offer." His demeanor turned serious. "You have to eat, Sam. You can't—"

"Take care of Amy if I don't take care of myself. All right, *Mom,* you win." He glanced at the closed door of her room. "I just hate to leave her alone."

"She needs to sleep. The nurses will keep an eye on her. Especially after what happened earlier. And once Dr. Yamana has had a chance to completely examine her, we'll have a better idea what we're dealing with."

Casey's words echoed Sam's own thoughts. After dropping by the nurse's station, they headed down to the cafeteria.

WHEN ADRIENNE WOKE for the third time, she felt as if she'd been asleep for weeks. A glance at the clock on the bedside table told her it had only been thirty minutes. The pain in her head had faded to a dull ache.

The panic she'd felt had faded, too. Once she told the people here about Vaughn, they wouldn't have him near her. And even if they didn't believe her, once she told Vaughn about her proof, he wouldn't dare hurt her, despite what he'd threatened.

The door opened. Adrienne tensed, then relaxed when Dr. Yamana stepped into the room. *So much for my new confidence,* she thought wryly.

"Well, you look like you're feeling better." The doctor moved to her bedside. She took out the same black instrument and once again shined the light in Adrienne's eyes. "How's your head?"

Seeing this as her chance to get herself released, Adrienne smiled. "The pain is all gone."

Dr. Yamana studied her skeptically. "All gone?"

"Well, it does ache a little," she admitted. "But not nearly enough to keep me in the hospital overnight."

"Anxious to leave, are you?"

So anxious she'd gone AWOL. Evidently the doctor hadn't heard about her little escapade. "There's no reason to stay if I'm feeling so much better, is there?"

The doctor smiled. "Why don't you let me finish my examination before you go running off, all right?"

Adrienne nodded reluctantly.

The doctor took the chart from the end of the bed and pulled up a chair. After she sat down, she opened the chart and took a pen out of her pocket. "As I started to explain before, in cases where there's been an injury to the head, sometimes there's a memory loss. So I'll ask you some basic questions, and you answer them to the best of your ability. Are you ready?"

Memory loss, Adrienne thought, maybe that's the answer. Sam had called her Amy, the doctor Mrs. Delaney. Delaney was Sam's last name. Was it possible he'd meant what he said, that he was only trying to make sure she got better? Maybe he knew the danger she'd been in the other night. Maybe this was his way of helping.

"Mrs. Delaney?"

Adrienne looked at the doctor. "What?"

"Are you up to answering these questions?"

Making a decision, Adrienne nodded.

"All right then, let's start with something easy. Can you tell me your name?"

Sending up a brief prayer for strength, Adrienne looked the doctor straight in the eye and lied, "Amy Delaney."

Dr. Yamana smiled. "How about your age?"

"Twenty-seven." Adrienne gave her real age reluctantly. She hoped it meshed with Sam's information.

"What is your birth date?"

This she knew she shouldn't answer. The age she might be forgiven. A wrong birth date would raise all sorts of suspicions. Now was the time for amnesia to set in. She paused, then tried to look puzzled, "I can't remember, Doctor."

"That's okay," Dr. Yamana said gently. "It will come back. Let's try something else. Can you tell me your address?"

Adrienne shook her head.

"What is your husband's name?"

Adrienne crossed her fingers under the covers. "Sam."

Dr. Yamana nodded. "Do you know the date of your anniversary?"

"No," she said, then made herself laugh. "I guess Sam won't be too happy with that."

The doctor smiled. "I'm sure he'll forgive you. He's very concerned about you. All the nurses are dreamy-eyed, wishing their husbands or boyfriends would show such devotion."

Which meant that they could be as easily fooled as she, Adrienne thought, or else he really was the caring man he seemed to be. Which one?

"Please try not to worry," Dr. Yamana said. "All the test results came out fine for you and the baby."

The mention of the baby she carried caused all other thoughts to vanish. Adrienne still had a hard time believing she'd been pregnant for several months and never had a clue.

"Since the tests came out so well, does that mean I can be released?" Adrienne asked.

"Well, we do have this memory loss to deal with," Dr. Yamana said.

Happy the doctor had bought her fake amnesia, Adrienne continued her act. "How long will it take me to remember?"

"That's hard to say. Different head injuries act differently. It could take days, weeks, or even months."

Dismay filled her. What have you gotten yourself into

now, Adrienne? she asked herself. "I can't stay in the hospital for months!"

The doctor laughed. "In a rush to get back to that handsome husband of yours, are you? Relax, Mrs. Delaney, your injury is relatively mild. You'll probably only be here overnight."

Adrienne didn't have to act out her relief. "That's wonderful, Doctor."

The other woman smiled. "I'm sure your husband will be happy about it, too."

Adrienne started at the term "your husband," then she realized the doctor was talking about Sam, not Vaughn.

"I'm going to go talk to him now," the doctor continued. "Get some rest. I'll be back as soon as possible." Dr. Yamana rose, and left the room.

Adrienne stared at the closed door. What would Sam say when the doctor told him about her "amnesia"? Would he give her away, or would he realize she'd decided to take him up on his offer of protection?

Adrienne sat up. It didn't matter what he'd said. There was no way she was going to wait around to find out. Moving more quickly than she knew she should, she made her way over to the closet. At least this time all she'd have to do was put on jeans and shoes.

She opened the door, then stood staring at the empty space inside. No jeans. No shoes. Only three clothesless hangers.

Damn them! There was no way she could leave now. Anger and fear made her sway. She moved back to the bed, muttering, "I can't faint. I can't faint." If she lost consciousness again, they would keep her here for days. That would only give Vaughn more time to find her. She was sure now he had no idea she'd landed in the hospital. If he knew, he'd be here.

Huddled under the covers, she tried to think, to plan, to

come up with anything she could to convince them to keep
Vaughn away from her once he arrived. And she thought
of the big blond man who'd regarded her so tenderly.
Could she really count on his help?

THE ELEVATOR DOOR whooshed open. Sam stepped into
the corridor, then turned to his brother, who had followed.
"I can't believe you stuck me with lunch again."

"I thought I had a twenty in my wallet."

"Yeah, right." Sam strode quickly down the wide hall
toward the nurse's station.

Casey moved to catch up. "I said I'm sorry."

"Yeah, you sound sorry." Arriving at his destination,
he leaned on the counter and returned the smile of the
nurse on duty. He figured there must have been a shift
change, since he didn't recognize her. "I'm Sam Delaney.
Is Dr. Yamana back yet?"

"Yes, sir, she returned a few minutes ago. I believe
she's in with Mrs. Delaney."

"What do you mean she's in with Mrs. Delaney?"

The nurse's eyes widened at his terse tone, but Sam
didn't feel in the least guilty. He'd told them he needed to
talk to the doctor before she saw Amy.

"The doctor needed to finish her examination," the
nurse said.

"But I told the other nurse I needed to talk to her first."

"Kathy gave Dr. Yamana the message. But you weren't
here, sir, and the doctor is very busy."

"If you had called the cafeteria when she arrived, I
would have been here in two minutes," he said between
gritted teeth. "Was she too busy to wait two minutes?"

Casey touched his arm. "Calm down, Sam. It's not this
young lady's fault."

Sam glared at him. "No, it's mine for letting *you* talk
me into going with you."

Casey smiled, not in the least intimidated by his brother. "Wanna beat me up?"

"Yes," Sam growled. "But I don't have time right now. I have to check on Amy." He pushed past his brother, only to stop abruptly.

Striding down the hall toward them was Dr. Yamana, looking as concerned as he felt.

He moved to meet her. "Dr. Yamana? Is my wife okay?"

"She's fine, Mr. Delaney, physically. But there's something we need to discuss." She took his arm. "Let's go down to the waiting room."

Sam scowled at her emphasis of the word *physically*. What did that mean? Had she found out about the amnesia? He looked at his brother. Casey shook his head.

The gesture to be cautious was unnecessary. Sam knew as well as Casey the value of remaining silent until you knew the whole story. He let the doctor lead him to the little room he'd grown to hate. Casey followed.

Inside, he sat down next to her on the cranberry couch. Casey took a chair across from them. "What's going on, Doctor?" Sam asked.

"I'm afraid your wife's concussion has left her with a bit of amnesia."

"Amnesia?" Sam said, trying to buy some time.

The doctor nodded. "I asked her some questions about herself. It's part of the procedure when a patient has suffered a head injury. She couldn't tell me her birth date or your anniversary. All she knew was that her name is Amy Delaney and that you, Sam Delaney, are her husband."

Sam felt rocked to his soul. If she knew she was his Amy, why had she told him her name was Adrienne Winston? What about this Vaughn person, had she mentioned him? One look at the closed expression on his brother's face told him not to ask. "She actually told you, Doctor, that her name is Amy Delaney?"

The doctor nodded. "Yes, but that's about all she could tell me. She became very concerned that her amnesia would keep her in the hospital, but I assured her that we would probably only keep her overnight. Her head injury is relatively minor. With rest, she should be herself in a few days."

Sam tried to be relieved, but Casey's doubts kept going through his mind. Maybe she really was Adrienne Winston. Maybe she lied about being Amy Delaney for the same reason she ran away.

"Can I see her, Doctor?"

"Of course, but try not to stay for long. She, and your baby, need her to rest as much as possible."

Sam nodded, but he was only going through the motions of understanding the doctor's words. The fact was, he didn't understand anything that had happened in the past few hours.

A beeper went off. Both Casey and Dr. Yamana checked their devices. Dr. Yamana smiled. "Duty calls. I'll check on your wife in a couple of hours, Mr. Delaney. Try not to worry. These things are usually temporary."

After she left, Sam looked at Casey. "Temporary? Is this the end, Casey? Has Amy finally remembered who she is after all these years?"

Casey's shrug was anything but casual. "We won't know for sure until we talk to her."

Sam half laughed. "Then why aren't I running down that hall right now?"

Casey regarded him with compassion. "Because you're afraid you've lost your wife, Sam. But you have to stop thinking that way. The woman you've spent the last three years loving loves you, too."

"Does she?" Sam wondered.

Chapter Three

"Of course she loves you," Casey assured him.

Sam appreciated his brother's loyalty, but he was practical enough to face reality. Amy hadn't recognized him. If she told the doctor her name was Amy Delaney, it wasn't because she'd remembered. And if she didn't remember being Amy, she wouldn't remember loving him either. A deep anger stirred inside him. He'd be damned if he'd allow one stupid accident to take his wife away from him!

He picked up a newspaper he found lying on a table, turned and left the room.

"Sam, wait up!"

Ignoring his brother's call, he strode down the hall toward Amy's room.

Casey caught up to him outside. "What are you going to do?"

Unable to discount the alarm in Casey's voice, Sam took a couple of calming breaths before answering. "I have to tell her who she is."

"You don't know who she is, Sam," Casey reminded him.

Sam shook his head in denial. "She's my wife. She's carrying our child. No matter what happened in her life before I found her that night, that will never change."

"Maybe you should wait until the doctor gets back," Casey said reasonably. "She thinks Amy has a simple case of amnesia. Even you and I don't know exactly what we're dealing with. Amy might need a doctor nearby."

Sam seriously considered his brother's suggestion. He didn't want to make things worse for Amy. She was already scared enough. That thought decided him. "I have to tell her now, Casey. If the danger she's so afraid of did happen three years ago, she has a right to know it's long in the past."

Casey nodded his understanding. He put a supportive hand on Sam's shoulder. "You want me to go with you."

Sam shook his head. "Wish me luck," he said and pushed open the door to his wife's room.

Adrienne watched Sam warily as he walked into the room. The doctor had left to talk to him. What had she said? Had she seen through her act?

Sam set the newspaper on the side table, then pulled up a chair and sat. "Hi."

Adrienne returned his greeting, but left it at that. For now, she would let Sam lead the conversation. Once she knew what he'd been told, she'd handle it from there.

"You must have gotten some rest. You look a lot better."

She nodded. "Thanks, I feel better." It was obvious he was stalling. She wondered why.

Sam cleared his throat. "The doctor says you have amnesia."

Adrienne nodded again, then, to avoid his intent gaze, looked down at her hands. Her fingers were clenched together, an obvious sign of nervousness.

He reached over and separated her hands. "Relax, honey, everything is going to be just fine." Laying them gently on the blanket, he touched her left ring finger. She'd taken off her ring before she left Boston, but the mark from it remained. "Dr. Yamana said you only remember that your name is Amy Delaney and that I'm your husband."

She opened her mouth, but she couldn't think of a thing to say.

Sam smiled. "It's okay, you don't have to talk." His smile faded. "There are some things you need to know about your accident."

His comment surprised her. "I was running, and I fell." It seemed simple enough.

"Yes." He nodded. "Into the road, right in front of my truck. It scared the hell out of me. Thank God, my brakes were good or I might have hit you."

The anguish in his eyes touched her. She reached out to him. "I'm sorry."

He took her hand in his and smiled. "You've more than made up for it in the last three years."

Shocked, she drew back. "Three years? What are you talking about?"

"The accident you remember took place three years ago," he said gently.

"But..." She reached up and touched the bandage on her head.

"This was caused by something entirely different. You were vacuuming. You slipped on the cord and hit your head on the vacuum."

"I was vacuuming!" This had to be a joke. She hadn't vacuumed in years. She and Vaughn had always been too busy for housework.

Vaughn. This had something to do with him. Was he trying to prove her insane? Crazy people weren't reliable witnesses. The police wouldn't believe a word she said.

She looked at Sam, deeply disappointed. She'd hoped he was different, that his gentleness was genuine. Now it seemed he was just someone Vaughn had sent to do his dirty work. Maybe he was the one she'd heard coming after her the night of the accident.

She hoped Vaughn had paid him well. His acting ability appeared to be top-notch. He'd almost had her fooled.

Well, one thing was clear. She couldn't let him know she'd figured out their plan. She decided to test him.

"Where was I vacuuming?"

"At our house."

That threw her. "*Our* house?"

"Yes, yours and mine."

"We live together?" She'd never seen this man before in her life. How could he possibly claim they lived together? How could Vaughn believe he'd get away with such an outrageous lie? How did they plan to prove it?

Her stomach dropped when she realized she might actually have helped them prove it, when she'd told the doctor she was Amy Delaney and Sam was her husband.

"Yes, we do live together." Sam looked at her closely, as if waiting for a reaction. "We're...married."

Adrienne saw red as anger overwhelmed her. She'd told the doctor this man was her husband, and now he was actually trying to prolong the charade. This man wasn't here to protect her. He was using her.

She stared at the man who claimed to be her husband, trying to figure him out. What made him think he could get away with this?

What she saw in his expression confused her. His blue eyes held more than a hint of concern. In fact, he looked almost afraid.

Which was just as ridiculous as everything else that had happened in the past couple of hours. What did he have to be afraid of? She was the one who didn't know what the hell was going on!

"Amy, are you all right?" Sam asked, reaching out.

She jerked her hand back before he could touch her

again. Anger and confusion warred inside her. Anger won. "I'm just ducky. I love being called by somebody else's name. I never saw you before today and you're claiming I'm your wife. On top of that, you're actually trying to tell me that I fell in front of your truck three years ago and I got this bump on my head tripping over a cord in 'our' house. How could I not be all right? I've stumbled into some damn rabbit hole!"

Sam stared at her as if she'd turned into the rabbit. "You don't believe me."

Trying to rub away the pain once again pounding against her forehead, Adrienne felt suddenly weary. "Of course I don't believe you."

He reached over and retrieved the newspaper he'd brought with him. He laid it on her lap. "Look at this."

She glanced down at the paper. The headline dealt with some foreign political problem. "Look at what?"

"The date," he said.

She read the date. She read it again. "This can't be real." Frantically, she searched each page for some sign this was a mocked-up version of the newspaper.

She looked at Sam. "Tell me this isn't real."

"I can't, honey. It is real."

"How can it be?" Her head began to swim. Tears threatened. She swiped them away. "How can I have forgotten three years of my life?"

"Oh, sunshine." Sam gently wiped the tears that refused to be stayed. "You did more than that."

Adrienne felt so tired she couldn't even raise a protest at this intimacy. "What do you mean?"

"Until you woke up in the hospital today, you'd forgotten everything about yourself *and* your past."

"What?"

"You didn't know who you were or where you came

from. You had identification that gave us your name and your address, but—''

''Wait!'' she interrupted. Putting her hands over her burning eyes, she tried to think. She'd had identification? That couldn't be right. She'd been running away. She'd left her driver's license and credit cards behind, she knew it. A vague memory prodded her brain. A man handing her something, her handing him a thick envelope in return. She looked at Sam. ''What name was on the ID?''

Sam gazed at her searchingly before he answered. ''Amy Nichols, from Los Angeles, California. Casey tried to find your phone number, but it was unlisted. He had a friend go to the address listed, but they had never heard of Amy Nichols.''

Of course they hadn't, Adrienne thought. Because she had never lived in Los Angeles, and she wasn't Amy Nichols.

''We ran your picture in the *L.A. Times,* as well as the local paper,'' Sam continued, ''but no one came forward.''

''No one?'' She needed the clarification. She needed to know the fake ID had worked.

Sam shook his head. ''I'm sorry.''

The words were so simple and heartfelt, she knew they were the truth.

I'm safe!

The words burst into her brain. He hadn't been following her that night. The accident had been just that. Vaughn hadn't insisted on seeing her in the hospital for no other reason than he wasn't here. She laughed out loud. She was *safe.*

Adrienne could hardly believe it. Because of the ID she'd bought before she left Boston, they'd only run her picture in California. Vaughn never would have seen it in Boston. Of course, that's why she'd chosen the Golden State. Vaughn thought it an intellectual wasteland. It never would have occurred to him that she would choose to live here.

Fast on those thoughts came another, more fantastic than the ones before.

"The baby?"

Sam nodded.

"It's yours?" *Please, God, let him say yes. Let it be anybody's but Vaughn's.*

Sam smiled.

Again, Adrienne laughed, then immediately burst into tears.

Sam moved to sit on the bed. Putting his arms around her he held her tight. "It's all right, sunshine. I promise. I'm a great guy once you get to know me. You don't have anything to be afraid of."

Adrienne heard his crooning words and knew she had to tell him. "You don't understand."

"I do understand. This has all been too much for you. Finding out about the amnesia. Learning you're living with a stranger, and pregnant on top of that. I know how upset you are."

Adrienne's tears turned back to laughter. The poor man was so intent on comforting her he didn't understand at all. She pulled away. "I'm not upset!"

Sam looked at her as if she'd lost her mind.

"And I'm not hysterical, either."

His expression turned skeptical.

She didn't blame him. If what he'd told her was true, and it seemed it was, her head and her emotions had been playing tricks on her for a long time.

She smiled wryly. "All right, maybe a little hysterical, but wouldn't you be, under the same circumstances?"

Sam returned her smile. "I'd be a blithering idiot."

Adrienne doubted that. In spite of all that she'd put him through during the past few hours, Sam's actions had been sure and steady. She suspected she was very lucky to have Sam as her baby's father. "I'm just so glad the baby's not Vaughn's."

"Vaughn?"

"He has no hold. He can't hurt us." As long as she and the baby belonged to someone else, he couldn't do a thing.

The truth was he probably never had. She'd been so careful. It was only once she'd arrived at her destination that she'd become afraid again. One strange noise had sent her running. How foolish!

"Amy."

And how wonderful to know that the noises she'd heard on her walk had been only that. Not Vaughn. Noises. But that night, the fear had been so real, it had sent her flying through the trees and onto the road where she'd fallen.

"Amy."

Even now, some of the fear remained. She'd lived with it for so long it was hard to let go. But she would, now she knew three years had passed. Three years in which she'd met a man, fallen in love, gotten married, *gotten pregnant,* and she remembered none of it! Incredible.

"*Amy!*"

It took her a few moments to realize he was talking to her. "I'm sorry. There is just so much to take in."

"I understand that, but there's something I have to know."

She looked at him curiously. His tone seemed almost angry. "What is it?"

"Who's Vaughn?"

She grimaced. "My husband."

Sam scowled. "Your *husband?*"

"Actually, my ex." She guessed. "It's been three years. I'm sure he went through with the divorce."

Sam's eyes went blank. He moved off the bed and walked over to the window. He stood for a moment staring out. "You're sure he went through with the divorce," Sam repeated as if by rote.

Adrienne watched him shake off whatever he'd been thinking. He turned back to her. "Why would your ex-husband want to hurt you?"

She shrugged. What use would it be to go into all that now? "He's probably forgotten all about me by now." At least, she hoped he had.

He held her gaze. "That doesn't answer my question."

The intensity in his blue eyes made her shiver. In the last few hours, she'd seen him gentle, concerned and hurt, but this fierceness surprised her.

"Amy, why would he want to hurt you?"

The husbandly sternness of his question reminded her he had a right to know. "Because he's a cold selfish son of a—" Anger flared in Sam's eyes, and she stopped. "What does it matter? I've obviously made a new life for myself. I'd rather talk about that."

"So would I," Sam said. "But if you're in danger..."

"I'm not!" If Vaughn had known where she was, he wouldn't have waited to do something about it. But he hadn't. So that meant she didn't have to be afraid anymore. Now all she wanted to do was forget him. *Selective amnesia. I wonder how that works.*

She looked at her "new" husband. "Sam, sit down, please." She waited until he sat in the chair by the bed. "I feel funny asking this since we've been married for..."

"We celebrated our second year together three months ago," Sam informed her. "Around the same time the baby was conceived."

A blush warmed her cheeks. "Oh." She'd never been a shy person, but the thought of making love with this virtual stranger unsettled her. Her brain certainly worked in mysterious ways. First she'd forgotten her first husband. Now she'd forgotten her second.

"Are you okay?" He leaned forward and reached for her hand.

"I'm fine," she said, although it seemed an anemic word to use for how she felt.

Sam was so big and strong. Sitting so close, he made her feel almost delicate. Yet, he hadn't tried to intimidate her physically like other men had. He'd made her feel safe and protected. That's what had scared her so much when she'd believed he'd been sent by Vaughn, that he could have taken her in so easily. When she'd finally accepted that not only wasn't he involved with Vaughn, but that he was her husband and the father of the baby she carried, she'd felt relieved and somewhat vindicated.

Now she felt curious. Not only about him, personally, but about her life with him. She moved restlessly. "Sam, for all intents and purposes, we've just met. I know nothing about you beyond these last few hours."

He released her hand and sat back, as if reading her need for a little space. "I'm not sure I know where to start."

Start with why you married me. The thought came full-blown to her mind, but she didn't voice it. She'd asked Vaughn that once, and he'd answered with the required pretty words. But it hadn't taken her long to realize pretty words meant nothing. Or that she wouldn't have wanted a man like Vaughn to love her, even if they had.

Sam seemed like a good, honest man. But she wanted to know him a lot better before she asked him a question whose answer she'd have to analyze. So, she decided to start with something simple.

"I know your name is Sam Delaney. How old are you?"

"I'll be thirty-five April third. That's about three months from now."

It seemed impossible so much time had passed. Like some modern Rip van Winkle, she'd gone to sleep and woken up over three years later. But old Rip hadn't gotten married and pregnant during his nap! Thinking about the time that had passed, another thought occurred. ''I missed my thirtieth birthday,'' she said. There were probably women who'd rejoice at such a fact, but she only felt strange to have missed such an important milestone.

''When is your birthday?'' Sam asked. ''We've been using October seventeenth, the day of the accident.''

''December thirty-first.''

''Well, we didn't know it was your birthday, but we did celebrate.''

She laughed. ''Us and the rest of the world. It *is* New Year's Eve.''

His blue eyes sparkled. ''I bet when you were a kid you thought the celebration was all for you.''

''You win.''

But that hadn't lasted long, she thought. People had been quick to tell her the celebration had nothing to do with her. Just like Vaughn had been quick to tell her their success had nothing to do with her. It was his work, his brains that made their advertising company a huge success. The campaigns she'd designed, he'd told her, would never have gotten off the ground if it hadn't been for him.

''Hey, what's wrong?'' Sam interrupted her dismal thoughts.

Adrienne rubbed her eyes. Suddenly, she felt very tired and emotional. ''What could be wrong? I've forgotten three years of my life. I'm pregnant with a child I don't remember conceiving with a man I don't remember marrying.''

Seeing the stricken look on his face, she regretted snapping at him. ''Look, I'm sorry. My head is aching again. Would you mind if we postponed this question-and-answer session for a while?''

For a moment she thought he was going to refuse. There was a stubborn look on his face that told her he wanted to. Instead, he got up and moved the chair he'd been sitting on back next to the wall.

Grateful for his compliance, she felt a need to reassure him. "I just need a little rest, Sam. It's been a big day."

Sam managed a smile. "That's putting it mildly. Get some sleep. I'll be down the hall if you need me."

"You don't have to stay."

He looked a little hurt. "Yes, I do."

Adrienne was glad. She liked the security she felt knowing he would be near. Even though she knew Vaughn lived a couple thousand miles away, in blessed ignorance, she couldn't quite shake the fear that he'd come running should he ever learn of her circumstances. Then, she suspected, there would be no more safety. No matter how big and strong Sam was.

SAM LEFT THE ROOM reluctantly. Something was wrong, but he couldn't figure out what. He walked down the hall toward the waiting room, though he already hated the sight of those rose walls and cranberry couches.

He understood that Amy had been through a lot. She probably just needed some time to assimilate what she'd learned so far. He certainly did.

But he also suspected there was something she hadn't told him. Something about her ex-husband. Why else would she be worried about whether he had a hold on her and the baby?

Once in the waiting room, Sam found it difficult to keep still. He sat. He stood. He paced, then sat again. Had he made a mistake letting her distance him like this? What else could he have done?

He picked up a magazine and leafed through the pages, but never saw one. His mind never left the woman lying in the hospital room down the hall. He couldn't force her to talk to him. He knew that. So he stayed where he was, knowing also that if he pushed, she'd run. She'd already done it once.

Twice, if what he suspected about her arrival in California had any validity.

So, he'd wait. Because next time he might not find her so easily. Frustrated by his own logic, he threw the magazine across the room.

Casey strode in as the magazine settled itself on the floor next to the couch. "Hey, big brother, what are you doing here?"

"Amy needed some rest."

"Told her you were her husband and she kicked you out, huh?"

Sam glared at him. "That's not funny."

Casey sat down beside him and slapped a hand on his back. "It ain't gonna happen, either. So quit worrying. You're much more interesting than that stiff she left in Boston."

That got his attention. "Her ex-husband's dead?"

Casey laughed. "Not that kind of stiff. You've been hanging around cops too much."

"How did you find him so fast?" He'd just found out the Vaughn she'd kept mentioning was related to her himself.

Acting insulted, Casey moved to the chair across from him. "Will you ever stop underestimating your little brother? I put the names Vaughn and Winston together, called a friend who's good at tracing people. Winston's in advertising. Has a big company in Boston called Advon Inc. He and Adrienne started it five years ago. Right after they got married."

"So the ID was fake," Sam said, only surprised that Amy hadn't made that clear when he'd talked about trying to find her next of kin.

"Yep," Casey said. "A good fake, too. She must have paid a bundle for it."

Restless, Sam picked up a magazine, then put it back down. "I can't believe Amy has her own advertising company. Why would she leave it to run to California?"

Casey sat forward. "Had. She signed it over to him right before she left town."

"What?" That made less sense than her running away from it. "Why?"

Casey shrugged. "Maybe that's the price she had to pay to get rid of him."

Remembering his own comment about survival skills earlier, Sam felt a shiver of fear. "She must have wanted to do that pretty badly to give up a company she founded." That fact should have made him happy. After all, it was easier to deal with an ex the woman you loved hated. You never had to see him. But the desperation of it made him uneasy. "What else did you find out?"

"Not much. Actually, what I did find was pretty weird. Nobody seemed to know she'd been missing."

"A woman disappears for three years and nobody notices?" This was getting stranger by the moment.

"She has no family. Nobody filled out a missing-person's report. All she had was Winston, who evidently didn't care if she disappeared. The private detective suggested that Amy might have wanted to be lost, so he's being very discreet. We don't want to alert the wrong person to her presence."

Sam's fear took form. How would they know who the wrong person was? Of course, it was probably her ex. If so, what had he done to make her turn over her half of their company and run all the way to California?

His mind jumped to the obvious: abuse. "Come on." He grabbed Casey's arm and dragged him out of the room.

"Where are we going?"

"To talk to Amy."

Casey pulled away. "And ask her what?"

So many questions filled Sam's mind, he couldn't begin to list them. Instead, he focused on his brother's doubt-filled expression. "Are you saying we shouldn't ask her what made her come out here three years ago?" It had to be the ex. He must have hurt her, threatened her. Something had driven her away. How could Sam protect her if he didn't know what that was?

"I'm saying you can't go charging in there and demand answers."

Sam gave a short laugh. "That's pretty good coming from the original bull in a china shop."

Casey smiled wryly. "You spent a lot of time trying to teach me patience. Maybe the lessons finally got through my thick head."

Sam paced up the hall a few feet, then back. "It's easy for you to be patient. She's not your wife."

"She's not yours, either."

His brother's tone was so mild, Sam almost missed the import of what he'd said. Fire filled him. He grabbed Casey's shoulders and held him against the wall. "Don't ever say that again."

Casey didn't fight him off. "Use your head, Sam. You're not dealing with Amy anymore. You said yourself she doesn't remember you. It's Adrienne Winston you're going to be questioning. Not the woman you've been married to the past two years."

Sam slowly released his brother. Frustration and anger had driven him, but he had no desire to hurt a man who spoke only the truth. "I'm sorry."

Casey straightened his jacket. "Forget it."

"So what do we do now?" He really had no idea. He'd lived with Amy for the last three years. Even before they'd fallen in love, she'd stayed in the home he and Casey had shared. To him, she was one person. Sweet, loving, talented, hardworking, intelligent Amy. To think of her as another person, one who didn't know him, who didn't love him, seemed impossible.

"I think we should do nothing," Casey said.

It was the last answer he'd expected. "Nothing?" No questions? No answers? "How can I keep her safe if I don't know what I'm up against?"

"She is safe." Before Sam could protest, Casey rushed on. "I'm beginning to think you're the one with amnesia. This isn't three years ago, Sam. She didn't just fall into the street in front of your truck. She tripped vacuuming, for God's sake!"

Casey's voice had risen so loud, a passing nurse shushed him.

Sam laughed. "So much for patience."

Casey's eyebrows lowered. "You're a jackass."

Amy would have said "headstrong and stubborn," Sam thought. And as usual she would have been right. He had to get a grip. He was in love with, and expecting a child with, a woman who no longer knew him from Adam. That was enough of a problem to solve, without having to worry about what happened in the past.

"All right, you win."

Casey looked at him in surprise. "I do? What do I win?"

Sam shook his head at his brother's clowning. Casey never could hold a grudge. "My patience."

"Ah." He nodded sagely. "Well, that was more for you than for me."

"Amy's here. She's safe." For now, he couldn't help thinking. "She and the baby are my top priorities." He started to move down the hall, then turned back. "But that patience won't last forever. Tell that P.I. friend of yours to get to work. I want to know every move Vaughn Winston makes.''

"Sam…''

Sam saw the uneasy look on his brother's face. "He hurt her, Casey. I don't know when or why or how. But he hurt her. If he comes anywhere near her again, I'll make him pay.''

Casey covered the space between them in three strides, grabbed his arm. "Sam, you have to let me handle this. You're not trained…''

Sam shook him off. "She's mine, Casey. Divorced or not. Married or not. She's mine. And *I* am going to make sure no one hurts her again.''

Chapter Four

In her hospital room the next morning, Adrienne put on the clothes Sam had brought for her. If she hadn't already been ambivalent about going home with him, the clothes would certainly have given her some doubts. The ankle-length gauze skirt of watercolor pastels and the long pink cotton sweater definitely belonged to Amy.

She looked in the mirror and studied the woman she'd become. Her hair, which she normally kept chin length, fell below her shoulders. The curl she'd tried to tame had obviously been allowed to take its natural course. Without the mousse she usually applied, the golden-blond color appeared lighter and shinier somehow.

Since Sam hadn't brought any, Adrienne assumed she no longer wore makeup either. She didn't really need it. Her lashes were dark enough. She could have used some blusher, since her face was still pale. Lipstick would have been nice. But overall, still okay.

The parts were different, but taken as a whole she looked soft and womanly. It didn't exactly displease her, but it wasn't at all the effect she usually tried for.

Her colleagues would have interpreted soft and womanly as weak and less than bright. She would never have worn anything so obviously feminine. The clothes she'd chosen had been boldly colored and of modern design.

Suits that emphasized her strength and creativity. Dresses that showed her to be innovative and intelligent. They were more than power suits. They were armor.

This…froth…would protect her from nothing.

Of course, the argument could be made that she didn't need to be protected. Not from business associates. Not from rival firms. And not from Vaughn.

She had a new life now as Amy Delaney. She was wife of Sam Delaney, soon-to-be-mother of this child she carried, and…what else?

Who *was* Amy Delaney? Had her loss of memory really changed her as much as her choice of clothing indicated?

In the end, it was that question that decided her. She would go home with Sam. She would learn about Amy Delaney. But she would do it as Adrienne. She didn't want to hurt him, but Sam would just have to understand that she wasn't the woman he'd been living with the past three years. She had to go with what was familiar to her.

Adrienne, the survivor.

SAM PACED the hallway outside Amy's room. He refused to set foot in that waiting room again. This had been the worst two days of his life.

But I'll get through it, he thought, taking a deep breath to ease the panic that kept threatening to overtake his usually rational mind. Once he had her home and safe, Amy would remember what they'd had together and everything would get back to normal.

"Sam?"

Sam turned. "Amy. You look beautiful."

"Adrienne."

"Excuse me?" She looked so familiar, the lack of a responding smile confused him.

"My name is Adrienne. It's the name I lived with for

twenty-seven years. And since I don't remember the last three, I'd rather you call me by that name."

He didn't like it. It put too much distance between him and the woman he knew. If he let her distance him now, how could he ever make her understand what had been between them? The refusal was on his lips, but one look at her set face made him realize he had to keep it to himself. This wasn't the woman he knew. "All right. Adrienne. Are you ready to go?"

She nodded.

Not exactly enthusiastic about the prospect of going home with me, Sam thought as they walked silently to the nurse's station to sign the final release papers. And who could blame her? In Adrienne's mind, she'd known him barely two days. She didn't have any idea how much they'd shared.

But he knew. Seeing the lack of true recognition in her eyes hurt more than he dared admit. To tell her would be to lay the responsibility for his feelings in her lap. And this wasn't her fault.

It was his. If he'd been there, she never would have been vacuuming. If she hadn't been vacuuming, she never would have fallen. *What next?* he asked himself. *If she hadn't fallen, she never would have remembered? Is that what you wanted?*

"Hi! Are you ready to go?"

Sam nodded at the girl who'd interrupted his thoughts. Hospital policy dictated that patients being released ride to the exit in a wheelchair. With the young student nurse accompanying them in the elevator, they made the descent to the lobby without saying a word.

Once outside, he directed the nurse to his truck where he'd parked in a patient-loading zone. Conscientious to the end, the girl didn't leave her patient until she saw her securely seated in the passenger seat of the dark blue pickup.

Beside her, Sam took in Adrienne's nervous movements. Poor kid. "I don't blame you for being scared, sunshine. But I promise everything will be okay."

His effort to comfort her failed. She bristled like an angry porcupine. "How can you promise any such thing?"

The sharpness in her voice shocked him. Such a tone had never crossed Amy's lips. Though they'd had the normal adjustments to deal with, the fights that many newlyweds suffered had bypassed them.

"Well?"

Sam saw the fear behind the impatience. "I can't." Normally, he would have taken her into his arms and kissed her concerns away. With circumstances being what they were, he decided on a different tack. "Would you rather I said, 'Everything isn't going to be fine'?"

She rewarded his light sarcasm with a smile. "No, but it might be more honest."

Her reaction relieved him greatly. At least she hadn't lost her sense of humor. The statement that followed did make him curious, however. "Why would being negative be more honest? Don't tell me Adrienne Winston is a pessimist." Amy had been an optimist. Could a loss of memory change a person that much?

"No," she said. "I'm a realist." She hadn't liked thinking that way. Once she had been optimistic as any young girl could be. Experience had taught her to believe differently. If Sam hadn't learned that lesson by now, he must have been very lucky indeed.

"What do you mean by a 'realist'?"

She gave him a glance that questioned his naiveté. "Just that everything is fine only if you work very hard at making it that way, and you don't run into someone who's just as determined to do the opposite."

"Sounds like you've run into a few of those people."

"Too many."

Even one was too many when it came to his Amy. It broke his heart to know she had experienced pain he couldn't ease. "Well, I'm not one of them," he assured her. "I'll work for you all the way."

"And if I decide that Amy Delaney's life is not for me?"

He was being tested. He knew that, as surely as the sun rose in the east. This time, he refused to let her goad him. "We'll cross that bridge when we come to it."

He started the ignition and drove slowly through the parking lot to the exit. At the stop sign, Adrienne watched him give strict concentration to the oncoming traffic. His thick golden eyebrows were drawn down, his quick smile had disappeared completely and his knuckles had gone white from holding the steering wheel too tightly.

It didn't take a genius to see he was upset, which made Adrienne feel mean and petty. She shouldn't be taking her frustrations out on Sam. He didn't deserve it. He'd been unfailingly kind and caring. Her guardian angel. Suddenly, she felt an intense desire to make it up to him.

"The sign on your truck says Delaney Landscape. Are you a gardener?"

His tense expression lightened. "Sort of. I do landscape design."

"You mean telling people where they should plant their flowers and shrubs?" She was hopelessly out of her league here. She hadn't killed the plants she had in her condo, but that was the most that could be said for her gardening skills.

"Yes, plus planting trees, putting up fences, building decks, laying sprinklers. That kind of stuff."

Well, that explained the muscles. She ran her gaze over Sam, who wore snug faded jeans and a baby blue sweater.

Without being tight, the sweater emphasized his wide shoulders and chest. The sleeves had been pushed up, revealing muscular forearms, tanned and covered with golden hair.

Hours of physical activity had honed his body, and she couldn't help thinking how envious Vaughn would be of Sam's physique. He didn't give a damn about her life or anyone else's, but he'd spent hours in the gym trying to keep himself fit.

Thinking back over the last two days, Adrienne realized that Vaughn couldn't begin to hold a candle to Sam Delaney. Not in looks or personality. Sam was good. Vaughn was evil. Thank God she was out of his hands.

"Adrienne? Are you okay?"

Adrienne looked over at Sam, whose concern shone clearly from his eyes. She smiled. "I'm fine." It was true. For the first time since she woke up in the hospital that first day, she felt relaxed and free of fear. And, she realized, her head had stopped aching.

Suddenly, she longed to know everything about this man who was her husband. "Tell me more about your business."

Sam sensed more than saw the change that had come over Adrienne during the last few minutes. Had she finally decided to trust him? He almost asked what had changed, but decided not to push his luck.

Instead, he filled her in on his company. "In addition to private contracts, we also do a lot of commercial landscape design. The people in this area are very conscious of ecology and aesthetics. The Monterey Bay area is very beautiful. The people who live here want to keep it that way."

"I don't blame them. Spending most of my life in Boston, I would never have believed the natural beauty I found here. The windswept cypress trees, all the brightly colored flowers, the waves pounding against the rocks.'' She laughed. ''I'm beginning to sound like an advertising campaign.''

He smiled at her enthusiasm. ''Most people who've spent any time in the area do.''

''Yes, but I've only been here a few days, and most of it I've been in the hospi...''

Adrienne's sudden silence made Sam glance over at her. She sat staring out the side window, biting her lip as if to keep from crying. He eased the truck over to the side of the road. Though they were only a short distance from home, he couldn't bear to see her so miserable.

Disregarding any protest she might make, he pulled her into his arms and held her tight. ''It's okay, sunshine,'' he murmured over and over, stroking her hair.

Unnerved, he didn't know what else to say. One minute she sounded just like Amy, who loved Monterey and could go on for hours about how beautiful the trees and flowers were and how much she loved the beaches. The next minute she was clearly this Adrienne person who was hurt and confused and felt like Alice who'd been set down in a crazy world called Wonderland.

''How can you say it's okay?'' She pulled out of his arms and leaned back against her door, scrubbing tears away from her cheeks. ''Your wife doesn't remember you. Doesn't that make you angry? I don't remember living with you. I don't remember falling in love or your proposal or our wedding. I don't remember making love. I'm carrying your child right now, and I have to keep reminding myself that I'm pregnant! Why do you keep saying everything's okay?''

The pain and fear grew with each word she screamed at him, until he couldn't keep it in a moment longer. ''Because if I stop saying it, I might have to accept the fact that you'll never remember, that's why! Are you happy now? I'm just as afraid as you are.''

He paused a moment to calm himself. ''I got involved with you knowing your memory might come back one day, but I never expected it to happen. You'd been here a year before we considered moving into a house of our own. I've known you for over three years, and there hasn't been one inkling of insight about your past.''

''Until now,'' she said quietly.

He nodded. ''Until now.''

''What are we going to do, Sam? How are we supposed to live with this?''

The tone held anger, but underneath he heard a plea in her voice that cut him to the quick. She asked for answers he didn't have. Because he could do nothing else, he asked the question he'd been dreading. ''Do you want to go back to Boston?''

''No!'' The answer came quickly and with such adamancy he almost laughed.

''Then I guess we live with it one day at a time, and hope to God your whole memory returns.'' *Or, barring that, that you fall in love with me all over again.* Because he could not imagine a life without her.

When she didn't say anything else, he started the truck and drove on.

One day at a time, she thought as they drove through the streets of Pacific Grove toward the home in which she didn't remember living. What else could they do? She didn't want to go back to Boston. There was nothing left to draw her back. She'd signed the company over to Vaughn in return for a quick divorce. The home they'd shared hadn't meant anything to her since the day she'd learned about his philandering.

But was it fair to put Sam through this? He'd really done nothing to deserve it. Except be unwise enough to marry her, a woman whose past had suddenly reared its ugly head.

Unfortunately, she couldn't see any other way. To leave would mean taking his child with her. And that she would not do. The baby inside her had been conceived in love. Just because she didn't remember that love didn't mean it hadn't existed. He'd loved her and taken care of her for three years. She owed it to him to try to make the best of things.

Still, she couldn't help feeling that living with a man who had married another self would bring its own pain. She wasn't Amy. She didn't know anything about her, except that she'd fallen in love with and married Sam.

Adrienne had only drawn Vaughn, a man who had pretended to love her, because he needed her money and her creativity for the advertising empire he wanted to build.

It had taken her years to figure out that her creativity as a designer had been all that had interested Vaughn. And in the end, he couldn't even give her credit for that.

It wasn't enough that he'd had affair after affair behind her back, with her being too stupid to know. No, he'd had to take her confidence in her work away from her, too. He'd chipped it away piece by piece. Telling her she'd be nothing without him to guide her. Letting her know that their clients only accepted her ideas because he'd convinced them she could do better with his help.

But what she'd found out at the end had been so much worse. All her other complaints paled in the shadow of his horrendous deeds. Afraid of what he'd do to her, she'd taken the evidence and run, hoping that someday she'd find the nerve to turn him in.

"We're home." Sam's voice broke into her thoughts.

"What?"

He smiled. "I said, we're home."

She'd been so involved in her dark thoughts, she hadn't

even noticed they'd stopped. Now she looked around. "Oh my," she breathed.

When she'd tried to picture their home, she'd assumed they lived in a nice tree-lined residential neighborhood. Instead, she found herself in a small enchanted forest. All around her were trees and flowers. Though she caught a glimpse of another house through the pines, the quiet and peace that enveloped her made the nearest neighbor seem miles away.

Sam got out of the truck and moved around to open her door. She took the hand he offered and stepped out. Taking in her surroundings, she saw the house. Made of warm wood, rustic rock and soaring windows, it was at once natural, homey and, oddly enough, elegant. "It's gorgeous."

Sam laughed, and she turned to look at him. "What?"

"You had that same look on your face the first time we saw it."

That surprised her. "You didn't live here before we met?"

He shook his head. "Casey and I shared a house in Monterey. Once you and I admitted how we felt, we needed something of our own."

Something of our own, she repeated in her head. This beautiful place belonged to her. Paid for with Sam's money, a voice inside her head insisted. The voice sounded very much like Vaughn's. *"You really think you had something to do with making this company a success?"*

She looked away from the house, disappointed that her joy had been taken away so soon. Spoiled by the voice of an evil man she couldn't get out of her head.

"Now, why do you look so sad all of a sudden?" Sam asked.

She didn't even consider telling him a lie. "The house belongs to you. I did nothing to help buy it."

He grinned. "Who says?"

A memory exploded inside her head. The money! Could she have given it to Sam? Surely, he would have mentioned it if she'd had it when he found her.

"Adrienne?"

She looked back at Sam. How on earth was she going to tell him his beautiful home had been bought with money Vaughn had laundered for a cocaine dealer?

"What exactly do you think you've been doing the past three years?" he asked.

She shrugged, buying time. "I don't know. Keeping house?" It seemed strange to think of herself as a homemaker. Some women thrived on it, and more power to them. She, on the other hand, had never been very domestic.

Which she'd proven quite effectively by hitting her head while vacuuming.

"Keeping house, huh?" Sam burst out laughing.

"What's so funny?"

He held out his hand. "Come in the house. I want to show you something."

She was dying to see the interior, so she went with him. There would be time enough later to tell him about the money she'd taken from Vaughn's safe.

He led her up wide flagstone steps to the double front doors, flanked on each side by large windows. While he put the key in the lock, she took a moment to admire the carving of pinecones that embellished the wood.

Pushing open the door, he again took her hand. The gentle warmth that filled her at his touch made it easier to believe she belonged here.

Inside, he pulled her down a long hallway without giving her a chance to admire anything else. "Where are we going? I want to look around."

"You'll have plenty of time for that." He stopped at a

door near the end of the hall and opened it. Inside, sunshine filled a large room with high ceilings. Opposite, a wall of windows looked out on a small grove of Monterey pines and, in the distance, the blue waters of the bay.

"This view is incredible," she told him, unable to keep her eyes off it.

"I didn't bring you here to look at the view."

She turned to him, and that was when she saw them. Paintings. Large and small. Oils and watercolors. They covered the walls, the floors, the chairs. She looked around and saw this was an artist's studio. She glanced back at the paintings. "Are those mine?"

Stupid question! Of course they were. She didn't need his nod of confirmation. She'd painted many similar ones when she'd first gone to college, before she'd realized that commercial art would be much more lucrative and switched her focus.

But these showed one happy difference. These displayed more emotion and better technique than anything she'd ever done. The artist's maturity and sensitivity shone through every one. Away from Vaughn's influence she'd been allowed to grow. If only she'd known years ago the effect leaving him would have on her.

"I didn't bring you here to show you those, either," Sam said from right behind her.

She turned to him, confused. He put a pile of books into her arms. "You had plenty of money of your own, from the paintings and from these."

"What?" She looked at the books. Children's books, all of them, written and illustrated by Amy Delaney. She looked at him. "I wrote these?"

She'd never told anyone, not one person, her secret desire. From the moment she'd read her first book, she'd wanted to write them for herself. But she'd learned early to keep whatever hopes she had hidden. Terrified she'd be laughed at, she'd buried this hope so deep that she'd forgotten it herself. Until she fell and hit her head.

"When did I start writing these?"

"You were in the hospital for a while after that first fall. You used to sneak down to the children's ward to tell them stories. One of the candy stripers, who had several younger brothers and sisters, heard the stories and started copying them down. She gave them to you the day you left the hospital."

"What a wonderful thing to do." It amazed her she'd had that kind of effect on another person. When she'd learned about Vaughn's infidelities, she hadn't been able to find one person willing to lend a shoulder or a hand.

"When the first book got published you dedicated it to her, and gave her half the advance."

"I did that?" The employees at Advon had called her dragon lady behind her back.

He nodded. "After we brought you home, you asked us to get you some art supplies so you could illustrate them. It took six months to sell the first one, but after that there wasn't a problem at all. The books are immensely popular. You have another due in April."

So the money hadn't come from the stash she'd stolen from Vaughn. She wished she could remember the thrill of selling that first book. She took the books over to a long table and started to look through them. "Who's us?"

Sam joined her. "What?"

"You said I asked 'us' to get art supplies."

"Oh, Casey and me.' He settled into the chair next to her.

"I lived with both of you." He'd said something of the sort when they'd arrived, she now remembered, hating the fact her head was still fuzzy. Would she ever be normal?

"Yeah." He cut into her thoughts with a grin. "We chaperoned each other."

The picture that conjured up made her laugh. "Are you telling me you two needed to be chaperoned?"

"Are you kidding? Bringing a beautiful...addled... young woman into the house puts ideas in a man's head," he teased.

"I can imagine," she said primly. "But I refuse to believe I was ever *addled*."

"Well, that's true." He grinned. "You did choose to fall in love with me, after all."

Unable to resist, she grinned back, then because she felt suddenly shy returned her gaze to the book.

"Are you hungry?"

She looked up and smiled. "Now that you mention it."

He stood. "I'll go make some sandwiches."

"Do you want some help?"

"Nah, you go ahead and look at your books. This is as good a place for you to rest as any."

Because she did feel a little tired, she didn't argue. The house wasn't going to disappear. She had plenty of time to explore. For now, she would content herself with looking at her youthful dream come true.

One by one, she looked through the four books Sam had given her. Each page she turned, each drawing she studied told her more about the woman she'd been during the past three years.

Fanciful creatures danced across the pages and, surely, into children's hearts. The characters were depicted in fairy-tale illustrations with a delicacy of technique and a lightness of spirit that made her envy the self she didn't remember.

Amy Delaney had been a relaxed, happy person, eager to share that happiness with others. Clearly, the amnesia had been the best thing that ever happened to her.

Too bad she'd had to wake up.

The thought made her want to cry. There was so much

uncertainty now. What would happen to her? Would she be able to be as happy now as she was as Amy? Or would knowledge of the past interfere?

"Here we go." Sam entered the room carrying a tray laden with food. He set it on the table. "Turkey and avocado on twelve-grain bread okay with you?"

Adrienne pushed away her thoughts. Sam deserved for her to make an effort. "Sounds great."

She reached for one of the plates. Even if the food hadn't been her favorite, she wouldn't have turned it down. For the last half hour, her stomach had growled like an angry lion.

Sam took the other plate and sat down opposite her. He popped the top on a can of caffeine-free cola and handed it to her. "I guess even amnesia can't fool the body when it comes to food preferences."

"Did I know which foods I liked and didn't like?" she asked, then took a bite of her sandwich. Her favorite sandwich and soda seemed to indicate she did.

He shook her head. "No, but once you tasted something, you reacted immediately. Sometimes you only had to smell the aroma to know."

"It must have been interesting the first time I tasted coffee." She loved the smell, hated the taste.

He smiled. "You looked like a six year old who'd just been tricked into taking a mouthful of spinach."

"I love spinach."

He turned up his nose. "I know. You make me eat it once a month, whether I want to or not."

As they ate their lunch, they discussed food likes and dislikes. Adrienne felt strange sitting there, conversing in such a casual, familiar way. Sam listened to her opinions and made her laugh. She and Vaughn had never shared a meal without him silencing her with his sarcastic comments, made under the guise of sophistication.

Unwillingly, she thought of Vaughn now. He'd been her husband. She'd loved him, then she'd hated him. Even that emotion had cooled once she'd realized that the man she thought she knew had turned into a loathsome stranger. Now, knowing what he'd done, knowing what he was capable of doing again, she despised and feared him.

That fear didn't make her proud. She should have had the courage to turn him in the moment she realized she had proof of his crimes. Unfortunately, the memory of their last encounter had stopped her.

She shivered, remembering how cold his eyes had been, almost inhuman. "If you ever breathe a word of what you just heard," he'd whispered in a voice as bleak as a Siberian winter, "I'll kill you."

"A penny for your thoughts."

She jerked at the sound of Sam's voice, as warm and caring as Vaughn's had been cold and cruel. She forced a smile. "Sorry." Sell her dark thoughts to him? Not on your life. She was safe here in California. If Vaughn hadn't found her by now, he never would. Once she got some time to herself, she'd turn the tape and the money over to a private detective to take care of. Sam would never have to know.

"Hey! Where are you?"

Bringing her attention back to him, she tried to think of an excuse for her silence. "I'm in awe," she said finally. "I just can't believe I sold four books in the last two and a half years."

"Six, including the one coming out."

She glanced at the pile of books. "But there are only four here."

"Really?" He got up and walked over to a bookshelf beside the door. He searched for a moment. "Here it is." He took the book out, then walked over and laid it on the table in front of her. "This one was just released last week."

She read the title. *The Little Cabin in the Woods*. Then she saw the picture on the cover. *Oh my God*. She leafed quickly through the inside illustrations. *Oh my God*. She turned back to the title page. With dread, she read the publisher's name.

She wasn't safe. She wasn't safe at all.

Chapter Five

"Sam, could you…" In spite of her effort to remain calm, words caught in her throat. She cleared it, then started again. "Could you show me where the bedroom is? I'd like to lie down."

"Are you all right?" Sam dropped to his knees at her side and smoothed her hair from her face.

She flinched from his touch, then immediately felt guilty. Sam was a good, caring man who only wanted to protect the woman he loved. To hold the truth back from him seemed cruel. But not as cruel as Vaughn would be if he found out about Sam. He wouldn't hesitate for a moment to take advantage of that vulnerability. He might even…no, it was too horrible to contemplate!

"Adrienne?"

She looked at him, regretted the concern on his face. She had caused this. She had run away from one man and into the arms of another. If she had gone to the police immediately, Sam never would have been involved. He didn't deserve the trouble knowing her would bring. "I'm sorry."

He smiled gently. "For what?"

For hurting you, she thought. But she wouldn't say the words out loud. Sam wasn't dumb. He'd be sure to question a statement like that.

"Honey? What's wrong?"

She shook her head. She knew she'd eventually have to tell him about the horrors he might have to face, but not now. She forced a smile. "Nothing's wrong. I'm just tired."

"Of course you are." He helped her up. "Come on, the bedroom's right next door." He led her out to the hall. Immediately to the right was another door. He opened it, then guided her into a large room almost entirely encased in glass.

She stood and stared in awe at the most beautiful room she'd ever seen. Curtains were unnecessary. Foliage from trees and shrubs ensured their privacy. The canopied queen-size bed had been fashioned out of willow branches and draped with lace. White eyelet throw pillows embroidered with wildflowers every color of the rainbow graced the snow-white bedspread.

"A bed for a princess," she said softly, quoting the first fairy tale she'd ever written as a fanciful ten year old. In spite of her amnesia, parts of her old self had remained. First the cabin, now this. She'd remembered her dreams, but not the danger that threatened her.

Not too smart for someone who prided herself on being a survivor. But the intervening years must have been pretty wonderful if Sam had always been this romantic.

She looked at him. Tall, handsome, ruggedly built *and* sentimental, he was the man of her dreams. Suddenly, waking up seemed more a nightmare than ever. It must have seemed so to him, too. The woman who'd inspired this had disappeared, possibly never to return.

In just a few hours, Sam's life had changed completely. She knew the feeling intimately. Empathy swept over her. It made her want to hug him, as he'd done with her, and tell *him* everything would be all right.

Unfortunately, it might not be true.

Instead, she touched his arm and smiled up at him. "You had this bed designed for me, didn't you?"

He nodded, his eyes bright with emotion. "For your wedding present."

"Thank you." No one had ever done anything like that for her. It touched her heart that this man cared so much. And it made her even more determined to protect him.

It was odd, she thought, this feeling of wanting to keep someone safe.

Sam cleared his throat. "You'll probably want to get out of your clothes. The closet's through here."

She followed him through a doorway that led to a short hall in which there were two more doors. He opened one. "This is the closet. The other door leads to the bathroom."

The large walk-in closet held both his clothes and hers. None of them looked familiar, and once again it hit her that she'd been living a completely different life for three years. Would she ever remember those years?

"Do you want me to help you?" Sam asked from behind her.

She turned to him. His face showed a tinge of red indicating his embarrassment.

"You just look so tired."

She smiled. "It's okay, Sam. I realize you've probably helped me undress hundreds of times."

"I didn't mean...I wouldn't..." He took a breath. "Maybe I should just leave. Call me if you need anything."

He almost ran from the room. Adrienne couldn't help grinning after him.

Moving as fast as her exhausted body would allow, she took off the boots she wore, then stripped off the rest of her clothes. Standing naked, she caught sight of herself in a full-length mirror. Feeling a little curious, she searched her reflection for changes.

The last three years had brought many things to her life, including pregnancy. A warm glow began at that thought. A baby. Had she begun to show yet? She turned sideways, looking for any deviation from her normally flat tummy. She thought she saw some. Her breasts certainly looked fuller. But it could be her imagination.

Laughing at herself, she turned from the mirror to find something to wear. A baby. Who would have thought? She'd always wanted children. But she'd soon learned that Vaughn was too much of a workaholic to be a good father. She'd hoped that would change after the business became a success. It hadn't. So she'd taken birth control pills until the day she left him.

Thank heavens, he had no claim to this child.

Finding a warm-looking, long-sleeved nightgown, made of a soft emerald green material, she removed it from its hanger and slipped it on. She hung up the clothes she'd taken off, then went back into the bedroom.

Her breath caught as she once again took in the beautiful bed Sam must have designed from her description. She gently set aside the lovingly embroidered throw pillows, wondering who had spent so much time on them. She'd always wanted to learn embroidery. It was an old-fashioned craft, conjuring up images of less stressful times. Not at all suited to the ambitious career woman she'd been.

She pulled back the quilt and climbed into bed. In spite of her fatigue, she couldn't relax enough to sleep. The fear that Vaughn would find her overrode everything else, including her pregnancy.

Vaughn could be looking for her even now. Their advertising firm had handled quite a few projects for Wishing Starr, the company that had published her children's books. She had no hope that Vaughn wouldn't know it was her grandparents' cabin. Her grandfather's talent as a woodcarver would be easily recognizable to Vaughn. He would be elated to learn she'd been practically under his nose all this time.

Her thoughts in turmoil, she lay staring up at the branches of the trees through the glass. It seemed as if they'd been woven with the willow branches of the bed. Watching a blue jay hop from tree to tree, she felt as if she floated above the world in a tree house built just for her.

If only it could be that easy.

With a sigh, she closed her eyes. But, still, her exhaustion brought no sleep. She had to protect Sam and the baby. She had to find a way to turn Vaughn in to the police before he found them.

But how? Three years had passed. He could have covered his involvement in the money-laundering scheme by now. But would he? As arrogant as he was, wouldn't he keep on going, figuring he had nothing to fear from her, that she'd been too cowardly to tell the police what she knew?

She sat up abruptly. The tape! How could she have been so stupid? The tape would give enough cause for the police to investigate. All she had to do was turn it over.

Thank God, she'd been smart enough to pay five years' fees on that safe-deposit box. She didn't want to think what would have happened to the evidence if she hadn't been there to pay the fee.

First thing tomorrow she'd go get the tape. The sooner she got things going, the safer her family would be.

Her family. The feeling of elation she'd felt briefly before returned. That's what Sam and the baby were. Her family. She might not remember the beginning of the relationship, but that didn't mean it was any less legal. Did it? She'd have to ask Sam.

Sleepiness began to creep over her. A family. She and Vaughn had never been a family, though that was what she'd started out wanting. It hadn't taken long to find out Vaughn had no such intention. He hadn't needed her. All he'd needed was his money and his power.

Well, soon he'd lose those, too. Tomorrow she would take the key and go down to the bank and… The key! On the brink of sleep, she was suddenly wide awake. Where was it? She hadn't seen it for three years. She didn't even know where to start looking.

She threw back the covers and sat on the edge of the bed. Where was the key? She tried to think back to the day she'd rented the safe-deposit box. Nothing came. She knew she would have wanted to put the key somewhere safe.

She picked up a pillow and hugged it tightly, trying to concentrate. What had she done that day? What had she worn?

Jeans, she knew. Vaughn had loathed them. She'd worn them in defiance. A sweater. It had been autumn, a chilly day. What color was the sweater? Green? No, blue, she thought in triumph, aquamarine. The jeans had been black.

She closed her eyes, trying to picture herself. That's right, black. They'd matched her jacket.

Oh my God, the jacket! She jumped from the bed. Nausea and dizziness came at her like a buzzing locomotive. She fell into a black hole.

SAM RAN WATER in the kitchen sink, glad to have something to do. If he hadn't been so worried about leaving Amy alone, he would have used the time to start clearing the vegetable plot she'd made him promise to work on the minute he got back from the trade show. She'd been adamant about them growing their own fruit and vegetables, so they could make baby food.

He put the dishes in to soak and wondered if *Adrienne* would still be interested in canning their own baby food.

As a partner in an advertising agency, he doubted she'd spent much time in the kitchen.

As Amy, she'd spent a great deal of time cooking. Could a woman really change that much? he thought as he moved to put away the items left from lunch.

The counter was dotted with mayonnaise and avocado and crumbs. Seeing it, he had to smile. That was something he and Amy had always had in common, he thought as he wrung out a sponge. Whether they were preparing a simple lunch or a five-course meal, they always left the kitchen a big mess.

Not that they'd minded. It had been just as much fun to clean up as it had been to dirty the place. But it had driven Casey crazy. He was one of those "neat" cooks. He would make some woman very happy one day.

The phone rang. Throwing the sponge into the sink, Sam answered. "Hello."

"Hi, big brother. How's it going?"

Sam smiled. "Well, speak of the devil."

"You two must be bored if you're discussing me."

"Am…Adrienne's napping." The name took some getting used to, but that's what she preferred. "I was just thinking how happy you'd make some woman someday."

Casey snorted. "Now you're starting to sound like Mom. I'll tell you what I told her. Don't hold your breath."

Sam laughed. He'd said the same thing, about a week before he almost ran over Amy. "Did you find out anything else?"

"I tried to call the private detective, but all I keep hearing are busy signals."

"Well, keep trying. The more I know about this guy, the easier it will be to protect her." Just the thought of having to protect her made him angry. What kind of man would instill such fear into his wife that she'd run so far away?

"Believe me," Casey said, "I'm sticking to the phone. I've seen too many of these domestic situations go bad. Last week we had to book a woman for attempted murder of her husband, even though he'd been beating her for years."

"Thanks, little brother, that's just what I needed to hear."

"It won't do either of you any good to hide your head in the sand, Sam."

Sam just stopped himself from snapping back. His brother was right. "Believe me, Casey. I've considered every possibility."

"Good. I'll let you know as soon as I know anything else. And you do the same."

"I will, but I can't push her to tell me, Casey. She's too fragile right now. And if I upset her, she might run again." From him, this time. He couldn't stand the thought of it.

"Just play it by ear, big brother. I'll be in touch."

"All right, I'll talk to you later."

He hung up the phone feeling more unsettled than ever. The thought of anyone trying to hurt Amy scared him to death. He turned and walked out of the kitchen. He had to check on her. Now.

Opening the door slowly so the hinge wouldn't squeak, he peeked in. The bed was empty. "Adrienne?" He moved into the room.

Then he saw her. She lay crumpled beside the bed, unconscious. "Amy!" Alarm raged through him though the doctor had warned him she might feel dizzy. Wanting to kick himself for leaving her alone, he scooped her gently into his arms and laid her on the bed.

Once he had her settled, he talked to her quietly until

she opened her eyes. Her gaze unfocused, she struggled against him.

"Relax, honey, you fainted. You need to stay still."

His calm tone didn't have the affect he'd hoped for.

She continued to struggle. "Let me go. I need to find it. I need…" Her voice was weak, almost inaudible.

He put his arms around her and felt her trembling. "I'm here, sweetheart. I'll take care of you." He leaned back to look at her. "Can you tell me what happened?"

There was a strange look on her face, as if she'd just realized who he was. She moved out of his arms to lean against the pillows. He could almost feel her withdraw emotionally. "I guess I got up too fast."

"Did you need something?"

"Just some water. I was thirsty," she answered quickly.

Too quickly, he thought. The suspicious response galled him. They'd been together for three years, and he'd never felt an inkling of suspicion. Now he wanted to question everything she said.

He rose from the bed. "I'll get you some now." He walked out of the room to the kitchen. Adrienne was lying. He took a bottle from the refrigerator and poured the water into a glass. After all these years, she was lying to him. He put the bottle back into the fridge. Why, damn it?

He strode back to their room, moved to the side of the bed and stopped. She lay with her eyes closed, her golden hair fanned out on the white pillowcase, her cheeks flushed pink from tears. All his anger died.

She looked just like the illustrations of Sleeping Beauty he remembered from his childhood. He wanted to kiss her awake. He wanted her to look at him with recognition in her eyes. He wanted her to remember everything about her past and their life together.

He set the glass on the bedside table and sat on the edge of the bed. Adrienne didn't stir. He decided not to disturb her slumber. The doctor had told him sleep would be the best thing for her. So, he would be patient. It wasn't easy, when just two days ago they'd been laughing and loving together and making wonderful plans for their child's future.

With a sigh, he rose from the bed and left the room, promising himself it wouldn't be for long. He had a couple of phone calls to make, then he would begin his all-night vigil. He had no intention of letting her out of his sight for more than a few minutes at a time.

NIGHTMARE IMAGES flashed across her brain like a strobe light gone crazy. Eyes of arctic gray, icy as a glacier, yet hot with the fires of hell. Vaughn smiling a smile that wasn't a smile at all. Vaughn laughing with no humor. Vaughn threatening. "I'll kill you. I'll kill you. I'LL KILL YOU!"

She wanted to scream, but she couldn't make a sound. If she did, she'd give away her hiding place. She had to be quiet. She had to move, to run. Too late! He caught her. "Sign this paper. Sign it!"

She did what he said. She had to. Then she'd run. Vaughn laughed. "Watch your back, Adrienne. You never know when I'll be there. You'll never be safe again."

"Never be safe, never be safe." This time the words were hers. She was running, running, and then there were lights attacking her, blinding her. She screamed. She had to find it. She had to keep the baby safe.

"Adrienne." Hands grabbed her arms, shaking her slightly. Oh, God, he'd caught her. She screamed and screamed. "Adrienne, it's Sam! Wake up, darling. You're having a nightmare."

She opened her eyes, the nightmare still with her. Those eyes, so cold, so malevolent. Nothing like Sam's. Sam's were warm, blue as a sunlit sea. He wasn't Vaughn. He wouldn't hurt her. He would help her.

She grasped his arms. Under his sweater, they felt so solid, so strong. "Sam! You have to find the jacket. I need it. You have to find it!"

"Jacket? Adrienne, honey, what's wrong? What's scaring you so much?"

Releasing her tight hold, she took a deep breath, trying to calm herself. But her heart raced as if she were still running. The fright was too close, too real. If Vaughn saw the illustration he'd know where to find her. She had to keep her family safe. "The jacket, Sam. I need the jacket I was wearing the night of the accident. Do you have it?"

"Honey, you need to rest. We'll find it in the morning." He smoothed back her hair with gentle hands, making her feel coddled and safe. But she knew the feeling wouldn't last. As long as Vaughn stayed out of prison, her family was in jeopardy. She couldn't just go back to sleep as if the whole nightmare had never happened.

"I need it now, Sam." When he seemed reluctant, she didn't blame him. He probably thought she'd gone crazy. "I promise I'll go back to sleep as soon as I have it in my hands."

"Adrienne…"

She gazed into his eyes, letting the urgency he must see there convince him. *"Please."*

"All right, I'll find it, but I wish you'd tell me why it's so important. You don't remember our life together, but you can trust me, sunshine."

Words from the past intruded. *"You can trust me, Adrienne. I promise I won't ever hurt you."* Spoken on her wedding day, she'd soon had cause to regret believing them.

It wasn't fair to put Sam in the same category as

Vaughn. Sam had been nothing but kind and caring. She knew she should explain.

Yet, she couldn't bring herself to do it. "Everything is so unfamiliar," she told him finally. "I just need something from my past to hold on to."

He gave her a sad smile. "I guess I can't blame you for that. You must be feeling a little like Alice in the looking glass."

He rose from the bed and went to the closet.

Coward, she berated herself. Just like Vaughn predicted. *"You're too much of a coward to go to the police. If you do, you know what will happen. No one in the world will be able to keep you safe. And if they try..."*

Sam would try. And he'd be hurt. But if she could handle things herself, Vaughn would never have to know about her new husband. Or her child.

Sam walked back into the room carrying a flowered storage box. He set it on the foot of the bed and took off the lid. "We put everything you had with you that night in here. The psychiatrist suggested you look at them every now and then to see if they brought back any memories."

She moved over to look in the box that had held all she had known of her past for the last three years. She took out the aqua sweater, black jeans and matching jacket that spoke of her defiance toward Vaughn.

He'd hated denim, so when she'd seen the outfit, she'd bought it. He'd hated California, so that's where she'd headed, in as roundabout a route as she could manage.

In spite of his cruel prediction, she'd been proud of the intelligence and courage she'd shown in avoiding his every trap. Then she'd lost her memory and set her own trap, by remembering a small cabin in the woods.

She ran her hands over the jacket, feeling for the small bump that would prove the safe-deposit key was safe and sound. When she felt it, she held in her sigh of relief.

She glanced up at Sam, who was looking at her with curiosity and concern clear on his face. "Thank you." It wasn't enough to express her gratitude, but any more would make him suspicious.

There was a strained silence, as if he wanted to say something, then he smiled. "You're welcome." Leaving the jacket with her, he put the other garments in the box, replaced the lid and set it at the end of the bed. "Now, will you get some sleep?"

She returned his smile. "Yes, sir." She lay back under the covers, taking the jacket with her.

He moved to her side, then bent down and gave her a soft kiss on the cheek. "Good night, sunshine."

The kiss made her skin tingle, a pleasant sensation she thought she could get used to. "Good night, Sam."

He turned and walked over to a sky-blue club chair with matching ottoman and settled himself in it.

She frowned. "You aren't sleeping there, are you?"

"I want to be close in case you need something."

So that was how he'd come to her so quickly when she'd screamed. "How can you sleep? It's way too small for you."

"I'm fine, sunshine. Quit worrying."

She couldn't. It wasn't fair to make him spend the night in a chair, when he was obviously used to sleeping with her in this wonderful bed. The thought made her feel nervous and excited at the same time. Before she could lose her nerve, she said, "This bed is more than big enough for the both of us."

He sat up. "Are you sure?"

She licked her suddenly dry lips. "Well, we *are* married."

He looked at her closely. A strange expression crossed his face, there for a moment then gone. "I'm still a stranger to you. If it's too awkward…"

"I'll manage," she said. It was nice of him not to push it. "As long as you're going to be keeping watch over me, the least I can do is let you do it comfortably."

"That's the best offer I've had all day." He got up and moved back to the bed. "You want to close your eyes?"

She blinked. "Why?"

"Because if I'm going to lie under the covers, I should probably take off my pants."

Her first reaction was to say no, she didn't want to close her eyes. After all, it would be her first look at the husband she hadn't known she'd married.

Embarrassed by the thought, she looked the other way. She waited until she felt his weight hit the bed and the shift of the quilt covering him before she turned back. He'd taken off his sweater as well as his jeans and was lying against the pillows grinning at her.

She scowled at him. "What are you smiling about?"

"I was just thinking what an interesting situation this is, having the woman I've shared a bed with for two years suddenly acting like a virgin on her wedding night."

She turned to lie the other way with a flounce. "Just don't go getting any ideas." Immediately, she wanted to kick herself. She sounded exactly like what he'd accused her of.

Sam moved to lie against her, putting a possessive arm around her waist. "Believe me, sunshine, any ideas I have have been there since the first day we met. It will take several more lifetimes together to get rid of them."

"Sam…"

He kissed the side of her neck. "Go to sleep, sweetheart. I'm not going to do anything about them tonight."

Surprised by the luscious feeling that had gone through her at the touch of his lips, Adrienne found herself wondering, long after Sam had gone to sleep, what it would have felt like if he'd done more.

HOURS LATER, Adrienne woke to a morning as peaceful as she'd ever known. The fog and the forest had muted the sun's light to a soft dove gray. No traffic outside, no jet engines overhead, not even the chirp of a small bird intruded on the silvery silence of her fairy-tale bedroom.

The quiet unnerved her. She was used to noise, people yelling, doors slamming, the constant bustle of the city. The silence made her think.

Actually, it made her want to stop thinking.

It made her want to lie here in this warm bed, with her husband's strong arms wrapped around her and the tiny baby growing in her womb, and forget everything she ever knew about Vaughn Winston.

Sam's breath stirred her hair, his chest rose and fell evenly against her back, and she felt comforted. It would be so easy to sink into the love Sam seemed so eager to give.

And it would be so foolish.

She slipped carefully from Sam's arms to sit on the edge of the bed. A coward she might have been, but never a fool. Vaughn was a problem that wouldn't go away without a fight. And she had every intention of seeing him put in prison where he belonged.

Spying her jacket on the floor where it had fallen during the night, she bent to pick it up. The action caused no dizziness, making her feel more confident. She rose from the bed, slowly, not wanting to push her luck. Then she made her way to the bathroom, taking the jacket with her.

Her head still ached, but she decided to chance a shower anyway. Sam wouldn't approve, but the sooner she returned to normal the better.

She stood under the spray, eyes closed, willing the warm water to wash away the headache and fatigue left over from her stay in the hospital. She needed all the strength she could muster.

Her stomach growled, reminding her that her first order of business should be to feed her baby. Poor little thing hadn't eaten since lunch yesterday. Its mommy had slept away the afternoon and the entire night.

Smiling at the thought of being anyone's mother, she turned off the water and wrapped a large blue towel around her damp body. Tucking the end between her breasts, she stepped out of the shower. The jacket she'd dropped on the floor caught her eye.

Her stomach growled again. She patted it gently. "Breakfast will have to wait a few minutes, little one. I have something to do first."

She searched some drawers until she found a pair of nail scissors. Sitting cross-legged on the soft blue carpet that covered the bathroom floor, she carefully picked at the stitches that had held her secret for the past three years. Once loosened, she took out the fabric-wrapped key and began to unwind the padding.

The key dropped into her hand. The dull brass finish looked pretty much the same as it had the day she'd sewn it into the lining of her jacket.

"What is that?" Sam's voice came from behind her.

Startled, Adrienne dropped the key. It fell to the carpet, landing silently on the plush blue surface.

Chapter Six

This isn't Amy. The thought jolted Sam. Until that moment, he hadn't realized that he'd been denying the differences between the woman he'd married and the woman he'd brought home from the hospital. But there was no denying it now.

Amy's green eyes had never sparked defiance at him. The jut of Adrienne's jaw and the set of her shoulders nearly shouted out courageous obstinacy. This woman would do whatever she needed to do to protect herself.

She picked up the key, closing her fist around it as if it were a talisman. Then she rose to her feet with as much grace and dignity as her slipping towel allowed.

The end that she'd tucked between her breasts loosened, revealing far more of her anatomy than she'd intended. His breath caught as she made a grab for it. Desire blazed. But he quickly tamped it down. Even her actions weren't Amy's. Her movements were quicker, yet more sensual, as if she was aware of the picture she made and had no intention of giving him reason to act on whatever ideas he might have.

This was a woman who had some experience with men. The realization ate at him. His Amy had been a complete innocent. She hadn't been a virgin, of course. But no thoughts of other men had invaded their love life.

Adrienne's glare made him put his speculations away. It was clear their love life was the last thing on her mind.

"So, what's going on?" Sam tried to fill the awkward silence between them.

"It's a key."

Hearing the stubbornness in her voice, he knew he had to step carefully. "I can see that. A safe-deposit key."

Something flashed across her face. Guilt, maybe. He couldn't be sure since it was quickly replaced by her now-familiar obstinacy.

"Do you want to talk about it?" he asked gently. He would have to be an idiot not to know she didn't want to talk about it, but he was curious. And concerned.

"No."

Hurt, he glanced away. Amy had never kept secrets from him. Not deliberately. Unwilling to let it go, he looked at her. "Adrienne, that key must have been pretty important for you to hide it inside your jacket."

"It was...it is." This time she looked away. "I just don't want to talk about it right now."

Sam stepped forward and cupped her cheek. She flinched away. Again, hurt coursed through him. "I understand it's hard for you to trust me. I'm a stranger to you. But I'll do whatever I can to help you, sweetheart."

She gazed at him. The stubborn glare had disappeared. For long moments he thought she might be considering sharing her problems with him. Then a shutter came down. He didn't need words to tell him she'd decided against it. And though he glimpsed a small spark of regret, she said nothing else.

With a sigh, he retreated. "You must be starving. I'll go fix us some breakfast."

In the kitchen, Sam could barely hold himself in. He stormed around the room making breakfast preparations. He slammed drawers, threw mushrooms, peppers and an onion onto the counter, muttering curses all the while, taking out on innocent vegetables and cutlery the frustration he hadn't been able to express to the stranger who now shared his life.

Who was she?

Hurt and anger warred so violently within him, Sam hardly knew where one left off and the other began. Who was this woman who'd taken the place of the woman he loved? Who kept secrets and told lies?

He and Amy had always been completely honest with each other. He'd learned the hard way that lies ravaged a relationship. Was he to learn that lesson all over again? And at whose expense?

As he cut up vegetables, an action he usually found soothing, his mind turned to the not-so-soothing picture of Adrienne trying to keep up a towel that insisted on falling. That emerald green glare of hers had seemed to dare him to try anything. He was glad he'd resisted. Of course he was. But he found the whole thing intriguing. Amy had never challenged him to take her. Yet, it seemed that was exactly what Adrienne had done.

Sam reached for a handful of mushrooms. It felt strange thinking of Adrienne as a separate woman from Amy. But he couldn't deny that she had a mixture of competence and vulnerability he found appealing. Amy had been open and as confident as a child once she'd gotten over her initial fear. Adrienne seemed more grown-up. More womanly. Sexier. The thought stopped him cold. Sexier?

He looked down at the mushrooms he'd nearly pulverized and grumbled in disgust. "You're lucky it wasn't your fingers." He grabbed a bell pepper and started chopping more carefully. But his mind had trouble concentrating on his actions.

Adrienne's refusal to confide in him hadn't doused his passion. She'd treated him like a stranger, pushed his patience to its limit. Yet all he'd wanted was to drag her back to bed right then and there. Once they made love again, she'd remember the fires that burned between them.

The feeling made him uncomfortable. Wanting Adrienne so much seemed almost a betrayal of Amy. He kept telling himself they were the same person, but his reactions to her weren't the same. He slammed the knife on the cutting board. "God, Amy, where are you?"

"I'm right here."

Startled by the sound of her voice, he gazed at the woman who stood on the opposite side of the cooking island. He hoped against hope that her comment meant she'd remembered their life together. But as he took in her outfit of black jeans and blue sweater, he knew he'd hoped in vain.

Her green eyes looked directly at him, but the arms wrapped around her waist betrayed her nervousness. "As hard as it is for me to believe, I know it's true," she continued. "I couldn't spend a half hour in that bedroom without seeing the connection. The clothes are all my size. The decor, the books, the paintings, every one something I would have picked myself. And the bed…"

Sam couldn't help but smile as she trailed off. Maybe their love life wasn't as far from her mind as he thought. He caught her gaze in his, trying silently to let her know he understood. For a moment, a green flame blazed. Then she looked away.

"Anyway," she blurted, "I know that I'm your wife and you're my husband and because you are, there's something you need to know."

The sudden hardness in her voice worried him. "What something?"

She deliberately unclenched her fist and placed the key on the counter. "Right after I arrived in Monterey, I rented a safe-deposit box and put some things in it."

"What *things?*" he prodded gently.

She gripped the edge of the counter. "Would you mind if I had a glass of orange juice? I'm feeling a little light-headed."

"What an idiot I am. Of course." He moved quickly around the counter and guided her to a chair at the antique trestle table they'd given each other for their six-month anniversary. "Sit down. You haven't eaten since yesterday afternoon. Your head must be pounding."

His words must have been spilling over themselves. Adrienne looked at him with a bemused smile. "Slow down, Sam. My head is fine. I'm just hungry."

He shot over to the refrigerator to grab the pitcher of orange juice he'd made earlier, then to a nearby cabinet for a glass. It didn't matter what she called herself. She was still his pregnant wife, and he was doing a pretty lousy job of taking care of her.

"I'm sorry." He handed her the glass. "I'll have your breakfast ready in no time." He rushed back to the refrigerator for eggs and turned so fast one went flying out of his hand onto the flagstone floor. When he stopped to pick it up, another followed, landing on the hard surface with a dull crack.

Adrienne moved over to touch his arm. "Sam, stop! The juice will be fine for now. Keep on at this pace, we won't have any eggs left for breakfast."

Sam looked down at her hand on the sleeve of his sweater and wanted more than anything to drop the rest of the eggs and take her into his arms. The gesture had been automatic for her, the actions of a wife.

Then she took her hand away.

"I'm sorry. You've had so much to deal with, and all I've been thinking about is myself."

He regarded her ruefully. "Breaking eggs on the floor isn't exactly a nervous breakdown."

She smiled. "So, you always do it this way? I know you can't make an omelet without breaking a few eggs, but…"

Unable to help himself, Sam grinned. "That was bad."

The joke eased Sam's tension. "Go drink your juice," he ordered. "I've got a mess to clean up and a meal to prepare."

She gave him an amused look.

"Slowly and with care," he said.

She raised her eyebrows in a comical skepticism.

"I promise," he added.

Adrienne smiled. "All right. As long as you've promised." She walked back to the table and sat down.

Sam grabbed a roll of paper towels and crouched down to wipe up the broken eggs. Thank heavens they'd sealed the stone. Otherwise, there'd be signs of his clumsiness for years to come.

The floor clean, he went back to the refrigerator for more eggs. This time he broke them in a bowl. He glanced over at Adrienne, who sat drinking her juice like a good girl. He waited until she'd emptied half the glass before he spoke again. "Why don't you tell me about this safe-deposit box? What's in it?" He figured it held the papers that would have told them who she was three years ago, had they known it existed.

She took another drink, then set the glass down with more care than was warranted. "Evidence."

That surprised him. "Evidence?"

She nodded.

"You mean of a crime?" She wasn't a criminal. There was no doubt in his mind about that. "Your ex-husband?"

She nodded again.

"Adrienne, you're driving me crazy. Are you going to tell me about it or not?"

After a long pause, she sighed. "I found out not long

before I ran away that Vaughn had been laundering drug money through our agency for a big-time cocaine dealer.''

''Was he arrested?''

She shook her head.

''Why not?''

''Because the only person besides me who knew about it isn't talking.''

''Why not?'' he asked, then it hit him. ''Because he's dead?''

She nodded.

Sam turned off the burner under the omelet pan and moved over to the table. He pulled out the chair next to hers, sat down and put his arm around her, though she gave no indication she'd welcome it. ''Oh, honey, I'm sorry.'' No wonder she'd been so scared. No wonder she'd run away from the hospital. When they mentioned her husband, she must have thought Winston had caught up with her.

''I overheard an argument between Vaughn and his assistant, Barry Owen,'' she continued with terrifying calm. ''Barry was trying to convince Vaughn to call off the deal. He said they'd made enough, that they had to stop before someone found out. He didn't want to spend the rest of his life in prison.''

''Winston didn't go for it, I take it.'' The man must be an idiot, taking a chance like that.

''Vaughn thought he was invincible. It seems he grew up with this dealer. He figured he didn't have anything to worry about.''

''But this assistant thought so?''

She nodded. ''I was scared to death they'd realize I was home, so I didn't hear everything they said. But it sounded like Barry thought they had a good reason to worry. That he knew about someone else who'd been in the same situation and had gotten killed.''

Adrienne rubbed her eyes. "Vaughn laughed, and then he said in the coldest voice I've ever heard, 'Solorio deserved what he got. He was a coward who didn't know how to handle a sweet deal when it was handed to him on a silver platter. He got in their way. Don't you do the same, little boy.'"

"Did you call the police?"

She raised her face to his, her gaze imploring. "They were in the den at home. I ran to the phone. Vaughn must have heard me. He caught me before I could dial the first number." She stopped abruptly, as if it was too painful to continue.

Disgust and anger overwhelmed him, but he knew he had to hold it in check. Adrienne had more to tell him. She had to be his first concern. "You have to tell me, Adrienne. What did he do to you?"

"He didn't have to do anything." Shame filled her voice. "I was so terrified all he had to do was touch me and I fell apart."

"You're too hard on yourself. You'd just heard your husband threaten his assistant."

"He said he'd kill me," she said. The lack of emotion chilled him to the bone.

"Unless I did what he said. No matter where I went he'd find me. I wouldn't even know what hit me."

Sam held her to him. He rubbed her back and made soothing noises, trying to relax the stranglehold she had put on her emotions. She needed to cry. "It's all right, honey. I'm here. I'll take care of you. You can let go now."

She never shed a tear, but gradually she relaxed enough to wrap her arms around him. He never wanted her to let go.

He moved back a little, so he could see her face. "You're safe now, honey. I'll keep you safe."

Her smile held little humor. "That's one of the reasons I didn't tell you immediately. I wanted to keep *you* safe. I thought you'd never have to know about my sordid past."

"Your past isn't sordid. You ex-husband's is." Something she said clicked. "Just how were you going to keep this from me?"

She looked away. He touched her chin and held it so she had to look him in the eye. "Tell me."

She took a breath. "I was going to send the evidence to the police in Boston. Once they find out what kind of man Vaughn is they'll investigate."

As a cop's brother, the plan sounded sort of naive to him, but he refrained from saying so. "What made you change your mind?"

"When I realized the impact my past could have on my new family, I wanted to protect you." She touched her tummy with wonder on her face. "You and the baby. I never felt like that before."

He gave her a gentle smile. "I can understand that. I feel the same way."

"I know. When I refused to answer your questions earlier, you looked so hurt and angry. That's when I realized it wasn't fair to keep this from you. A man has a right to know when his family's in jeopardy."

Her sentiments touched him, but there was something he didn't understand. "Why are you so sure we're in jeopardy? You've been living under a different name for years. Winston probably thinks you've dropped off the face of the earth."

She pushed back her chair and got up. "He won't once he sees the illustration." She walked over to the meal preparations he'd abandoned, turned on the burner, then began to whip the eggs he'd cracked into a copper bowl.

He didn't protest. She seemed to need the action. "What illustration?"

"*The Little Cabin in the Woods.* It belonged to my grandparents."

"So, the cabin's real."

"Vaughn and I spent several weekends there when we were first married." She poured the chopped onion and bell peppers into the pan to sauté them.

"Which means Winston would recognize it if he saw the illustration in the book." There didn't seem much chance of that, he thought.

She added the mushrooms to the mixture. "Not 'if,' *when.*"

"This guy reads children's books?"

She poured the eggs into the pan. "This guys owns an advertising company that does publicity for publishing companies."

That got him moving. In a moment, he was next to her, once again holding her chin so she couldn't look away. "Including your publishing company?"

She nodded. "The only advantage we have is the fact that I've been writing under another name."

He relaxed a little. "Your agent only knows you as Amy Delaney. She's the one who deals with publicity and such. Even if he asked, she wouldn't give away your address."

She turned back to the stove to flip the omelet. She placed the pan back on the burner, then looked at him. "He'll find us."

"He's not omnipotent!"

"No, he's diabolical," she replied in a voice filled with cold fear. "Once he sees that illustration, he'll leave no stone unturned in locating me. I'm the only thing standing between him and twenty-five years to life."

"He can't…"

"He can." Absolute confidence radiated from her.

"He's cold and calculating and..." She threw down the spatula and moved away from the stove.

He reached over to turn off the burner. Adrienne had gone to stand by the large window that looked out on the forest, with the blue of the bay beyond. He walked over to stand behind her. "And?"

"Ruthless."

The hardness in her voice hurt him. He'd had no idea his wife had been through so much. "What did he do to you?" he asked again, sure there were volumes she hadn't told him.

She gazed out at the trees. "I already told you he didn't do anything to me. He didn't have to."

Something in the way she said it gave him a clue he couldn't quite grasp. "Then he did do something..." He grasped her shoulders and turned her around to face him. "You said you were the only one between Winston and prison. What about this assistant you heard him talking to?"

"He can't do anything."

The finality in her statement raised the hairs on the back of his neck. "Why not?"

"He's dead. I told you that before."

"You think Winston did it?"

She went into his arms. "I don't know. I'll never know. It might have been suicide. That's what the authorities found as the cause of death."

"But you believe differently?"

She nodded against his chest. "Right after I heard the news on TV, I got a phone call from Vaughn."

"What did he say?"

She gazed up at him, her eyes wide with a horror he couldn't imagine. "'You have your proof now, don't you?' I left town the next day."

Just a few words, Sam thought. That's all it had taken

for the devil to make her believe that he would kill her if she went to the police. The terror she'd felt must have had something to do with her forgetting her past so thoroughly.

Until a knock on the head brought it rushing back.

Anger and fear washed over him. He wanted to find Vaughn Winston and beat him within an inch of his life. In all his years, he'd never felt the need for vengeance.

Afraid his feelings would spill over, he turned from Adrienne and walked back to the stove. "Let's eat breakfast."

Silence reigned for a few minutes as he divided the omelet between their two plates, popped some bread into the toaster and filled two glasses with milk.

"Is that all you can say?" Adrienne's incredulous voice finally accused.

He buttered the toast, put one slice on each plate, then carried their breakfast over to the table before he dared look at her.

She stood gazing at him with an expression that tore at his heart, the hurt look of someone who'd just been betrayed. "No, honey, there's a lot I can say. And obviously a lot more you have to tell me." She jerked at that. She still didn't realize he knew her better than anyone else could. Not knowing her past had never mattered to him. She was his other half. As Amy she had known that. As Adrienne she would have to learn. "Sit down. We can talk while we eat."

She didn't move. "But I'm—"

"Stop right there." He went over to her and guided her to her seat. "It doesn't matter whether you're hungry or not. My appetite seems to have disappeared, too."

Seeing the look on her face, he regretted his disclosure. He recognized guilt when he saw it and had no intention of letting her feel responsible for her demon of an exhusband. He grinned to lighten the mood. "But since you have to eat, I'm going to make the ultimate sacrifice and join you.''

Adrienne forced a smile at his jest. "Some sacrifice. I'm the best omelet maker east of the Mississippi."

He pulled out her chair, then kissed her on the cheek. "West, too."

Adrienne's reluctance to eat didn't last past the first bite. She obviously hadn't lost her touch when it came to omelets. Where before she'd wondered about the differences between herself and the woman she'd been the last three years, now she wondered at the similarities. They said alcohol couldn't alter your true self, maybe amnesia worked the same way.

She and Sam ate in companionable silence, both hungry in spite of the emotions that had filled up the morning. After eating everything on her plate, she pushed it away and picked up her glass of milk.

"Did you want more toast?" Sam asked.

She almost said yes. Her emotions had calmed during the past few minutes. Another piece of toast would prolong the moment she had to stir them up again.

Unfortunately, she couldn't eat another bite. "No, thanks. But I could get you some." She went to stand, but Sam stopped her, circling her wrist with two fingers.

"Relax, sweetheart, I'm fine."

Relax? He had to be kidding. "Sam—"

"Adrienne," he interrupted gently. "I know this is difficult. You must feel like you're reliving your past. But I need to know the rest of the story. Otherwise I can't fight this guy."

Sam fight Vaughn? The very thought filled her with horror. She pulled her arm from his hold. "I don't want you to fight him, Sam. You have to stay away from him."

Vaughn was vicious enough to use Sam for revenge

against her. He wouldn't even care how much he hurt Sam in the process.

Sam reached out to touch her hand. "Adrienne—"

"No!" She pulled away. "You can't say something like that then pet me like a child. You have to promise to stay away from him."

"You're overreacting, sweetheart. I'm not planning to go out and beat up the guy."

But she could see from his expression that was exactly what he wanted to do. "Vaughn will be turned over to the police."

"Of course he will."

The firmness in his voice didn't fool her for a minute. "You have to promise, Sam, or I'll handle everything myself."

That shook him. "I'll be damned if I'll let you go up against a monster like that."

"You won't have a choice if you don't promise to stay away from him." She wouldn't have Sam hurt. He'd loved and taken care of her for three years. Even if she couldn't remember those years, she knew how precious that kind of commitment was. And how lucky she'd been to fall into this man's life.

He glared at her for a full minute. "What if he shows up on our doorstep?"

"He won't." Her tone had been as confident as she could make it. Quite an accomplishment since Vaughn showing up was exactly what she feared most.

She looked at Sam, who seemed to be in the middle of some inner struggle. "Sam?"

Her voice spurred him to action. He stood and started clearing the table. "You're right," he said. "He won't. Because as soon as you're ready, we're going down to the bank to retrieve your evidence, and then we're going to take it to Casey."

"Casey?" She got up and took her dish and glass over to the sink. "Why would we involve your brother?"

"He's a cop, remember?"

No, she didn't remember. That was the hell of it. She'd finally regained her memory only to forget everything she'd known the past three years. She watched Sam move around the kitchen. Already she felt close to him, but she suspected that was more in reaction to his protectiveness than any residual memory of their marriage.

Oh well, she thought, once they got Vaughn out of the picture, she'd feel more relaxed. Maybe then she'd be able to concentrate on the man she'd married, instead of the man who'd filled her life with fear.

"I think that's good enough for now."

Deep in thought, Adrienne started at the sound of Sam's voice. She looked around and saw he'd filled the sink with their dirty dishes, wiped off the counters and put away the bread and butter. She grinned at him. "How nice to have a husband who cleans up after himself."

Rinsing out a sponge, Sam laughed. "If you think this is normal, you certainly don't remember, do you?"

She walked over to him. "What are you saying? That you just did all this to impress me?" Her flirting came as a complete surprise to herself. After all Vaughn put her through, she'd thought she'd lost any bit of playfulness she'd once had.

Blue eyes twinkling with laughter, he put his hands on her waist. "Of course, it's not every day a guy gets a chance to impress the woman who's come to know him as a complete slob."

"Oh, I doubt that," she said and meant it. There was something about Sam that told her his protectiveness wasn't something new. "You're just not the type of man to turn his beloved wife into a drudge."

He laughed, a little awkwardly, she thought. It seemed

Sam wasn't as confident as he tried to appear, which made her feel bad. The man didn't deserve to have his life turned upside down like this.

"You wouldn't have let me if I tried," he continued. "One thing you made very clear to me and Casey when you moved in was that just because you were a woman didn't mean you were going to act like a live-in maid... What's wrong?"

Boy, the man didn't miss a thing. He'd notice the change in her expression immediately. "Nothing," she told him. "It's just that that sounds so much like me."

He pulled her to him and gave her a quick hug. "Well, of course it does. You might have forgotten your past, but that doesn't mean you changed your basic personality."

She shook off the strange feeling that had come over her at the sound of her own words. Words she'd spoken in just that way several years ago. "So, it never occurred to you I might be a serial killer or a drunk or something."

He lifted her chin so she had to look him in the eye. "It occurred to me that you were the woman I'd been waiting for my whole life and I'd be nuts not to hold on to you."

His eyes glowed with an intensity that scared and excited her at the same time. Slowly, he lowered his mouth to hers. She knew she could back away. But a strange trembling that began deep inside her signaled the basic anticipation a woman felt when the right man touched her. His kiss began gently, a sweet caressing movement that asked politely to continue his exploration.

She couldn't have said anything but yes. Warmth poured through her as his tongue traced the outline of her lips, then dipped inside to taste, to touch, to explore. Curious, her hands reached up, almost of their own accord, to caress his softly whiskered cheek. Her fingertips tingled with sensation. He pulled her closer, his hands at her back, molding her body to his.

Curiosity turned into voracious need. Her fingers buried in his hair, she pulled him into a deeper kiss, devouring and begging to be devoured. He answered her invitation by taking possession of her mouth in a kiss that seared her with its burning mastery. She met fire with fire, giving as good as she got, challenging him and being challenged, loving and being loved.

"No, stop!" The words tore from her lips, wrenching her heart with their denial.

Sam held her hard against him, his face buried in her hair, his breath coming in strangled gasps. "Sam, please…"

"I will…I will…I just need to hold you for a minute." The harsh words grated in her ears, building her guilt to towering proportions.

"I'm sorry." How awful to call a halt during such an emotional moment. "I shouldn't have pushed you."

Sam gave a short laugh, then set her away from him. "Pushed me? Surely you know that all it takes is a glance from your emerald green eyes to put me over the edge."

Her feeling of gratification couldn't be denied. The passion Sam had felt for her hadn't changed when her memory had returned. All the trouble with Vaughn had been as nothing to the feeling between them. It would be so easy to lose herself in the life she'd made as Sam's wife. But… "We can't do this, Sam. We can't hide away like newlyweds who don't have a care in the world. Vaughn is out there, waiting. He won't care that we've found each other. He'd laugh at the very thought that you might love me."

'There is no *might*," Sam said. "I do love you."

"It doesn't matter."

The hurt expression on his face ripped her heart in two.

"Don't you understand! It can't matter. Nothing matters until we put that man behind bars. If we don't, we'll be dead!" All the emotion she'd been holding inside came rushing at her like a flash flood, and she broke down.

Sam pulled her back to his arms. No matter how she fought he wouldn't let go. "Listen to me, sunshine. We aren't going to die. We're going to get our jackets, get in the car and go to the bank. Then we'll go see Casey. He's a good cop. He'll handle everything."

She wished she could believe it would be that easy. She wished it with all her heart.

"Come on, sunshine. Go get your jacket." He gave her a gentle shove away from him.

She moved around the counter to where she'd left the key. She stood for a moment, staring at it. "Oh my God."

Sam was beside her in a second. "What's wrong?"

She couldn't take her eyes off the key. "Oh my God."

"Adrienne?"

She picked up the small metal object and held it in her palm. Just a normal safe-deposit key, she thought, turning it over. Nothing written on it but a number. So much for wishes.

"Adrienne, what's wrong?"

The insistence and worry in his voice brought her out of her trance. "The bank, Sam."

"What about it, sunshine?"

She gazed up at him. "I can't remember."

His thick golden brows drew together in confusion. "What?"

"The bank where I rented the safe-deposit box, Sam. I can't remember the name of the bank."

Chapter Seven

"Don't get upset, Adrienne," Sam said in a calm voice destined to cause the opposite reaction. Men could be so dense sometimes.

She glared at him. "Don't get upset? I can't remember the name of the damn bank!"

"I understand…"

"If you understand so much, tell me how we are going to get the evidence against Vaughn if I can't remember where I left it?" She knew Sam didn't deserve the spurt of temper she'd just thrown at him, but she couldn't help it. The terror she'd lived with since she'd left Boston returned in Godzillion proportions.

Sam took her arm. "Sit down, sunshine."

"I don't want to sit down." Why did men always want you to sit down whenever something upset you?

"I don't care. Sit down anyway." He pulled out a chair and pushed her into it.

"Sam—"

"We have a problem, and your panicking isn't going to help."

"I'm not panicking," she snapped. But directing her anger at Sam wouldn't help anything. So she shut up and took a couple of deep breaths. The extra oxygen helped. She immediately felt calmer.

''That's better.'' He took the chair next to hers and reached for her hand. ''Now, close your eyes.''

''What—''

''Don't argue. Just do it.''

She didn't like his tone, but she closed her eyes anyway. Maybe he knew something about retrieving lost memories that she didn't.

''All right,'' he said softly. ''We know the memory is in there. You've remembered so much else about your past. You'll remember this. Just concentrate. Try to picture the outside of the bank, the lettering in the sign.''

He stopped talking, and she tried to travel back in time. She sat with her eyelids shut and concentrated, while he sat silently stroking her fingers. Little tingly sensations went up her arm.

She took another deep breath and doubled her concentration. His touch was as soft and gentle as a butterfly's. She'd loved watching them flit from flower to flower as a child. If she was lucky, and very still, sometimes they'd land on the back of her hand. Their tiny legs would tickle her and she'd laugh, then they'd fly away.

She opened her eyes. ''This isn't working.''

''It's only been about a minute and a half,'' Sam protested.

She had to smile. ''I mean your stroking my hand. You're distracting me.''

He drew his hand back. ''Sorry.''

''It doesn't matter.'' She stood up. ''This isn't going to do it anyhow.'' She put her fingers to his lips before he could argue. ''No, listen to me. I've gotten most of my memory back as Adrienne, but forgotten everything I saw as Amy. For all intents and purposes, I haven't seen anything of this area in three years.''

He stood to join her. ''And you can't picture what you

don't know. Which puts us back where we were a few minutes ago.''

"And where's that?"

"Getting our jackets."

She couldn't see any point to going out if they didn't know where they were going. "Sam..."

He pointed her in the direction of their bedroom. "Quit arguing and go get your coat."

She started toward the door, then turned back. "Did you use this 'I'm the boss' tone with Amy?" She still couldn't stop thinking of herself as two different people.

Sam affected a scowl. "No, I didn't have to."

She stuck out her tongue. "Too bad I'm Adrienne then, isn't it?"

He strode over, pulled her into his arms and claimed her lips with a soul-shattering kiss she felt to her toes and back. A heat wave of desire engulfed her body, sending fire through her veins.

Abruptly, he released her, only to cup her face in his big hands. "Not too bad at all. Amy didn't have all your memories, but she had your temper."

Adrienne could hardly breathe. All the torrid emotions she'd felt in his arms reflected in his eyes. "Sam..."

He opened his mouth to say something, then closed it as if he'd had second thoughts. Instead, he turned her in his arms so she faced the doorway, and patted her bottom. "Be good and go get your jacket."

She walked out of the room on shaky legs, wondering what Sam would have said, what she would have said in return. Knowing this wasn't the time didn't make it any easier to walk away. But they had things to take care of.

Once they were on their way, Adrienne felt much more confident about their quest. Being with Sam helped. And it surprised her. Life had made her a loner. Sam made her appreciate having a partner.

She took a moment to study him. His very size made her feel safe. Dressed in jeans and a multi-hued sweater, his blond hair tamed, his jaw set, he exuded masculinity. He handled the dark red Lumina with an ease that spoke of his confidence.

She forced her gaze away from the man whose kisses heated her to boiling point. He was much too distracting by far. She looked around the car, running her hand over the seat. Her fingers seemed to recognize the feel of soft leather. "Was this my car?"

"This *is* your car. I thought it might seem more familiar than my truck. I gave it to you for Christmas last year."

"Nice Christmas present." She smiled. "Thank you."

Looking out at the cypress trees that lined the narrow lane they traveled, she wondered how many times she'd been on that road before and why she couldn't remember any of them. She understood forgetting Vaughn and the rest of her past. She had no reason to want to remember.

But the life she'd lived the past few years seemed the answer to every dream she'd had as an adolescent. A wonderful man like Sam didn't deserve the trouble she'd brought him.

Yet here he was, offering love and support to the woman who could get him killed. Again she wondered why he'd taken the chance of marrying a woman who had no memory of her past.

Someday she'd learn the answer to that question. But for now they had to find out where she'd left the tape. Talking about what happened after she lost her memory would only bring up emotions they didn't have time to deal with.

"Adrienne, I've been thinking." Sam glanced over at her briefly, then gave his attention back to the road.

"About the bank?"

"Sort of. Maybe you should go over, in detail, how you

got to California. Maybe talking about it will jog your
memory. If we're just driving around looking at banks,
you'll drive yourself crazy.'' He grimaced at his phrasing.
''No pun intended. Talking will keep you distracted
enough so you don't put too much pressure on yourself.''
He stopped at the end of the road, checked for traffic, then
turned onto a wider boulevard.

''That's a good idea,'' she said. Heaven knew she
needed help. Maybe this would do it.

''Do you want to just tell me or would it be more help
if I ask questions?''

She thought for a moment, then said, ''Go ahead and
ask questions. It will help organize my thoughts.''

''Okay, but first we should decide where we're going to
start our search.''

''I don't know. I was only in town a couple of hours
when I fell.'' Running from someone? Or just from her
own imagination?

''We know you ended up in Pacific Grove, since that's
where you had your accident. How did you arrive in Monterey?''

''By plane.'' By a lot of planes, she thought.

''Did you take a taxi into town?''

''No, a bus.'' A taxi would have been too easy to follow, although by that time she thought she'd lost Vaughn's
shadows.

''Which probably took you to downtown Monterey,''
Sam suggested.

''You're probably right.'' She remembered being let off
in front of a beautiful, large hotel and told Sam so. She'd
even entered the lobby, though she had no intention of
staying there. It had been another ploy, and there'd been
many, to fool whoever might be following her.

Sam nodded. ''Then we'll start there.''

The wide boulevard turned into a main thoroughfare she thought she recognized. "Are we still in Pacific Grove?"

"Yes." They stopped at a red light. He gave her a searching look. "See anything familiar?"

She took in the myriad of stores, restaurants and other businesses. "Nothing specific. I just have a vague feeling that I've been here before." She looked back at him to catch a strange expression on his face. "I suppose that sounds pretty silly to you since I've probably been on this street hundreds of times."

"It doesn't sound silly at all," he said as the light turned green. He accelerated along with the rest of the traffic. "Quit being so hard on yourself. It's not your fault you can't remember the last three years. With all you've been through, I'm just grateful you're here."

She reached over to touch his arm. "I'm grateful you're here, Sam."

The emotion that filled his eyes at that moment was a wonder to see. She swore that one day she'd show him just how grateful she was he'd been the one to find her. But for now...

She sat back. "Okay, Sam. Question time."

"Where do I start?" He stared ahead thoughtfully. "Well, there is something I have been meaning to ask you. What exactly is this evidence you have hidden away?"

"Some papers. Mostly having to do with Vaughn's illegal business practices. And a tape." And two hundred fifty thousand dollars in drug money, she thought. She wasn't quite ready to share that information yet.

"The tape is the most important part, isn't it?" he asked, misunderstanding her silence. "What's on it?"

Since the tape was important, she answered. "The conversation I overheard between Vaughn and Barry."

He put on the right blinker and quickly pulled into a vacant parking place. He put the car in Park, then turned to face her. "You taped it? Does Winston know?"

The fear in his expression equaled every bit of the fear she'd felt that day. "*I* didn't even know till I was packing to leave two days later."

The fear she'd felt came back vividly. Just that morning Vaughn had made her sign the paper turning over the company in return for the divorce she wanted. She was surprised he'd let her go home alone after the meeting with the lawyer. But she'd soon found out why. Counting on her habit of turning on the TV news, Vaughn had known what she'd hear. Barry had been the son of a man high up in Massachusetts government. The local stations were sure to run a story on his death.

"Adrienne, what's going on? Did you remember something?"

Sam's voice brought her back to the present. "I'm sorry. The conversation took place in our office at home. I had a voice-activated tape recorder that I used to record ideas as they came to me. Evidently, I'd left it on."

He pulled her to him and held on tight. "God, when I think what could have happened if he'd found out, if he'd known how much you had on him."

"It didn't happen, Sam." She found herself comforting him where before he'd been the one to comfort. It felt good, putting someone else first for a change.

She'd spent so many years just trying to survive, always looking out for number one. Now Sam and the baby were number one in her life. She'd do anything to keep them safe and happy. The strength of her emotions surprised her. She didn't remember being Amy. Why did she feel so much? How could her emotions remember, but not her mind?

He set her back so he could look in her face. "Forgive me, honey, but I don't understand why you didn't immediately go to the police."

"I planned to drop off the tape at the police station on

the way to the airport. A few minutes after I got in the taxi, the driver asked me if anyone would have a reason to follow me.'' A shiver went through her, remembering the terror of wondering how she'd get away from Vaughn.

''He didn't know about the tape. He was just making sure I wouldn't be foolish enough to go to the cops.'' *''It will be your word against mine,''* he'd told her the last time she saw him. *''And you'll never make it out of the station alive.''*

She'd wanted to tear him apart with her bare hands. Instead, she'd stood tall and told him if he killed her they'd know.

He'd laughed in her face. *''A busy police station is a powder keg. Thieves, murderers, drug addicts, you never know when one of them will blow, taking innocent people with them.''*

She told all this to Sam and watched the anger and fear war on his face.

''I told the cabdriver to take me straight to the airport. I figured that would be the easiest way to lose whoever Vaughn had hired to follow me.''

She paused for a moment, knowing the impact the rest of her story would have on Sam. But she also knew it had to be told. ''Unfortunately, I hadn't counted on his already having people at the airport.''

''If they touched you…''

''They didn't,'' she said quickly. *''They''* were women. The way Vaughn had with women, I should have known. But I didn't even realize it until I was on a jet headed for Chicago.''

''How?''

''On the way to the rest room, I saw an attractive dark-haired woman dressed in a vivid sapphire blue suit, talking on a cellular phone. I thought I recognized her, figured she worked for one of the firms we represented. I glanced at her again on the way back to my seat. That's when I realized what firm she'd worked for. Not one of our clients'. Ours. She worked for Advon.''

''But that means there's another person who knows what Winston did.''

His naiveté endeared him to her even more, but she couldn't let him think the existence of that woman changed things for a second. ''Vaughn didn't confide in her. He hired her. That's why she looked so familiar. The day before I left, I went to the office to pick up some personal items. I saw her in his office.''

''So you don't think she knew?''

She shook her head. ''He probably told her to follow me to make sure I didn't meet anyone to give out company secrets. By the time I got to Chicago, he had more shadows in place.''

''How did you get away?''

It gratified her that he thought her smart enough to get away from Vaughn's goons. She hoped his confidence wasn't misplaced. ''From Chicago I took a plane to Dallas. From Dallas a plane to Denver. In Denver I got on a flight to Minneapolis. Just before they closed the doors, I got off and ran. The woman following me was seated far enough back that she couldn't catch up. Her high heels didn't hurt my chances either. My flight to San Francisco left ten minutes later, with no shadows.''

''Whew!'' He cuffed her on the chin. ''You sure are resourceful.''

She returned his grin. In the safety of the car, it seemed more like an adventure than a run for her life. But the feeling of security didn't last long. Vaughn was more than just a shadow. Once he knew where she lived, he'd make sure she couldn't show up one day to ruin his life. ''We have to go, Sam. We have to find that bank.''

He started the car, and they made the rest of the trip to

downtown Monterey in silence. She could tell from the expression on Sam's face that he'd been deeply affected by her story. What a thing to hand a man who only a few days ago had only the normal concerns for his pregnant wife's health and that of their unborn child.

To have her memory return after three years without a hint about her past must have been a great shock to him. She'd had such a bad headache when she woke she hadn't paid attention to his reactions in the hospital. "Sam?"

"Yeah."

A block ahead lay a tunnel. Sam put on the right-hand blinker and took the exit that pointed toward downtown. Her heart raced as they got closer to their destination. She was glad to have Sam by her side, but at the same time… "I'm sorry I got you into this."

He shot her a look. "Don't be ridiculous."

She wasn't being ridiculous. She cared about him, and she didn't want him hurt. But it only took one look at his set face to keep her quiet.

Sam didn't seem the type of man given to macho posturing, but he would protect his family at any cost. To ask him not to would be like asking the sun not to shine and the sea to dry up.

Sam pulled into the parking lot of the nearest bank. "Does this look familiar?"

She looked at the dark glass facade with its bright red logo and shook her head. She turned toward him and tried to smile. "I guess it's asking too much that I recognize the first bank we pull up to?"

"No, it's not asking too much." He leaned over and kissed her cheek. "Quit worrying. We'll find it."

She wished she could be as optimistic. A tense knot had formed at the back of her neck. She reached up a hand to rub it, hoping Sam didn't notice. If he had any idea how much her head still hurt, he'd take her home. "So, where do we go next?"

He settled his back against the door. "I don't think we should go anywhere until you finish your story."

"What good will that do?" Now that they'd arrived, she wanted to get on with the search. "I don't remember the bank. Telling you about it isn't going to make its location come back to me. I have to *see* it."

She didn't need Sam's indulgent gaze to tell her she sounded like a petulant child. She took a deep breath to calm herself before she spoke again. "Look, I'm sorry I snapped at you, but I really don't think talking is what we need to do right now. If it was going to work, it would have by now."

"What happened once you got to San Francisco?"

He'd completely ignored her! She stared at him in disbelief.

"Did you fly straight to Monterey?"

"No, I flew to Phoenix, then to San Di…" What was wrong with her? He'd ignored her wishes again and here she was answering his questions. She glared at him, only to get a grin in return.

"I can't believe I answered you!" The next thing she knew she was giggling like a schoolgirl. Within seconds his laughter joined hers.

Finally quiet, she gazed at the handsome man she'd been smart enough to marry. His color had heightened with his laughter, giving him a healthy outdoors look, even though he'd spent the last couple of days indoors with her. His blue eyes shone like a moon-lightened midnight sky. His lips curled up, revealing strong, even teeth. Reluctant though she was to admit it, that few minutes of mirth had been just what she needed to relax.

Just like Sam had been what she needed to grab the life she should always have wanted. Desiring career goals she could share with her spouse had only brought her a greedy husband and life on the run.

"So, what happened once you got to San Diego?"

She shook her head. "You're impossible!"

"Au contraire," he said, shaking a finger at her. "I'm very possible. But I am incorrigible. So, you might as well answer my question."

She had to smile. Even the strictest nun couldn't have kept a straight face at such an unrepentant mischief maker. And she was no nun. "All right, you win. Once I got to San Diego, I bought a used car from its owner and drove up to Orange County. I left it at John Wayne Airport and flew to Monterey."

"I left instructions inside to contact the owner. He wouldn't have had time to change the registration. The money I paid him would more than cover any parking fees. And he could sell the car again."

"He must have been happy," Sam said and smiled.

She'd hoped so. She'd wanted to know somebody was happy.

Sam took her hand. "You know, when we found you, you didn't have anything but the clothes on your back. No purse, no identification, some money. But no more than a hundred dollars. Even after we put your picture in the paper, no one came forward with your luggage."

Adrienne nodded. "Luggage would have slowed me down. I had to move fast."

He looked at her searchingly. "But all those tickets must have cost plenty."

"I had some money stashed in a secret account that I opened about a year before I found out about Vaughn's criminal activities." She hesitated for a second, considered telling him the rest, then decided against it.

"I knew it might be a long time before I could safely open a bank account or work at a job. I put the cash into a knapsack, the kind that can fold down to almost nothing. When I got to Monterey, I put all but a couple hundred dollars in the safe-deposit box.''

Sam started the car.

"What are you doing?"

He checked the rearview mirror and backed the car out of the parking place before answering. "I'm taking you down to the police station."

"But you agreed—"

He glanced at her confused face. "I was wrong. This is a police matter. What if you never remember where this evidence is? Do you think we should let Winston get away with his crimes just because you can't hand the proof to the police on a silver platter?" Or get her, which was his real concern. Just the thought of the vengeance the man might wreak on Adrienne had Sam speeding toward his brother's precinct as fast as the congested streets would allow.

"Sam, what if the police don't believe me?"

The quiet question was almost his undoing. How many abused wives had asked the same question in just that tone? To hear it from her was more than he could stand. "They will," he told her.

She looked away from him, out at the busy streets. An indication that his attempt to build up her confidence had failed. When she turned back to him, her set expression pierced his heart. It was almost as if she'd resigned herself to disbelief.

Seeing the station ahead, he pulled into the left-turn lane and stopped to wait for the green arrow. He reached over and grasped her hand. "The guy's a sleaze. Why would the police take his word over yours?"

"He's only a sleaze to you because I told you what he did. To others, Vaughn Winston looks like an upstanding member of the business community. Who would believe an award-winning advertising executive would risk his livelihood to launder drug money? Or that he would have his assistant killed because he wanted to back out of the deal?''

''Casey will believe you.''

''Just because I'm his sister-in-law? I'm sure his superiors will love that.''

The light turned green. Sam let go of Adrienne's hand and made the turn into the parking lot. Once he'd stopped the car and turned off the engine he turned back to her. ''Casey will believe you because he knows you.''

Her green eyes darkened. ''He knows Amy.''

Sam cupped her face with his hands and fixed his gaze on hers. ''You *are* Amy.''

She shook her head in denial. But he didn't give in to her. ''Yes, you are.'' He leaned over and took her lips in a kiss meant to warm her soul. Yet he was the one who heated up. Abruptly, he broke off. ''Yes. You are.''

''But I don't know all of my past. I don't remember marrying you.''

He didn't know what to say. It still hurt to know that she'd forgotten the best day of their lives so completely.

''Half the time I don't remember being pregnant,'' she continued.

Sam laughed. He couldn't help it. She looked so mortified by her revelation. Seeing her scowl, he tried to stifle his laughter, failed, and pulled her into his arms instead.

She struggled against him. ''Let me go. It's not funny.''

He held her tighter. ''You want to know the great thing about this?'' She shook her head against his chest, but he didn't let that stop him. ''You can forget that pregnancy from here to eternity, and it still won't make you any less pregnant.''

He knew he had her when she smiled. This time when she pushed against him, he let her go. He gazed at her face, and thought he'd never seen her look so beautiful. "Well?"

She rewarded him with a grin. "I guess that was pretty silly. Babies have a way of making themselves felt whether you remember them or not."

"Have you felt the baby?"

She gazed at him blankly for a moment. "No, I don't think so. Isn't it too early?"

He shrugged, not knowing the answer any more than she did. "Maybe we should read that pile of baby books we picked up at the Thunderbird bookstore the other day."

She obviously didn't remember the shopping trip, but she nodded anyway. "Maybe we should."

"Are you ready to go see Casey?"

She took a deep breath before she replied. "As ready as I'll ever be."

Five minutes later, they sat in Casey's tiny office. While Adrienne told Casey her story, Sam sat silently at her side, holding her hand when he could, letting it go when she got up to pace the small room.

Her face seemed to grow paler with every question his brother asked. Questions he'd never thought of, but which Casey, with his experience in domestic situations, had to ask, uncovering the depths of emotional abuse Adrienne had suffered at the whims of upstanding businessman Vaughn Winston.

"I'm going to make a couple of calls." Casey stood up and moved to the door. "Why don't you go down the hall and buy Adrienne a soda, big brother? She looks like she's about to fall over. Don't you ever feed her?"

The comments had been made in typical bratty-little-brother manner, but that didn't make them any less serious. Adrienne did look as if she was about to faint. He gave her a kiss and exited with his brother.

Out in the hall, he put out a hand to stop Casey. "Are you going to be able to do something about this?"

"I'm going to try my damnedest. Let me make those calls, then I'll come back and discuss it with both of you."

Sam wanted to pin him down, but he knew his brother wouldn't say anything until he was ready. So he went to get Adrienne a drink, then rejoined her in Casey's office, where for the next half hour they waited.

By the time Casey opened the door to his office, Sam was hard put to keep his wife from bolting. In fact, she'd just reached for the doorknob when his brother walked in.

Casey stopped to give Adrienne a kiss on the cheek, then moved over to his chair and threw himself into it. "You two doing okay?"

Sam had had enough. "Of course we're not okay! We've been waiting hours for you to come back and tell us what you're going to do about this creep."

Casey looked at his watch. "I've been gone exactly thirty-two minutes."

Sam leaned over the desk and glared at him. "Casey..."

Casey just grinned. "If you don't sit down, big brother, I'm not going to tell you the good news."

Chapter Eight

Sam sat. "Good news?"

Adrienne knew his stunned expression mirrored her own. "What good news?" she asked, not bothering to hide the skepticism she felt.

"Advon no longer handles the advertising for Wishing Starr."

"You didn't find that out from Advon." If he had...

"Give me some credit, sis. I called the publishing company and asked who did the ads for the children's books. Creative has been their rep for over two years."

Adrienne let out a sigh of relief. It made sense. Vaughn had always considered that client small potatoes. She'd been the one to insist on keeping them. "I wonder how many others he's gotten rid of."

Sam took her hand. "The important thing is he dropped this one."

His expression became concerned. "Unless you think he'd see your book some other way?"

Her first impulse was to allay his fear. But to do that she would have to feel none herself. She considered his question seriously. "I don't think so. Vaughn has no interest in anything having to do with children. Or any book that's not connected to the business world, for that matter."

Unfortunately, by the time she'd learned either, they'd been married over a year. Vaughn was very good at keeping secrets.

"Don't you two want to know who else I talked to?"

Adrienne looked back at Casey. She'd almost forgotten he was there. "Who else did you talk to? Not Vaughn?"

Casey leaned back in his chair. "Just what kind of detective do you think I am? The perp is the last person you talk to."

"Perp?" Sam gave his brother a look. "You've been watching too much TV."

Casey's expression was unrepentant. "Can't help it. I love those cop shows."

Adrienne enjoyed the camaraderie between the two brothers. It was something she'd always envied the children she'd grown up with. Someone to share with, someone to fight with. As an only child, she'd known neither.

"I talked to a cop friend," Casey said. "Adrienne's right about us not being able to arrest the guy on her say-so. Money laundering is hard to prove in the best of circumstances. But Frank agreed to do some unofficial investigation for us. In the meantime…"

"I have to remember where I left the tape," Adrienne finished for him. And turn over the money. But there was no use mentioning that now. It would only worry Sam.

"That would help." Casey picked up the key she'd laid on his desk earlier. "But I have a little free time coming, so I'm going to see if I can find the bank for you."

"How are you going to do that?" she asked.

"I'll call the local banks, ask if they have a safety-deposit box by that number."

"Is that legal?" Sam asked. "Aren't there privacy laws?"

"They wouldn't be able to give out the name of the

renter, but they can tell me if they have that number or not," he explained. "That would narrow the field."

Adrienne hunched her shoulders, trying to ease the tension that wouldn't leave. She'd expected to feel better after their talk with Casey, but she couldn't help feeling that time was running out.

Sam stood. "Thanks, Casey. Now, if you don't mind, I'm going to take Adrienne home."

Casey rose, too. "Good idea."

Adrienne suddenly felt invisible. "But shouldn't we drive around for a while, just in case..."

Sam held out a hand to help her to her feet. "Casey will handle it, sunshine. He just looks irresponsible."

It went against the grain to turn this over to him, even if he was a police detective. Besides... "Casey hasn't seen the bank. I have."

"I know, honey, but Casey's not pregnant and recovering from a concussion, either. You need some rest. Maybe tomorrow, if he hasn't found anything."

Adrienne didn't like the tone of his voice. She wasn't a child, after all. *But you are with child,* her reasonable voice said, ending whatever argument she might have come up with. Whatever energy she'd had, drained out of her, leaving her feeling limp and weepy. The feeling was unfamiliar enough to make her suddenly agree. "All right, you win."

The combination of relief and smugness on the men's faces was comical to behold. In a different mood, she might have wanted to slap them. But how could she, when all they'd tried to do was take care of her?

AT A STOPLIGHT on Lighthouse Avenue, Sam glanced over at Adrienne, who had fallen into an exhausted slumber just minutes after getting into the car. She looked so beautiful, but sleep hadn't erased the tension from her forehead. She moved restlessly against the seat, murmuring softly.

The signal changed, and Sam drove through the intersection. At the next light, he turned left and parked on the street next to The Bagel Shop. After checking to make sure Adrienne still slept, he got out of the car, closing the door quietly so as not to wake her.

After he finished his errand, he drove to their favorite part of the long beach that lined Monterey Bay. Across from the foghorn, the rocky coast had been battered by waves, leaving shallow tide pools between the jagged rocks. They'd spent a lot of time on the white beach lately, so Amy could sketch the illustrations she'd planned for her next book. Her deadline was less than three months away.

Three months, he thought. In three months they'd be more than halfway through the pregnancy. Would she have remembered by then?

Sam sat for a few minutes, gazing out at the waves as they sprayed the rocks with white foam. Being by the ocean always had a calming effect on his nerves. He watched as a line of pelicans skimmed the water on their way to who knew where. He'd often wondered where the birds headed with such determination.

"Sam?" Adrienne sat up and looked around. "Where are we?"

Hiding his disappointment that she didn't remember their favorite place, Sam reached in the back seat for the brown paper bag. "I thought you might like a picnic."

Adrienne smiled. "I'd like that very much."

Sam retrieved a stadium blanket from the trunk, and they made their way down the path to the beach. After a couple of tries, they found a spot where sand covered sand, instead of the flat granite and sandstone rocks that liked to stub bare toes.

Sam spread the blanket out and watched her sink gracefully onto it. He knew that grace wouldn't last long and couldn't wait to see her stomach grow large with their child.

Kicking off her shoes, Adrienne regarded the bag he opened. "What did you buy for us? I'm starving!" She laughed. "It seems all I've done the last couple of days is sleep and eat."

He smiled. The short nap she'd taken had done wonders with her mood. "That's par for the course for a pregnant lady, you know." He handed her one of the paper-wrapped bagel sandwiches he'd purchased.

"You must play golf."

It took a moment to figure out that her comment had to do with the phrase he'd just used. "I do. I also play basketball. I could have said, 'That's the way the ball bounces.'"

She grinned. "I appreciate your restraint." She unwrapped the sandwich, took off the top to inspect the insides and smiled. "Turkey, avocado, tomatoes and sprouts. My favorite. But you forgot the red onion."

He wriggled his eyebrows at her. "I had them leave it out on purpose."

She laughed at that, too, relieving him greatly. She seemed so much more comfortable with him now. Almost as if she'd remembered their life together. Sam opened a cream soda and set it in the sand by her, then opened one for himself.

After taking a drink, he tucked into his own sandwich. Bagels and cream soda. He'd never had either until he'd met Amy. He supposed that should have given him a clue to her origins. But he'd grown very good at ignoring any clues that led to her past.

"I suppose I'll get used to strange places seeming familiar, sooner or later."

Her comment, coming so close to his own thoughts, startled him. "Do you remember this beach?"

She shook her head. "Not exactly. It's more a feeling of being comfortable here, as if I've spent a lot of time with the white sand between my toes, the sea breeze in my hair."

Sam decided not to mention the importance of this beach. It would just make her feel bad. He opted for the other reason instead. "It should be familiar. You've been spending a lot of time down here, sketching pictures for your new book."

Finishing her sandwich, she wiped her fingers and lips with a napkin. "I'm writing a new book?"

"Don't look so worried. The story's written. You're just illustrating now."

She stared at him. "Just illustrating? Sam, I've never illustrated a children's book in my life!"

"You've illustrated several."

"But not as Adrienne!"

Sam started gathering papers and bottles. "What difference does it make what you're called? You're an artist."

Adrienne hugged her knees and dug her toes into the soft sand. "I don't even know what story I'm illustrating. I assume it takes places on the beach. What if my style's completely different now? When is this book due anyway?"

Sam found her agitation amusing, but hid his smile. Amnesia or not, she wasn't so different from the woman he'd spent the last three years loving to distraction. If only she'd quit separating the old and new and accept herself as one person. "Amy, calm down."

He knew he'd made a mistake the moment he said it. His words drove her to her feet. He rose to stand beside her. "Amy."

Her first clenched. "I'm not Amy! I'm not the person who wrote those books and drew those pictures. I'm a completely different person."

"That's ridiculous." Not the most tactful way of dealing with her, but her complete denial of the woman he loved angered him in a way he'd never thought it would. The fact that her denial mirrored his own didn't help.

"It's *not* ridiculous, Sam. Amy didn't have my memories or my experiences." She moved a few feet away to stand by the water's edge. "She had to have been different," she continued, her voice reflective. "She never knew anything but her life here."

She was right. He knew she was. But fear of what she might do if he admitted it kept him silent.

Adrienne turned to face him. "I'm not Amy, Sam."

Her firm, quiet voice as much as said, "And that's that."

His mind cried, "No!"

He strode over to her and pulled her into his arms. "You are Amy," he growled, then claimed her lips in a kiss meant to show her exactly who she was.

Her instant response stirred the flames burning in his belly. He wanted this woman with every throb of his heart. He always had. He always would. Whether she remembered their life together or not.

His lips still on hers, he picked her up and carried her back to the blanket. Refusing to ease his hold an inch, he dropped to his knees, laid her down, then joined her, thigh against thigh, breast against breast, mouth against mouth.

Tongues dipped, teased, touched, devoured. Every thrust was met, every touch returned, every act of passion shared. With each kiss, his need became more intense. The tiny sounds of response she made drove him wild. "I want to love you. Please let me love you."

"Yes, yes."

His knee hit a rock under the blanket. The pain was minor, but it brought him to his senses. He rolled away from her. The effort made him groan. The blood still coursed through his veins. His heart pounded in his ears. "I'm sorry." It was all he could manage, and not nearly enough.

"Me, too." Her voice was small, breathless. "I didn't mean to make you angry."

He turned to face her, saw the guilt and uncertainty. "That wasn't anger, sunshine. Not once I touched you. That was passion. I love you. I want you."

"But I'm not—"

He stopped her with his fingertips. "Please don't say it again. It makes me crazy. You might not remember being Amy. But you are Amy, as much as you are Adrienne. The mind can play strange tricks on us, but some things are basic to a person."

She looked away from him. "Everything I've learned about her..." She glanced at him. "...about me, when I was Amy, seems so different from the way I am."

There was something going on here he couldn't quite grasp. She seemed almost sad. He waved away his own doubts to question hers. "Different how?"

"She seems softer, sweeter, more..." She shrugged. "...feminine."

The danger of losing control past, Sam moved once again to lay beside her. He reached out to touch her face. "Just as soft." Her shoulders. "Just as sweet." Her waist. "Just as feminine."

Her green eyes turned cloudy. "Oh, Sam."

He smiled. "Oh, Adrienne," he replied, earning a laugh. "Let's go home."

They packed up in silence and walked to the car. Settled inside, Adrienne's thoughts returned to their earlier conversation. "You'll have to tell me about this book I'm illustrating."

He started the ignition. "I'll find it for you as soon as we get home."

"Sam?"

The gentle tone of her voice and the touch of her hand on his arm caught his attention. "What, sunshine?"

"Thanks for the picnic."

"My pleasure."

The smile he gave her was so sweet she could hardly believe this was the same man who'd kissed her so passionately only moments ago. One more surprise in a man full of surprises. She hoped the women forced into arranged marriages through the decades had as much fun discovering the strangers they'd married.

Pushing the interlude on the beach to the back of her mind for later, she turned her attention to the passing scenery as they drove home. Sam took the scenic route along the bay. The rocks, the bird life, the gorgeous homes and abundant flowers delighted her. She could hardly take it all in. It amazed her how lucky she'd been in choosing this lovely area to call home.

Home. The beach where they'd picnicked had seemed like home, as if it was someplace special. Their passionate encounter had seemed so natural there. She hadn't felt embarrassed at all, only the hot fire of desire. She looked over at the man who was her husband. She knew something significant had happened between them on that beach, today and in the past. "Sam?"

"Hmm?"

"You took me to that beach for a reason, didn't you?"

"It's been a hectic couple of days for you. You needed to relax."

The hedging surprised her. Sam's openness and honesty had impressed her from the first. "You can tell me, you know."

He glanced over briefly then turned his attention back to the winding road they traveled. A moment later he pulled to the side of the road, turned off the ignition and turned in his seat to face her. "What's going on?"

"The beach means something special to us, doesn't it?"

The expression on his face told her he was trying to decide how much to tell her. If he had been her ex, she would suspect bad news. But Sam wasn't Vaughn. "Please, tell me why I feel such warmth for that place, Sam. I almost let you make love to me on a public beach."

He smiled, as if remembering, and she smiled back. "Well?"

He reached for her hand, intertwining their fingers. "All right," he said. "About three months after your accident, I brought you here for a picnic. Monterey's at its best in winter. Just like today, there was no fog. The sun was shining." So, now, were his eyes, she noticed.

Suddenly, he became serious. "You were so beautiful I couldn't hold back my love for you any longer. What made the day special was you telling me you felt the same."

A tingle went through her. She'd known. Somehow she'd known how important that beach was. But no pictures came to mind, no memories. She leaned over and kissed his lips gently. "I'm sorry I didn't remember."

He touched her cheek. "It's not your fault."

"It's not yours either, but you're the one suffering from it."

Sam laughed. "I'm not exactly suffering."

Suspecting he wouldn't tell her if he was, she couldn't let it go. "Maybe not, but I think this has been a lot more difficult on you than you're letting on."

His grip on her hand tightened. "I'm not exactly the prince of restraint. I grabbed you on the beach."

On the beach, in the car, grab me anywhere you want. The irreverent statement went unsaid, but Adrienne amazed herself. The passion she felt for a man she'd known two days amazed her. It also gave her hope. If her body still remembered his kiss so well, surely her mind would, too.

"Adrienne?"

She looked at her husband. At his concerned sky-blue eyes. At his strong nose and stubborn chin. At the gentle yet masculine curve of his lips. And she longed to remember every part of their lives together. "Why did you marry me, Sam?"

There it was…the question she'd been afraid to ask, the question she longed to hear the answer to. It lay between them like a package wrapped in brown paper. Mysterious, intriguing, yet you hesitate before opening it, because the outside gives no hint of the contents hiding within.

She wanted to see what was inside, yet she couldn't help but be a little suspicious. Why would a man marry a woman he knew nothing about?

"I wanted to share my life with you."

"But you didn't know if I was married or had a family somewhere else or, as you learned, on the run from a murderer. Or was a murderer myself, for that matter."

He shot her a look at that. "I knew you were the woman I was meant to spend my life with."

"But what if—"

"Stop it!"

The sharpness of his tone startled her and she jumped.

"I'm sorry." He immediately lowered his voice. "There's no sense in keeping it from you. You know anyway, and when you get your memory back…"

All her senses went on alert. Now she would know why he'd married her. Just loving her hadn't been enough. It hadn't been enough for Vaughn. Why should it for Sam?

"Before we met, I had two serious relationships. The first when I was in college. The second about five years ago. In both cases, I lived with the woman and we planned to marry someday. But someday never came."

Sam's gaze shifted out the window. With Amy, some-day had come. With Adrienne, it would come again. He refused to believe that she would never remember their life together and the plans they'd made.

"Barbara, my college sweetheart," he explained, "was a biology major who planned to enter environmental research. She knew she'd have years of graduate study ahead of her. Much of it included travel to foreign countries. She couldn't see being married when she'd be away so much."

"What happened?" she asked.

Thinking she always had had a vivid imagination, he smiled wryly. "Nothing as drastic as you're thinking, I'm sure. Eventually, we drifted apart. She was in South America for six months. I lived in San Francisco, building my own career. When she got back, it seemed we had nothing in common anymore. She finally admitted to being in love with a fellow scientist."

"Even if the two of you had drifted apart, you must have been hurt."

He appreciated Adrienne's sympathy, but he had to confess, "Actually, I was more confused than hurt. This was the woman I'd built all my plans around. Yet, when she told me she loved someone else, I felt *relieved*." He paused, wondering how he could ever have thought he was in love with Barbara. He'd never known what real love felt like until Amy came into his life.

"And?" Adrienne asked, bringing him back.

He smiled. "And at loose ends. I had a great job designing parks for an international firm based in San Francisco. But the rest of my life had revolved around Barbara. Once she moved her stuff out of our town house, I had an empty house and an empty life."

"That's when you met this other woman?"

He nodded. "In my quest to fill both, I met Marilyn. I needed an interior decorator, and a colleague suggested her company. She insisted her clients be very involved in the decorating process, so we spent a lot of time together.''

"And fell in love?"

She'd sounded almost jealous, Sam thought, and set out to allay the green-eyed monster. "I'm not sure love had anything to do with it," he said. "She'd just been divorced. I'd just left a long-term relationship. We were both looking for something and found each other." He shrugged without apology. "I liked and admired Marilyn. She was hardworking and fun to be with. We were physically compatible..." He trailed off, suddenly embarrassed. What a thing to admit to the women he was trying to convince he loved more than anything.

Adrienne didn't look too thrilled by his disclosure either. "How long were you together?"

"Two years." Too long, he thought. "Our relationship was so comfortable it took that long for us to realize we were better friends than lovers. We were easy together, but there was no romance, no real spark between us. Our parting was mutually decided and friendly."

At this statement, Adrienne stopped imagining Marilyn as a femme fatale and started seeing her as the girl next door. It made her feel better, and it seemed much more fair than being hostile toward a woman she didn't know. Or did she? For all she knew, Marilyn *was* the girl next door. "What happened to Barbara and Marilyn?"

He settled back in his seat, obviously more comfortable now that he'd told her about his past. For the second time. "Barbara married the scientist she met in South America. They're a research team for a company specializing in medicine made from plants that grow in the rain forest. I get a Christmas card every couple of years, but I haven't seen her since she moved out."

"And Marilyn?"

"A month after we broke up, she got swept off her feet

by a carpenter she'd hired to build some cabinets for a client. Three months later they were married and expecting a baby. Now they have three. We used to talk on the phone once in a while, but our friendship bothered her husband. I've only spoken to her twice in the last two years. Once to tell her about you, the other right after her third child was born."

"It's too bad your friendship had to end." *Easy for you to say when you know there's no chance of running into the woman,* she taunted herself.

But she couldn't feel completely guilty. It had become very clear that Sam was the best thing that had ever happened to her. She wouldn't relish old girlfriends showing up, reminding him how less complicated it was loving a woman who actually remembered making love to you.

Sam reached over and cupped her cheek. "I never understood Marilyn's husband's jealousy until I fell in love with you. I could never have a casual conversation with any man you'd once cared enough to make love to."

Adrienne had never understood jealousy either, until now. But it wasn't Sam's old girlfriends that bothered her. It was Amy. "Sam?"

"Shh." He put a finger to her lips. "I'm with you because I love you. It might sound funny after all I just told you, but you are the only reason I've ever wanted to marry."

It was Amy, Adrienne thought. It was Amy he'd wanted to marry, not her.

Sam traced her lips with his thumb. "I'm selfish when it comes to you, sunshine. I wanted you to be beside me at all times, and I wasn't about to wait for your memory to come back before I had you for my own."

Hearing the intensity of Sam's declaration, Adrienne didn't imagine Amy had put up much of a fight. That kind of love comes once in a lifetime. She'd found a safe harbor, even though she hadn't been aware of needing one.

Suspecting she needed him more than ever, Adrienne decided she wasn't about to give him up. "You took a real chance hooking up with a woman with no memory of her past. Thank you."

He gave her a strange smile, almost sad. "You're welcome, sunshine. Now, let's get you home. You could probably use a nap."

As Sam started the car and put it in gear, Adrienne smiled to herself. Well, a big, warm bed sounded wonderful, but a nap in it was the furthest thing from her mind. She wondered how much convincing Sam would need to take that nap with her.

The thought, coming out of nowhere, gave her hope. If anything could convince her that the woman she was and the woman she'd been for the past three years would one day converge into one personality, it was ideas like the one she'd just had. The playfulness it conveyed had been buried long ago by a husband who considered sex serious business. Passion he'd allowed. Laughter had only bruised his ego. No wonder her injured brain had been so eager to bury all memory of him.

She wished she could forget him now. But she also realized how dangerous her ignorance could have been. If Vaughn had known where she was, he could have done anything to her.

The fact that he hadn't hurt her made her feel safe. Or at least as safe as she could feel until he was behind bars. With Casey's help, they'd find the bank where she'd rented the box. Once she handed the authorities in Boston the evidence they needed, Vaughn would be arrested.

With Vaughn in prison, she and Sam could get on with their lives.

She looked at her husband, then at the house as it came

into view. This man, this home—she looked at her nearly flat stomach—this baby. These were what was important. How she ever could have thought of living a different life, she'd never know.

Sam stopped the car, got out and walked around to open her door. With exquisite gentleness, he helped her out, then held her hand as they walked to the front door.

Inside, he ordered her to go change into something more comfortable.

She grinned at his phrasing.

"For a nap, young lady," he admonished. "I need to make a couple of phone calls. I'll use the kitchen phone."

She watched him walk down the hall, wondering if he'd chosen to use that phone because he didn't trust himself to just let her nap.

Still smiling, she headed toward the bedroom. The doorbell rang, making her change her direction. Maybe this was Casey now.

She opened the door. On the porch stood a woman she'd never seen before.

The woman smiled. "Hi, I'm home."

Chapter Nine

Tall and thin as a fashion model, the woman who stood on the porch had a mane of bright red hair and a smile that didn't quite reach her bottle-green eyes. Something about the way she held herself struck a note of familiarity inside Adrienne's brain. Whether she recognized her from her life as Amy or as Adrienne, she didn't know. But it seemed more likely she was a friend of Amy's.

On that thought came another. Why would she even question if this was a friend of Amy's or Adrienne's?

"Well? What do you think?" the woman asked, affecting a low, sultry tone.

"About what?" The woman didn't seem to have noticed any difference, and Adrienne was reluctant to divulge her new identity to a stranger.

"The new suit, of course." The woman sidled past Adrienne into the hall. "I bought it in New York. They don't have anything like *this* in California."

That probably wasn't such a bad thing.

The skirt was too short. The tailored jacket looked uncomfortable. And the chartreuse color was unflattering, even on a redhead with green eyes. With matching tights and shoes, she was quite a sight.

Not that Adrienne would have said so. The woman who

chattered on before her didn't look the type to take criticism of her fashion sense lightly.

Sam walked into the foyer. "Did I hear the doorbell? Oh, hi, Ginger. Back again, huh?"

Ginger? Adrienne thought, amused. *How appropriate.*

"Hi, Sam, what are you doing home in the middle of a workday?" Ginger asked with the forwardness of a close friend.

"Amy had an accident, so I'm taking a couple of days off."

Adrienne gave him a grateful look.

"Oh my God, Amy! Are you all right? What happened?" Ginger touched her arm.

Adrienne started involuntarily.

"I'm sorry," Ginger said. "Did I hurt you?"

Adrienne forced a smile. "No, I'm just a little jumpy, I guess." She wondered at the strange reaction, but decided not to say anything.

"So, what happened to you?"

Adrienne glanced at Sam, whose expression told her he'd handle this if that's what she wanted. She didn't. Making her own explanations gave her more control of the situation. She forced a laugh. "I tripped over the vacuum cleaner. Can you believe it?"

"Unfortunately, yes," Ginger said huffily. "I keep telling you to get a full-time housekeeper. My Sonia's a dream." She moved down the hall toward the kitchen. "How about something to drink? I'm parched."

"Go pour yourself something," Sam called after her. "We'll be there in a minute."

"I know her from somewhere," Adrienne whispered so Ginger wouldn't overhear.

"She was the first woman friend you made. You've known her almost as long as you've known me."

''There's something about her.'' Something not quite real.

Sam put his arm around her. ''Ginger Zane's a character all right. She's an artist's model. Does a lot of nude posing for artists all over the world. We only see her every few months.''

Ginger posing nude? Yes, she could see it. What she had a hard time fathoming was the two of them being bosom buddies. Amy certainly surprised her this time.

''A penny for your thoughts.''

Adrienne looked up at Sam, who grinned down at her. ''Can't see the two of you together, huh?''

She laughed. ''I have to confess, Ginger is the first nude model I've been friends with.''

''I think you felt sorry for her at first. She seemed so desperate for a friend. After a while, you began to enjoy her quirkiness. Everything else about our lives was so normal.''

She gaped at him. ''Normal? How many people do we know who've lost their memories?''

He hugged her to him. ''Believe it or not, after a while even that seemed normal. During the past year, I don't think we talked about it more than once. And that was when you found out you were pregnant.''

She could just imagine how distressed she must have been. If you didn't know what kind of childhood you had, how could you know what kind of parent you'd be? Even now, knowing what she hadn't then, she had to wonder.

''Adrienne...'' Sam scowled at her.

''What?''

''You're a wonderful woman, and you'll make a wonderful mother.''

She stared at him in amazement. ''How did you know what I was thinking?''

"I *know* you," he said. His expression said more. "Now, why don't we go join our guest?"

"All right."

They moved down the hall hand in hand.

AN HOUR LATER, Adrienne wondered if Amy had kept Ginger around for her entertainment value. The woman was an incorrigible gossip. She knew everybody and had no qualms about telling their secrets. It was like having your own personal tabloid.

When Ginger decided it was time to leave, Adrienne didn't know whether to be sorry or relieved. Her friend's nonstop chatter, though extremely entertaining, had exhausted Adrienne. She definitely needed a nap.

Sam went to try Casey again, while she walked Ginger to the door.

"Well, I'm glad you dropped by, Ginger." It was nice to know she'd made a friend, even if that friend had turned out to be a trifle peculiar.

Ginger's expression became concerned. "Are you sure you're all right, Amy? You don't seem yourself."

A truer statement had never been said, Adrienne thought. But she didn't want to go into it now. Sooner or later, her friend would have to be told, but...

"Concussions have a way of doing that to you, I hear. I'll be fine in a few days."

"Well, you call me if you need anything. I'll be in town for at least a week, now that the holidays are over. Need to rest and recoup, you know." She turned and walked down the steps.

"I will. Drive safely," Adrienne called to her, watching the other woman get into a school bus–yellow sports car that clashed terribly with her chartreuse outfit.

She waited until the car drove out of sight, then walked

back into the house, shaking her head. Was the woman color-blind?

"Ginger gone?" Sam asked when she walked into the bedroom.

"Yes. Did you get a hold of Casey?" She sat on the edge of the bed and pulled off her shoes.

"No, they keep saying he's not available. I don't know if that means he's not there or that he is, but too busy to talk. I'd have to be a detective myself to get an answer out of the people who answer the phone at that station."

Adrienne felt his frustration, because it was her own. "Maybe we should have made some calls ourselves."

He sat down beside her, putting his hand to her cheek. "You're exhausted. The only thing you're going to look for right now is some z's."

She laughed. "Z's?"

"Call it whatever you want. You are going to take a nap, like a good little pregnant woman should."

"You want to take one with me?" The question she'd wanted to ask him coming home burst out unbidden. But she couldn't regret it enough to take it back. Every instinct told her this man loved her in a way no one else ever had.

He kissed her lips gently. "Thanks for the offer, but if I join you on this bed, neither of us will get the sleep you need."

So, who needs sleep? The irreverent thought went unspoken, but her expression must have given her away.

"You do." He kissed her again. "Now, lie down. I'll check on you later."

She did as he asked and watched him walk to the door. "Sam?"

He turned. "Yes, sunshine?"

"Thanks." For being there. For loving her. Even if the love was for Amy, she felt as if it was hers.

He smiled. "You're welcome." He shut the door quietly behind him.

AFTER TRYING to get in touch with Casey and failing again, Sam sat at the kitchen table staring out the window. Wind whipped the trees and sent the clouds flying. Birds flew by in frantic search for shelter. The storm he'd seen no sign of earlier was coming in fast. Not only outside, but also in his home. He'd always felt it was a safe haven for his family, and now Vaughn Winston was trying to take all that away. If he could.

Vaughn valued nothing but money. He'd thrown away his wife's faith and love without a thought. He'd laundered drug money. He'd possibly murdered his assistant. He'd had Adrienne followed day and night, for thousands of miles, to make sure she didn't get away. If he learned where she had been living these past three years, that she remembered what he'd done, there'd be no stopping him.

Sam only hoped the love he felt for her and their unborn child would lend him the strength to fight for them, that the brains God gave him would be powerful enough to outwit the demon.

A bolt of lightning electrified the garden just as the phone rang. Sam jumped a foot, then laughed at himself. When they were kids, he and Casey used to tell each other ghost stories on stormy nights, scaring each other so much they hadn't been able to sleep for hours.

The phone rang again and he snatched up the receiver before it disturbed Adrienne's nap. Hanging up a few minutes later, Sam shook his head. Life went on, no matter what. Other people had problems, too. If you ever had the nerve to forget the fact, fate stepped in to jolt you back to reality.

In this case, reality happened to be a fence his workers had finished the day before yesterday. A fence that had been blown down by the first twenty-five-mile-an-hour wind to hit the coast. A fence that would have to be nailed back together before the rain started pounding down. He made a couple of quick calls, then went to tell Adrienne he had to leave for a while.

SHE KNEW it was a dream. Everything was fuzzy, as if she watched through a camera with a lens slightly out of focus. A woman sat behind a desk, reading aloud a bunch of numbers that had no meaning to Adrienne. Her hair was a pale strawberry blond, drawn tightly back from her face, giving her a look of severity echoed in the glitter of her equally pale gray eyes. "You know something, Mrs. Winston," she hissed. "And I'll find out what it is. I'm the one who'll win. You'll see."

Her anger frightened Adrienne. It radiated from her, filling the room with a fiery orange light that threatened to burst into flames. Adrienne tore at her clothes, stifled by the heat. The odor of the woman's perfume filled her nose and her throat, choking her. She tried to breathe, struggling for the oxygen this woman seemed bent on denying her. She tried to back away, even as the woman pulled at her with a snakelike glare.

"Adrienne, honey, wake up. Come on, sweetheart, open those gorgeous eyes for me."

She woke abruptly. A man sat on the edge of the bed, his expression full of love and concern. "Are you okay? You were moaning in your sleep."

Sam. She rubbed her eyes, wiping away the last vestiges of the dream. "I had a nightmare." She sat up with his help. "A woman with pale hair and eyes. She was so angry at me. I don't know why. Vaughn's the only enemy I've ever had. But this woman wanted something from me, something I couldn't give."

Sam put his arm around her. "Was she someone you knew in the past, someone you worked with?"

"I don't know." With the close proximity, Adrienne couldn't keep from leaning against him, but action was only physical. If the dream had told her anything, it was that the past was very much a part of her present. She couldn't let her guard down for a moment.

"What's bothering you?" Sam asked, his tone as serious as her thoughts had been.

She gazed out at the forest beyond the window. The trees bent in the wind, but she knew she could never bend. She had to keep searching her mind for the memories it hid. "I thought my memory had come back," she told him, "but I keep running into walls."

"Maybe she was one of your shadows."

Adrienne closed her eyes, trying to focus on her scary flight across the country. "I remember a couple of brunettes. There was a blond, but her hair wasn't that pale. Of course, they were probably wearing wigs, so who knows."

Sam hugged her closer. "And they're all far away, sunshine. If Winston had known where you were, he would never have backed off."

"I know you're right, but..." A shiver went through her, fear and a feeling of imminent danger.

"But you're scared and hurt and feeling vulnerable." He kissed her cheek.

She shrugged him off, irritated. She didn't want to be coddled right now. "You don't understand. I'm worried, Sam. If Vaughn finds out about you, he won't hesitate to hurt you. And all this upheaval can't be good for the baby I'm carrying."

"The baby will be fine, and so will you. Because I'm going to take care of both of you."

She shook her head. "It's not that easy, Sam."

Sam grabbed her chin and turned her head to look at him. "I'm not an idiot, Adrienne. The more I learn about this guy, the more terrified I am that he's going to hurt you. But if you expect me to go hide in a corner, think again."

"I don't expect—"

"No," he broke in. "You don't. You don't expect anything, do you? Because you never had anyone to protect you before, did you? Well, you might as well get used to it. You're mine, whether you remember marrying me or not. And no one is going to get near you." He paused for a heartbeat. "Now, I have to go out, do you want to take a ride with me?"

After all that, she wondered if she dared say no. Not that she wanted to. The coming storm outside made her feel closed in. "Yes, I do."

Sam nodded abruptly and got off the bed.

She raised her eyebrows at the change in the man who'd been nothing but gentle and kind. "Do you mind if I ask where we're going?" A thought struck. She drew in a quick breath. "Did Casey find out the name of the bank?"

"No." Sam's gaze softened in apology. "I haven't heard from him yet. This is business."

Adrienne looked away from the tenderness of his gaze. "I knew it was too soon, but…" She trailed off. But not knowing put them in so much danger, she finished silently. Sam said he understood, but he couldn't possibly.

"Adrienne?"

She scooted off the bed. "You never said where we're going."

He took the hint. "I had a call from a client whose new fence blew down. I called the men who built it, but I have to go supervise. I thought you might like to come along for the ride."

"I do. The fresh air will do me good."

"The house is down the coast, south of Carmel Valley. It's right on the ocean, you'll love it." He headed for the closet. "I have to change. I'll be ready in five minutes." He paused and looked back at her. "Dress warm, okay. The wind's blowing up a storm."

SITTING IN THE TRUCK an hour later, Adrienne considered his words an understatement. This was a storm the likes of which she'd never seen. Wind and waves battered the rocks, sending foam high into the air. The clouds grew darker by the minute. To her left, Sam and his workers labored to right the section of fence that had collapsed. The rain hadn't started yet, but it wouldn't be long.

She watched Sam lifting boards, hammering the nails with forceful blows, and felt a timeless excitement. For millions of years women had watched their men struggle against the forces of nature, thrilled when they'd triumphed, mourned when they'd failed. That women had done plenty of their own struggling and gloried in their own triumphs didn't change the elemental desire generated by observing man versus nature.

She settled more comfortably in her seat, her gaze never leaving her husband. It was a strange thing, feeling such passion for a man she barely knew. Her heart and her body recognized and welcomed each touch of his strong, gentle hands, yet her mind still saw him as the stranger she'd woken to in the hospital.

Her conscious mind, that was.

Her subconscious insisted on pushing her toward him. She'd actually asked him to take a nap with her, though she'd had no intention of doing so. And sleeping had been the last thing on her mind!

Thinking of sleeping reminded her of the dream that had made her nap anything but restful. She searched her memory for the woman's face. Was she a former employee? A co-worker? A neighbor? The woman's anger indicated she might be one of Vaughn's mistresses. Sooner or later, she had met most of them. But if she had missed meeting this one, how could she know what the woman looked like?

Frustration coursed through her. How could she fight Vaughn if she couldn't remember half what she needed to know?

Sam jumped into the truck, two seconds ahead of a torrential downpour. His cheeks glowed red from the wind, and raindrops glistened in his golden hair. She'd been so involved in her thoughts, she hadn't noticed until now that the rain had begun.

He looked out the windshield at the deluge and grinned. "Great timing, huh?"

She smiled. "Were you able to finish the fence?"

"Yep. Let's hope it remains standing this time."

The way the rain was coming down, she wondered that anything remained standing. "I guess we'll have to stay here for a while." It obviously wasn't safe to drive.

Sam shrugged out of his wet jacket, laying it on the back seat. "I can think of worse things than being stranded in my pickup with a beautiful woman."

Adrienne raised an eyebrow at him. "*A* beautiful woman?"

He regarded her with serious blue eyes. "There's only one beautiful woman as far as I'm concerned."

She shied under the intensity of his gaze, saying the first thing that came to mind. "Ginger's very beautiful."

He pretended to think about it. "I suppose she is in a strange, kinky sort of way."

"Are you into kinky?" she asked haughtily.

He gave her a very sexy smile. "I don't know. What did you have in mind?"

She blushed, then laughed, knowing she'd set herself up for that. "Forget I said that."

He gave an exaggerated sigh of regret. "If I have to."

"Well, I can't be the only one around here forgetting things," she teased. Immediately awed that she *could* tease and flirt. She and her ex-husband had not had that kind of relationship. How sad for both of them, she thought.

"You haven't forgotten anything, sunshine. Your memories just decided to take a little vacation."

She smiled at his absurd comment. "Well, I hope they're having a wonderful time, because this is their last one!"

Sam caressed her cheek. "There's one memory that decided to stay behind."

Drowning in the whirlpool of his ocean-blue eyes, she could hardly come up with words. "What..." Her voice failed her. She swallowed and tried again. "What's that?"

His arm slipped around her, his warm hand on her back drawing her closer. His lips hovered a mere inch from hers. "Your response to my touch."

His mouth captured hers before she could speak. Not that it mattered. Even if he hadn't kissed her, she could only agree. What he'd said was true, so she didn't even try to deny it.

Instead, she gave herself up to the pleasure of his kiss, surrendering herself to the magic she felt with his every touch. Shivers of desire raced through her. The storm outside had nothing on the one the feel of his tongue raised inside her. She had a vague sense of his hands beneath her sweater. He released the catch on her bra, and she started at the heat of his touch on her breasts.

His hands felt so familiar, his movements so sure. They'd done this many times before, yet she remembered none of them. Suddenly, it felt very wrong to be doing this.

A bright flash of light startled her, a loud clap of thunder followed, sending them apart. Laughing at their reaction, they looked past the truck's windshield where the storm raged to its height.

Even as she marveled at the magnificence of nature's tempest, she thought it a mere trickle next to the feelings that had exploded within her. She'd reacted so strongly to Sam, who was as much stranger as lover. And she felt more than a little chagrined that even when she started to have doubts, she didn't think she would have stopped him.

"What's wrong?"

She looked at him, wondered how he'd known, but didn't ask. Because even as she questioned his knowledge, she knew. Manly, sexy Sam was as sensitive as he was desirable. He'd lived with her for three years. He knew every expression, every nuance of her being. It scared her, baffled her, thrilled her.

With that knowledge, she accepted what she couldn't before. Maybe she *was* Amy. She didn't have all Amy's memories, but perhaps she shared her identity.

"Adrienne? You're not embarrassed, are you?"

She smiled wryly. "Do you blame me? I know you're my husband, but my memory of you begins days ago in the hospital. I feel like I'm throwing myself at a stranger."

He scowled. "How can you say I'm your husband one minute then call me a stranger the next?"

Though she wanted to look away from the pain and anger warring in his eyes, she didn't. "I can say it because those are the facts. You are my husband, and you are a stranger." She shook her head in regret. "I know it hurts you. And I'm sorry, but it's nothing either of us can control. I may never remember the last three years. And I think it's time you started accepting it. Otherwise…"

He grabbed her hand and brought it to his lips. "I won't let you leave me, damn it!"

Seeking to comfort, she touched his cheek. "I'm not leaving, and I'm not giving up. But, barring a miraculous return of my memory, our relationship has to start from here.''

He jerked her against him, taking her lips in a searing kiss. Then another, and another until flames licked at her heart.

Abruptly, he pulled away.

She waited in silence for his harsh breathing to steady.

He looked at her, his heart in his eyes. "I'm sorry. I know you're right. I don't want to force things. But there's so much I *do* remember. I keep forgetting you're a stranger.''

It sounded so much like a rejection, she had to swallow back the tears that threatened. She should have known she could never measure up to the "perfect" Amy.

"There's something I have to tell you, Adrienne.''

A persistent ringing sound stopped him. "The phone.'' He reached in the back seat and grabbed his jacket. Finding the cell phone, he flipped it open, growling. "This had better be good.''

Chapter Ten

"Catch you at a bad time?"

Sam's frustration turned cold at the sound of his brother's voice. "What'd you find out?"

"Nothing, yet."

"Nothing?" Sam looked over at Adrienne and saw his disappointment mirrored on her face. "Why not?"

"In case you haven't noticed, big brother, Mother Nature has unleashed her rage, leaving us to deal with car accidents, flood warnings and power outages. All off-time has been canceled till further notice."

"I didn't realize the storm had gotten that bad."

The silence that followed made him realize how lame that sounded.

"Where have *you* been?" Casey finally asked.

"Dan Jacobsen's fence blew down, thanks to your friend Mother Nature and my workers' carelessness."

"Knowing Dan Jacobsen, he probably knocked it down himself."

"Just because he flunked you in that computer class is no reason to malign the man."

"It wasn't my fault his stupid computer ate my final project. And quit trying to change the subject."

"What subject?"

"The subject of why you haven't noticed all hell breaking loose. And don't tell me it's because of Jacobsen's fence. It's outside!''

''Well, I'm in my truck,'' Sam told him. He wiped off a small hole in the fog-covered window. Outside, the rain poured down in sheets. A gust of wind shook the truck. If he hadn't been so caught up with Adrienne, he would have notice the worsening storm.

''In the truck. Well, that explains it. Not! What the heck have you been doing that you—'' He stopped abruptly. Sam could almost hear the wheels turning. ''Oh, I get it. Brought the little woman along, did you! And when it started raining you just decided to, uh, *sit* out the storm.''

To deny it would only have brought more teasing.

Casey snorted at his telling silence. ''Well, wipe off the windows and come up for air. Unless you plan to move in with old man Jacobsen for a week or so.''

Sam scowled. ''Move in with Jacobsen? What the hell are you talking about?''

''The last time it rained like this the bridge washed out, remember? People on that side were struck there for days.''

Sam started the ignition and turned on the defroster. Covering the receiver, he looked back at his obviously curious wife. ''Look in the back seat and see if you can find something to wipe the windows with.''

She reached back, grabbed a small towel and handed it to him. He smiled his thanks and wiped the rest of the fog off the windshield with his free hand. ''I thought they fixed that bridge,'' he commented to his brother.

''They did. They also didn't think it was going to wash out last time, and look what happened. The romantic interlude is over, big brother, time to come home. Besides, I need you.''

''What for?''

''Did you hear anything I said?'' Casey shouted, causing

Sam to move the receiver away from his ear. "We've got a major storm here. There are flood warnings all over central and northern California."

"Sandbags. Sorry, Casey, my mind's been elsewhere. We're headed back now. I'll have Adrienne make some calls while we're driving. Give me the locations."

After finding out where to send his men, he hung up, then put the truck in drive. Before he released the brake, he reached over to squeeze Adrienne's hand. "Sorry, sweetheart, looks like it's going to be a busy few days."

She shrugged. "That's okay. You said sandbags. That means flooding."

He eased the truck onto the road. "The bridge we crossed earlier?"

She nodded.

"You don't remember, but a couple of years ago the flooding was so bad it knocked the whole thing out. It also closed the highways. Monterey was cut off from the rest of California for days."

"It was like living on an island."

Sam glanced over at her in surprise. Her expression was just as shocked. "You remember?"

"Not details. Just a feeling of isolation. As if we'd been separated from the rest of the world."

"It was a scary time," Sam said. "We had no electricity, no heat. And it seemed like it would never stop raining."

"Then it did. There was a rainbow. The biggest one I'd ever seen." She looked at him, eyes wide. "I painted it!"

"Yes, you did," he said quietly. Afraid of frightening the memories away.

"I can't believe it. Maybe I'm really starting to get my memory back." There was real hope in her expression.

He turned his concentration back to the road, but his mind wouldn't let him forget what he'd just seen. For years he had wished for her memory to return. The thought of her past, of what secrets it held, scared him. He'd been so afraid of losing her. But now he could see how unfair he had been.

"Sam?"

"Yeah, sunshine?"

"You said something about making calls."

He nodded. "I told Casey we'd try and dig up some volunteers. There's an address book in the glove box. Start at the A's and call everyone on the list. Most of them know who you are…" He stopped. Most of them knew who *Amy* was. But he couldn't bring himself to say that. Instead, he just told her the locations where they'd be working.

Listening in on the first call, he learned she'd understood without him having to say anything.

"Dave Arnold, please. Dave, this is Amy Delaney. Sam asked me to call for volunteers to fill sandbags…"

LATE WEDNESDAY MORNING, Adrienne stood in the kitchen staring out at the rain. Three days, and the rain still hadn't let up. She wouldn't have minded being closed in the house if Sam had been with her. But she'd barely seen him since he'd brought her home from Carmel Valley.

She tried to convince him to take her with him, but he'd been adamant. Between her recent concussion and her pregnancy, the last thing he'd allow was her out filling sandbags. The best thing she could do for both herself and the baby was rest and recover.

For someone used to working, resting and recovering grew old fast, but Sam wouldn't hear of her lifting a finger around the house. "Why don't you draw?" he'd suggested. But a brief foray into her studio had left her feeling out of her depth.

During her time as Amy, she'd developed into an award-winning artist and author of children's books. One reviewer had called her "the best thing to happen to children's literature since Chris Van Allsburg." How could she even begin to live up to that praise when she didn't remember doing a single story?

If Sam had been here, she knew he would have convinced her to try. Without him here to keep her spirits up, her thoughts kept going to Vaughn and what he'd been up to since she'd disappeared. What other lives had he ruined? She didn't believe for a moment he'd seen the error of his ways. If he hadn't come after her in the last three years, it was because he didn't know where she was.

Unfortunately, she couldn't shake the feeling he was still looking.

Turning from the window, she walked over to the phone. She couldn't draw, but she could take Sam's other suggestion. When she'd volunteered to make provisions for the volunteers, Sam had thankfully taken her up on it. "That's a great idea. I'll come by sometime after noon to pick them up. Why don't you call Ginger and see if she'll come over and help?"

Adrienne had spent the morning baking cookies on her own. Ginger really hadn't struck her as the happy-homemaker type. But anyone could make sandwiches. And Adrienne had long ago tired of her own thoughts.

Getting Ginger's number from the list taped inside the cabinet above the phone, Adrienne dialed her friend's home.

Ginger answered immediately, her tone eager.

"Ginger? This is Ad…Amy. From the sound of your voice I'd guess I'm not the only one with cabin fever."

"Oh, Amy. This rain is horrible. I haven't seen another soul for *days*. I was looking forward to some rest after the holidays, but this is ridiculous!"

Ginger's dramatics made Adrienne laugh. "I know how

you feel. So, how about dragging yourself over here and helping me make some sandwiches for the troops out filling sandbags and clearing debris?''

Ginger sighed audibly. "Well, it's not the best offer I've ever had, but if I have to go one more hour without seeing another person, I'll go mad!"

Adrienne's first reaction was to say "Gee, thanks." But she didn't. She was sure Ginger didn't mean that quite the way it sounded. Especially since they were supposed to be friends. "Then you'll come right over?"

"As soon as I get dressed. You don't need me to pick up anything on the way, do you?"

Not exactly an offer she couldn't refuse, Adrienne thought as she imagined what form Ginger's outfit would take this time. "No, Sam went to the store this morning. We have everything we need." And more. Sam had turned out to be a marathon shopper when it came to groceries.

Ginger showed up a half hour later wearing an outfit Adrienne could only describe as mind-boggling. She'd thought nothing could top the chartreuse suit Ginger had worn the first time they'd met, but this had done it. In spades.

And this one didn't clash with her school bus–yellow sports car.

No, indeed, this one matched it exactly.

Leggings, sweater, socks, ankle boots and thigh-length jacket, all the same bright color as school buses all over the country. With stop sign–red scarf, gloves and earrings, Ginger was truly a wonder to behold.

Adrienne figured she must have been staring, because Ginger struck a pose. "What do you think? Mr. Gary designed it exclusively for me. I told him I wanted something to brighten up a gloomy day."

Adrienne smiled. "It's bright all right."

"It's better than wearing gray all the time," Ginger snapped.

"It certainly is," Adrienne returned cheerfully. Since neither her light blue jeans, nor the long pink sweater she wore could be considered gray, Adrienne figured the comment hadn't been meant for her. She was curious who it had been aimed at, though.

"Come on into the kitchen, I've made some hot chocolate for us to drink while we work. I'll find an apron for you, so you don't mess up your new outfit."

Ginger followed behind. "Hot chocolate sounds great as long as you've put in a dash of brandy to make it interesting."

In the kitchen, Adrienne found the brandy and handed it to Ginger, then went exploring for an apron.

"What *are* you doing?"

Adrienne looked at Ginger. "Trying to find an apron."

"Really, Amy, this rain must have made your brain soggy. You keep the aprons there." She pointed to a long chest of drawers over by the table.

Adrienne knew the top drawers contained place mats and cloth napkins. She found everything else she'd needed the last few days in the kitchen cabinets. Since she'd never been much of an apron wearer, she hadn't felt the need to go looking for them.

Hoping she'd chosen the right one, she opened the third drawer. Aprons. Thank heavens, she still wasn't ready to explain her memory loss…memory return? Whatever. Not without Sam there to lend his support.

She handed Ginger a black-and-white striped full-length apron. Turning up her nose a little, her friend put it on. Now, instead of looking like a school bus, Ginger looked something like a giant bumblebee. Adrienne turned to the refrigerator to hide her smile.

"Sam suggested we stick to peanut butter and jelly. That

way if the crew doesn't eat the food right away, it won't spoil.''

Ginger sat at the raised counter, sipping her brandy and hot chocolate. ''Sounds dreadful. I'm just glad *I* don't have to eat it.''

Adrienne went to work, getting out the ingredients for the sandwiches, as well as utensils. As she moved around the kitchen, she glanced at Ginger, who sat where she was, not offering to help. The more she was around her, the more she wondered why Amy had put up with her. The woman was obviously a snob, not to mention someone with very strange taste in clothing.

Her entertainment value didn't seem enough to put up with her sarcastic comments. Maybe Amy really had felt sorry for her. In spite of the life she claimed to lead, Ginger didn't seem to have many friends.

Once Adrienne got the stuff together, Ginger pitched in making the sandwiches. While they worked, she regaled Adrienne with story after story of her strange life as an artist's model and party girl.

She made Adrienne laugh with her outrageous comments, but once in a while Ginger would get a look on her face that Adrienne couldn't decipher. It was almost as if she was waiting for something.

At twelve-thirty, Sam came by to pick up the provisions. ''Thanks for all your hard work, girls. The guys will really appreciate this.''

After he'd changed into dry clothes and gotten ready to leave again, Adrienne followed him to the door. ''When will you be home?''

He smiled at her. ''Miss me?''

''Yes.'' Besides Ginger and Casey, Sam was the only person she knew in California. But she didn't try to fool herself that that was the only reason she missed him. At night, while he slept exhausted from his labors, she'd lain awake beside him, her body aching. At first she'd put it down to her pregnancy, or her fall, or both. But the night before, when he'd pulled her against him in his sleep, she'd learned the real reason. It was Sam she'd ached for. It was Sam she wanted.

As if reading her thoughts, he pulled her into his arms and gave her a long, luscious kiss. "I'll be home by six. The weather bureau says the rain might clear later this afternoon."

Unable to stop herself, she hugged him back. "Thank heavens, I thought the rain would never stop." She kissed his whiskered cheek. He hadn't taken time to shave for days. "Take care of yourself, okay? I'll fix us something special for dinner tonight."

She stood on the porch and watched until his truck drove out of sight. With a sigh, she went inside and joined Ginger by the fireplace in the living room.

Her friend had helped herself to another drink. This time she hadn't bothered with the hot chocolate. "Sam's quite a hunk. You're lucky to have him, you know."

Her tone sounded almost spiteful. A shiver went through Adrienne. She tried to shake off a feeling of foreboding, but couldn't. "Is something wrong, Ginger?"

Ginger sat back in her chair, one leg crossed over the other. "No, why do you ask?"

Again, Adrienne felt strange. Ginger seemed to say one thing, but mean something different. "You're looking at me funny."

Ginger seemed to consider her answer, then said, "There's something different about you. Are you sure you weren't more affected by your fall than you've told me?"

Something told her to step very carefully here. "A concussion isn't exactly a walk in the park, you know."

"Maybe," Ginger said thoughtfully.

Feeling a little restless under her friend's scrutiny, Adrienne moved over to the fireplace to stir the embers, then add another log.

"Is it Sam?"

"What?" Adrienne turned to her.

Ginger smiled sweetly. "I'm your friend, Amy. You can tell me anything, you know. Are you having problems?"

Adrienne laughed. "Of course not."

"Amy…"

It was hearing that name again that convinced her. Ginger was her friend, had been for almost three years. Keeping her memory loss from her friend just wasn't honest. It certainly didn't make her act like a friend. She'd been questioning everything Ginger had said, imagining strange looks where there were none. That's what people who kept secrets did, suspected everyone else of doing the same thing.

"Ginger, there's something I have to tell you." She took a deep breath. "I'm not Amy."

Ginger's thin eyebrows rose. "What *are* you talking about?"

"You know that I lost all memory of my past three years ago?"

"Yeah, so?"

If Ginger's gaze hadn't sharpened suddenly, Adrienne might have believed she wasn't that interested. As it was, her eager expression, combined with her casual question, heightened Adrienne's curiosity.

"Well?" Ginger prompted.

"The blow to my head brought back my memory."

Ginger's look sharpened. "It did?"

Adrienne grimaced. "Well, sort of. I remember who I am and what brought me to California." Something on which she'd decided not to elaborate. "But there are still holes."

"What do you mean, holes?"

"In my memory. I can remember most of my past, but not all of it. And there was a side effect even the doctors hadn't counted on."

Ginger leaned forward, studying her intently. "A side effect?"

Adrienne laughed. "Quit looking at me as if you expect me to sprout horns. The side effect is I remember who I am, but not who I have been."

"Amy, what are you talking about?"

"Amy is who I'm talking about, Ginger. I don't remember anything about her. I don't remember marrying Sam or c…" She'd been about to mention the baby, but backed down at the last minute. The pregnancy was still too new. She'd had some morning sickness, but mostly she felt as she always had.

"You don't remember marrying Sam or…?"

She should have known Ginger would catch her slip. "No, or our life together. Once in a while I get some glimpses. A few days ago, I remembered what it felt like when Monterey got cut off by flooding. But other than that, the last three years are pretty much a blank."

Ginger looked enthralled, and more than a little wary. Adrienne just had to call her on it. "Ginger, why are you looking at me like that?"

Ginger almost jumped. "Like what?"

"As if you're expecting to see my hair turn into snakes or something. I admit this experience has pretty much scared me to death, but there's nothing for you to be afraid of. I'm not going to go berserk or anything."

Ginger sat back and drank down the rest of her brandy. "Don't be ridiculous, dear. I wasn't thinking any such thing." She set the glass on the table. "There is something I would like to ask."

Adrienne couldn't begin to imagine which part of her

story had captured Ginger's offbeat imagination. "Go ahead and ask."

"Did you remember me?"

The question seemed so loaded, Adrienne hardly knew how to answer. "Did I remember you?" she repeated, buying time, though she didn't know why she needed to. In the end, she had to answer honestly. "No, not really."

"Not really?" Ginger seemed almost relieved.

Adrienne decided an explanation was needed. "Well, when I first opened the door that day, I thought you looked familiar. But I didn't know your name or who you were. I was still too disoriented to give explanations, so I was very relieved when Sam came in and called you by name."

Ginger smiled. "This is truly amazing. You get back one part of your memory and lose another. How strange it must have been for you, waking up *married* to a stranger."

Better married to a stranger than the devil she'd known, Adrienne thought.

"So, what did bring you to California?" Ginger asked, almost as if she knew which way Adrienne's thoughts had gone.

"The need to get away," Adrienne told her, then left it at that.

Ginger didn't. "Get away from what?"

Adrienne half smiled. "From my past life, of course."

Ginger raised an eyebrow. "Well, you certainly did that when you lost your memory. But what are you going to do now that you've recovered?"

"I'm going to finish some business that I should have taken care of long ago." She didn't care how cryptic her words sounded. Ginger didn't need to know about Vaughn. As her friend, it would only alarm her.

"That certainly sounds ominous."

Adrienne gave her a smile. "It's nothing you have to worry about. Sam's helping me take care of everything."

"But, Amy..."

Adrienne understood her friend's protest. After all, if she had someone who'd told her such an incredible story, she'd want to help, too. But keeping Ginger out of it was keeping her safe. It was bad enough she'd put Sam in danger.

"Ginger, please don't press me on this. My past isn't that important. My present life is. Maybe you can help me remember what it was like."

"I'm not exactly a shrink, Adrienne."

"And I'm not crazy, Ginger. I've just lost a little piece of my life."

"Three years is quite a piece. You should really be more careful where you put things," her friend joked, though there was still a slight edge to her tone.

"You can say that again," Adrienne agreed, thinking about the missing safe-deposit box and the important evidence inside.

"So, darling, how can I help you remember?"

For a second, Adrienne thought Ginger was talking about the box. "I don't know. Why don't you start with how we met, what we've done together, things like that," she suggested.

"Sure," Ginger said. "I'll tell you anything you want to know."

"Good," Adrienne said. "I don't know about you, but I'm hungry. Why don't we go see what we can dig up in the kitchen that isn't peanut butter?"

Ginger smiled. "You're on. And while we're digging, I'll fill you in on the last three years."

THE NEXT HOUR with Ginger exhausted Adrienne more than she would have imagined. Ginger filled her in on their "friendship," which ended up being as strange as she'd expected. Ginger spent only a few weeks a year in Monterey, but she always dropped in on her and Sam when she was in town.

The really weird thing was that she seemed to resent it, Adrienne thought as she stood at the front door waving goodbye. It didn't seem as if Ginger liked her all that much. She was always making comments that bordered on insults.

She closed the door and went to straighten the living room, keeping in mind Sam's admonishment not to lift a finger. With more time on her hands than she knew what to do with, she wandered around the big house, checking out cupboards and closets, trying to gain her bearings as the mistress of the house.

Walking from room to room, she kept feeling as though she was missing something. She paused in the kitchen, where she stood looking out the big window at the storm. She'd had the same feeling while talking to Ginger earlier, she thought. God, she hated it. It was as if she had no control over her life. And as long as she didn't have her whole memory, she supposed she never would. People could tell her anything about her life as Amy, and she would have to believe them, because she didn't *know*.

What would she have done without Sam? She knew without a doubt that she could trust him. On that thought came an idea. She looked at the clock. Hoping Sam would come home soon, she got to work.

SAM DROVE into the driveway around six o'clock. Home at last, he thought wearily. He was tired and hungry and his feet and hands felt like blocks of ice. He sat for a moment looking at the home he and Amy had made. Soft light glowed in the windows, warm and welcoming.

He never thought he would have taken their life together for granted, but he realized he'd done just that. Amy's memory return had been the wake-up call he'd needed to remind him that love was just too precious and the man who didn't realize that risked losing it.

Treating her past as if it didn't exist could have put all of them in danger. As much as he'd like to think that Winston had no idea where she was, he couldn't afford that luxury. As soon as the storm cleared, he was going to hire as many private detectives as he needed to get the goods on Vaughn Winston and put him away for the rest of his life.

He climbed out of the truck and headed for the door. It opened before he reached the porch. Adrienne stood in the doorway, looking more beautiful than he ever remembered. Or maybe he was seeing her with his eyes open for a change.

"Hi, sunshine." The name never seemed so appropriate. She was his sunshine. If he lost her, there would be only darkness left.

She stepped back to let him in. "Hi. You must be frozen to the bone."

He was, but somehow he didn't feel it anymore. There was a glow in her eyes that warmed him. The expression on her face made him curious. She seemed shy and excited at the same time. "What have you been up to?"

She smiled. "I have a nice dinner planned, but it will wait until you've taken a long, hot shower," she insisted.

While Sam took his shower, Adrienne worked on the dinner she'd planned earlier. The act of fixing a meal while her tired husband bathed made her feel very domestic, a feeling she once would have scoffed at.

She was sure that as Amy she'd put together more complicated meals than steak, salad and garlic bread. But this and omelets had been the extent of her cooking skills most of her adult life.

Her life with Vaughn had revolved around business and socializing. Meals at home with just the two of them were rare to nonexistent. Back then, when she'd thought about the few women she knew who didn't work outside the home, she'd felt sorry for the poor drudges. It was only toward the end, when she'd been trying to decide what to do with the rest of her life, that she'd reconsidered her opinion.

Adrienne placed the salad on the already set table, along with the steak she'd broiled and a basket of garlic bread. She regarded the lot with an unfamiliar feeling of pride.

These few days with Sam had completed the process that had begun the moment she realized life with Vaughn could never satisfy the young girl inside her who had once dreamed of marrying a wonderful man and living happily ever after.

A fairy-tale existence she'd known might never materialize. But she'd had to try. The terror had come when she'd realized her husband was more wicked than any fairy-tale villain.

Striking a match, Adrienne lit the candles she'd found earlier. The result of her work was as warm and welcoming as anything Martha Stewart could have come up with. With a sigh, she walked over to the refrigerator to fetch the milk that would have to take the place of wine for the next few months.

Though she'd once considered herself quite a connoisseur, she didn't mind the substitution at all. She wanted this life very much. The kind husband. The beautiful home filled with warmth and caring. The baby growing inside her.

She ran a hand over her belly, smiling. Though others might not be able to tell yet that she was pregnant, she could. Her tummy was no longer quite so flat. Her breasts were fuller, firmer. More important, she *felt* pregnant, sort of serene and excited at the same time.

"Hey, where's my dinner?" Sam asked from the doorway.

Adrienne turned and smiled. "On the table, sir, ready and waiting."

He walked over and kissed her on the cheek. "That's what I like, a domestic slave of my very own."

She raised an eyebrow at him. "I beg your pardon?" It was one thing to choose to do things, quite another to have it expected of you.

Sam laughed. "I knew that would get a rise out of you. It always did."

It always did? What did that mean? Her confusion must have shown on her face.

Sam took the plastic bottle from her and slipped an arm around her waist. "Come sit down, sweetheart, and I'll explain."

He set the bottle on the table, saw her seated, then seated himself. He flipped the top off the milk and filled their glasses. "I see we're having white wine tonight. With red meat, too. What will they say?"

If she hadn't been just that snobbish about wine once, she might have laughed at his clowning. Instead, she placed her napkin on her lap and said, "Weren't you going to explain that incredibly chauvinistic remark you just made?"

He grinned at her, his blue eyes sparkling in the candlelight. "You seem to be sticking to this idea that Amy was some kind of boring hausfrau. I was just having some fun with you."

"Are you saying I didn't handle all the cooking and cleaning? That you're that rarity among men, a husband who actually helps with the laundry and other assorted chores?" She deliberately used her most baiting tone.

Sam helped himself to salad, then passed her the bowl. "I'm saying we did the housework together...naked."

"What?"

Sam started laughing. She didn't blame him. She must have looked shocked to her toes. Knowing she'd been had, she laughed along with him.

"You are so easy," he said, when he could finally speak.

She made a face at him. "Well, how would I know? I don't remember anything about our life together."

His expression became serious, his gaze holding hers with an intensity that set her heart pounding. "You remember."

Adrienne tried to picture them together, but nothing came. Disappointment flooded through her. "I'm sorry, Sam. I don't," she replied, her voice barely above a whisper.

"You remember you love me."

His words sounded so confident she didn't try to deny them. She stared into his sea-blue eyes, drowning in a pool of utter sensuality.

"Your body remembers our lovemaking."

With shaky hand, she picked up her glass and took a long drink of the ice-cold milk. Her whole body felt warm and flushed. If Sam had that effect on her sitting across the table, she couldn't help thinking how she would feel when they made love. *Why don't you just drag him off to bed now and find out?* a tiny voice prodded.

She returned her gaze to Sam, who regarded her with banked desire in his eyes. *Because I need more,* she told the voice. To Sam, she said, "I don't remember anything else."

"You remember the important things. The rest are just insignificant details."

His dismissal made her angry. "Our wedding? An insignificant detail?"

His expression became regretful at her words, but there

was no stopping herself now. "The conception of our child? An insignificant detail? How can you be so insensitive?" Hurt coursed through her. She threw down her napkin and stormed out of the room.

Sam caught up before she'd gone twenty feet. When he turned her into his arms, she didn't fight him. How could she when she wanted to be there more than anything? But if he thought she was some wimp who would cry in his arms, he could think again.

"I'm sorry, baby." Sam held her to him, knowing he couldn't possibly make up for his insensitivity. The fact that she held herself so tightly, refusing to cry, only made him feel worse. He'd provoked her on purpose, trying to spur the memories she'd hidden so well. He wanted her to remember.

Everything.

So he wouldn't have to explain. So they could get Winston. So they could go on with their lives.

So he wouldn't have to feel so guilty that this "new" wife of his intrigued and attracted him more than ever.

Chapter Eleven

"So, what did Ginger say when you told her?" Sam asked, scooping up a spoonful of her frozen yogurt now that he'd finished his own.

Adrienne hit his hand with her spoon. "You already had yours."

"But I want more."

She couldn't help but smile as her big, strong husband pouted like a four year old. "Then go to the kitchen and make yourself another bowl. This is mine."

"All right, I will." He got up and went to the kitchen.

A feeling of contentment washed over her. After their run-in earlier, they'd returned to their dinner, and Sam had set himself to entertaining her. He'd kept her laughing so much she couldn't finish her steak. Which had suited Sam just fine, since he'd quickly volunteered to eat it for her.

After, they'd done the dishes. Then Sam had suggested dessert. She'd fixed a bowl of Ben and Jerry's Coffee Almond Fudge for each of them, while Sam built a fire in the natural-stone fireplace in the living room.

Sam walked back into the room. "Remind me to get some more of this at the store tomorrow."

Adrienne smiled. "Keep that up and you'll look like the one who's pregnant."

He eased onto the couch beside her. "There'll just be more of me to love then."

Adrienne gazed into the fire, knowing she could love Sam a lot, wishing she could remember the beginning of that love.

"So, you never did answer my question."

She looked at him. "What question?"

"About Ginger."

She ate a spoonful of her dessert, thinking about the strange afternoon she'd spent. She couldn't get those funny looks Ginger kept giving her out of her mind. "Mostly she asked a lot of questions."

"Doesn't surprise me," Sam said between bites. "She was always fascinated by your amnesia. Said it reminded her of a soap opera."

Adrienne didn't appreciate the comparison. "Maybe she kept me around for *my* entertainment value."

Sam put an arm around her and gave her a smack on the cheek. "That was certainly my reason."

She jabbed him in the ribs. "No, you just wanted a domestic slave."

"Yes, but just anyone wouldn't do. It had to be someone who'd be willing to wear the proper uniform."

She laughed. "You're not going to start that again, are you? I don't believe for a minute I kept house in the nude."

Sam went back to his yogurt. "Oh, well. It was a nice fantasy."

Adrienne ate her own dessert and considered her own fantasy. Now that she thought about it, it might be interesting to see Sam doing the dishes without a stitch on.

The phone rang, bringing them both back to earth. Sam went to the kitchen to answer it, returning a couple of minutes later. "I think we just got our first prank phone call."

She smiled. "Don't tell me, they wanted to know if our refrigerator was running."

He shook his head. "No, whoever it was didn't say anything, but I could hear breathing. There was definitely someone there."

Vaughn! The name jumped into her mind with the force of a megaton bomb.

"Cut that out!"

Sam's outburst drew her gaze to his. "You thought the same thing, admit it. Otherwise, you wouldn't have known what I was thinking."

Setting her bowl aside, he took her into his arms. "I realize it's difficult for either of us to think of anyone else, but it's not him, sunshine. He's thousands of miles away. And as soon as we find your evidence, he'll be behind bars."

Adrienne wished she could feel as confident.

Sam rose from the couch, offering her his hand. "Come on, it's time for pregnant ladies to be in bed."

Adrienne smiled and let him help her up. "Okay."

"I'll take care of the fire. You put the dishes in the sink."

Adrienne wanted to ask him if she should take off her clothes first but decided that would cause a discussion she wasn't ready for. Instead, she took their bowls into the kitchen.

She and Sam had slept together in the big willow bed since she'd come home. That was all she could handle right now. Sam, bless him, had been sensitive enough not to push for more.

That didn't mean he hadn't wanted her. She could feel his tension as they lay next to each other each night. He'd told her it helped just to hold her. But knowing how it made her want him more, she no longer believed that.

If her life had been the soap opera Ginger had compared

it to, she would have pressed the issue. Unfortunately, her amnesia was all too real. Her body desired Sam. But her mind didn't remember him, didn't know him the way it should. Making love with him now would be like making love with an attractive stranger. No matter how much she wanted it, she couldn't do it.

She ran water into the bowls, then turned to leave. The phone rang. Hoping it wasn't someone calling for Sam's help, she answered it. "Hello."

The breathing was faint, but it was there.

A hundred things went through her mind. All of them having to do with Vaughn. He'd found her. He knew where she was, who she was. He was going to hurt her, hurt Sam, hurt the baby.

Sam took the phone from her limp hand and hung up. "It's not him, honey. You know it's not him. If he'd known where you were, he would have come for you long ago."

His voice was soothing. His words made sense. But fear, like love, was irrational. Everything inside her told her it *was* Vaughn. That he was toying with her, playing with her like a cat with a mouse. It might seem like a game to those who watched, but, in the end, the mouse became dinner.

"It's not him, Adrienne," Sam repeated firmly.

All the fear and doubts she'd tried to keep tied up exploded inside her brain. She turned on him. "You don't know that! You don't know Vaughn, and you don't know me!"

"Adrienne..."

"Don't!" she shouted. She couldn't stand this charade a moment longer. "Don't call me that. You don't see Adrienne. You see Amy! Your wife. The one you love. The one you want to make love to."

Sam opened his mouth to protest. She put her hand on

his lips. "Don't deny it," she begged. "I couldn't stand it." She took her hand away and stepped back. "All this time, I thought you were being sensitive to my feelings. After all, you were a stranger to me. It would have taken a complete Neanderthal to pick me up and carry me off to bed."

Sam knew. He listened to her rave, and he knew what she wanted. And it hurt every cell of his being to deny her. "We can't make love yet, sunshine."

She blushed. "Is that what you think this is about? That I'm begging you to make love to me?"

"I think you're scared. You're so sure that Winston is going to show up here that you're grabbing for all the life you can. Making love is the most life-affirming act there is."

She shook her head. "No..."

"Yes." He pulled her against him, knowing she would feel his desire. "Feel that? I do want you. So much my blood is boiling inside my veins. But knowing you want me isn't enough. You have to start remembering first. I need to know you want me as the man you love, not just as a buffer against the past."

She leaned back and gazed at him, her beautiful green eyes filled with longing and confusion. "You're more to me than a buffer, Sam."

Sam knew. He pulled her back against him, holding tight. He knew every time she looked at him. He knew every night when she cuddled up against him in her sleep. He knew she loved him with all her heart.

But she'd never said it. Not since the accident. And until she could give him the love he'd grown to need more than air itself, he couldn't take the body she offered so sweetly. Though he remembered every curve, every inch, every place that sent her to the moon. *She* didn't.

She'd said it herself. It would be like making love to a

stranger for her. And he refused to be a stranger to the woman he loved.

He ran his hand down her back, glorying in and dreading the telltale shiver he felt against him. "There's..." He stopped as emotion overwhelmed him. Clearing his throat, he tried again. "There's nothing I want more than to make love to you, my darling. But this is too new to you, to both of us really. And I think we need more time."

"You're right," she said against his chest, sounding almost hurt. "I know you're right, but..."

He leaned back so he could see her face. "Sunshine..."

Her green eyes had darkened, indicating clearly that she wanted him, too. "Kiss me, Sam. I really need you to kiss me."

Her request was so heartfelt that he didn't try to resist. He kissed her. Again and again. Devouring her soft, sweet lips like a bear devours honey. Taking, giving, holding back when his body begged for more. Contenting himself with her mouth, her tongue, then moving on to her nose, her cheeks, her eyebrows, her ears, then her throat.

Little moans erupted from her, answered by his own. His belly burned with a fire that would never go out until he could take her to bed and make love to her for days on end. God, he wanted her, needed her. If Vaughn Winston came within a mile of her, he'd kill him.

"Oh!"

Adrienne's short exclamation brought his head up. For a moment, he thought he'd uttered his thoughts about Winston out loud. But the wonder of her face told him her reaction was due to something else entirely.

A beautiful smile lit her face.

He couldn't help but smile back. "What? Have you remembered something?"

She shook her head. "No, it's the baby."

He looked down to where her hand rested on her stomach. "You felt the baby move?"

She nodded, tears in her eyes.

A warm glow filled him that had nothing to do with the heat of their lovemaking. "What does it feel like?"

She took his hand. "I don't know if you can feel it. It might be too small." Nonetheless, she put his hand against her. "It feels like a tiny butterfly fluttering inside me."

He kept his hand where it was, though every book he'd read on the subject said it would be a while before he could feel the movement, too. But it was Adrienne's face that he watched. The wonder and excitement had mixed, painting her cheeks with a rose glow, brightening her jewel-green eyes.

"Oh, Sam, I'm going to have a *baby*."

That made him laugh. "No kidding!"

She didn't seem to mind. "I knew. You told me. The doctor told me." She laughed. "My morning sickness told me. But until I felt that tiny baby fluttering inside me, I didn't really *know*."

He didn't think now was the time to mention that she'd known when she was only one day late. Even though her doctor had made her wait almost a week for her blood test, there hadn't been a doubt in her mind.

"Sam?"

A serious expression had replaced her smile. "What is it, honey?"

"You said something before about baby books, on having a how-to-take-care-of-them, things like that?"

He put his arm around her shoulder. "Piles, sweetheart. The minute we got the word, we raided every bookstore within a fifty-mile radius looking for exactly the right ones."

"Where are they?" She looked around as if she expected them to materialize before her eyes.

He smiled. "Under the bed. Which is where you're going right now?"

Her eyebrows raised. "Under the bed?"

He gave her a squeeze, then pushed her toward the bedroom. "No, under the covers. You can start reading tomorrow."

She stalled. "But…"

"No buts. Pregnant women need their sleep, and so do pregnant fathers."

"Oh, Sam, I forgot you'd been working since early this morning."

The concern in her voice was so much like the old Amy, he almost considered going back on his resolve not to make love to her. But by the time they reached the bedroom, good sense, and fatigue, had won out. He needed to hear her say she loved him. As Amy or as Adrienne, it didn't matter. He loved them both. But he needed to hear the words, and know she knew them to be true.

Adrienne turned and caught an expression in Sam's eyes she couldn't figure out. She wanted to ask. She wanted to know everything about him, what he wanted, what he felt, his every thought, his dearest dream. Things she probably already knew as Amy.

But not as Adrienne.

And that was what stopped her from asking, she thought as she put on a silky nightie. After the closeness they'd shared, the kisses, then the baby's first movement, she didn't want to remind him that she didn't have a clue as to how her husband's mind worked.

She moved into the bathroom and picked up her toothbrush. Someday, she would ask. Someday, she would tell him how she felt. But for now she just wanted to savor this newfound joy. To get in bed and be held, and to dream. With that someday in her mind, she brushed her teeth, then went to join her husband in the fairy-tale bed he'd created for her.

THREE DAYS LATER, the rain stopped suddenly. The clouds whisked away, leaving a sky as deep and blue as Sam's eyes.

And Adrienne was happy.

In spite of the fact that she still couldn't remember where she'd hidden the evidence. And in spite of the fact that the police couldn't do anything about him until she did, because they hadn't found anything concrete on him, either.

The wind that had swept the storm out of the sky had taken her fears with it. Though she couldn't completely disregard the threat that hung over her, it didn't seem so imminent either.

What did seem imminent was their baby.

The day after their conversation about baby books, Sam had once again been called to help clear some debris swept in by the flooding. She'd hardly seen him the next couple of days.

She'd considered working on the illustrations for the book she'd been working on before the accident, but she hadn't been able to put herself to the test. Instead, she'd read baby books, learning more than she'd ever dreamed about her body and the baby's.

But now, with the sun shining and her fingers itching to capture on paper the jays hopping among the Monterey pines, she wondered if it wasn't time to put aside her fears of not living up to Amy's talents.

She laughed as she turned away from the kitchen window and headed for her studio. "I've got to stop thinking of myself as two different women."

Entering the brightly lit room, Adrienne felt as if she were seeing it for the first time. Her fear of failing had kept her away from the studio since the first time she'd seen it. But an artist couldn't be kept from her art very long before going crazy.

Even when she'd been at her busiest, working on advertising art for her company, she'd always made time to paint or draw. She couldn't count the lunch hours she'd spent perusing the local galleries rather than eating. Actions that had irritated Vaughn, with his "meals seal deals" philosophy.

Adrienne shook her head. It was just that single-mindedness that had driven her ex-husband to get involved with a criminal who preyed on children, hoping to create a new generation of drug addicts. Wondering, not for the first time, what she'd ever seen in him, Adrienne resolved to put Vaughn Winston out of her mind.

She searched and found the pile of beach sketches Sam had mentioned, as well as a supply of pencils and a fresh sketch pad. Vaughn had never been good for her art in any way, she couldn't help thinking as she sat at the drawing table. If he'd had his way, he would have stifled every spark of individual creativity she had.

But he didn't, she reminded herself. *You got away. You made a new life for yourself. Even made a name for yourself as a writer and illustrator. Yet now that you remember your past life, you're afraid to take what you've earned and enjoy it. How long are you going to let him scare you away from everything you ever wanted?*

As if disturbed by her thoughts, the baby stirred inside her, tickling her with its butterfly fluttering.

She placed her hand on her abdomen and smiled. "It's all right, little one," she said aloud. One of the books she'd read had mentioned that babies were comforted by the sound of their mother's voice. "Your mama's been a very foolish woman. But not anymore. The future is what's important. You and your daddy and our lives together are what counts. And no boogeyman from the past is going to change that.''

Feeling a little silly, she decided she'd better get to work. If she kept talking like that, this poor little kid was going to think it'd chosen some kind of nut for a mother. It was bad enough she couldn't remember its conception! Not to mention its father, their wedding, their...

"Stop!" She was stalling. Her conscious knew it. Her subconscious knew it. Heck! Her unconscious probably knew it. It was one thing to say you weren't going to be scared anymore, another to actually do it.

Luckily, knowing it was half the battle, she thought as she glanced through the sketches. Amy's style was a little more delicate than her own. But then maybe the subject called for delicacy. A foggy day at the beach. Soft, shimmery colors. She'd do it in dots, like Seurat. Tiny grains of sand, each one different in tone or shape or color. Bits of sea glass sparkling in the mist-clouded sun.

She turned to the last sketch. Her breath caught. Her very vision lay before her. Every detail exactly as she'd imagined.

Though the others had been pencil sketches of different parts of beach life. This one Amy had expanded on. Combining millions of dots of colored pencils with the soft, misty watercolor, she had created a magical land where hermit crabs waltzed across the sand and pelicans glided inches above the lazy waves.

This was what she'd seen in her mind's eye. This was what she'd wanted to create. This was what she *had* created. A warm glow came over her at the realization. And she took one more step toward accepting that she and Amy were the same person.

HAVING WORKED all morning removing debris from the Pajaro River, Sam was glad to see the second shift of volunteers arrive. Taking his shovel and pitchfork with him, he walked back to his truck. He threw them in the back, then climbed into the cab. A car pulled up, blocking his exit. He looked over to see his brother getting out.

"What are you doing out here? I thought you were on duty today."

Casey stopped beside Sam's open window. "I'm pulling a split shift. I go back in at two. Why don't you come by the house before you go home?"

Surprised at his brother's brusqueness, Sam raised his eyebrows. "I need to change. Why don't you follow me to my place?"

"I'll give you something dry to wear. I really need to talk to you, Sam," he said, then walked back to his car.

"Wait, Casey, what's going on?" Adrienne. It had to be something to do with her.

"Just be there." Casey got in the car and drove off.

More than a little frightened by his brother's demeanor, Sam drove straight to the house he and Casey had shared. Seeing it brought back a flood of memories from the year Amy had shared it with them.

He strode up the walkway and went in without knocking. "Casey!"

His brother came out of the kitchen with two bottles of root beer in hand. He handed one to Sam. "I put out some clothes in the bedroom. Get changed and then we'll talk."

Knowing how stubborn Casey could be when he got like this, Sam didn't bother arguing. He took his soda and went in to change.

Five minutes later, he found his brother at the kitchen table. He dragged out a chair and sat across from him. "Now, will you tell me what the hell is going on?"

"Has Adrienne remembered anything yet?"

Sam knew his brother didn't mean minor things like a rainbow. "No, I would have told you if she had."

"I warned you about this three years ago, Sam. Adrienne isn't one of those stray dogs or cats we used to bring home all the time. She's a human being. We should have looked harder then."

"I know what you told me!" Sam said. He knew every word his brother said was true. Amy had clung to him like a lost little kitten. He was the first person she'd seen after her accident, and in her delirium she hadn't wanted him out of her sight.

It had been a long time since he'd seen her that way. Still, every time he thought of forcing her to remember, he'd balked. "If I try to force her to remember, she might withdraw into herself. That's what the psychiatrist said."

Casey shook his head. "That's a risk you'll have to take."

"God damn it, Casey! If I force her now, I take away whatever security she has."

"Maybe she'd be better off not feeling that security."

Fear rolled through him. "What does that mean?"

"As far as we know, Winston is still in Boston. But that's all we know. Does he know where she is? Will he come after her if he finds out? Or is he living in ignorance? But none of that matters, because in the end, he's going to know where she is. He's a murderer, Sam. He has to be put behind bars. And as soon as we have Adrienne's evidence…"

He didn't finish. He didn't have to. Sam knew she'd have to testify against him. He rubbed his eyes wearily. "Have you made any progress finding that box?"

Casey shook his head. "That's one of the things I'm going to have to discuss with her. There are no safety-deposit boxes rented under the name Adrienne Winston or Amy Nichols."

Which meant, Sam thought, she'd taken it out under a different name, something else she hadn't remembered.

''You're going to have to tell her, Sam. She has to remember now.''

Sam shook his head. ''She sees me as an ally. If I force her, she'll hate me.''

''That's ridiculous. She loves you,'' Casey protested.

Sam shoved back his chair and got up. ''Amy loved me. Adrienne just thinks she loves me. But she still has doubts.''

Casey came to stand beside him. ''Of course she has doubts. You're a stranger to her. Amy could read you like a book. Adrienne knows, even if she doesn't know it yet.''

''I need more time.''

''You can't have it, Sam. I've learned something else about Adrienne and her ex-husband you're not going to like.''

Sam didn't think he could take much more, knowing the woman he loved had been married to a possible murderer was bad enough. ''What is it?''

''There's no record of a divorce between Adrienne and Vaughn Winston.''

Chapter Twelve

"Adrienne!"

Adrienne looked up from her sketch pad to see Ginger standing in the doorway. "Oh, hi, Ginger."

"Oh, hi, Ginger?" Her impatience showed clearly in the tone of her voice and the expression on her carefully made-up face. "I rang the bell, knocked on the door, then finally let myself in." She moved over to stand behind Adrienne. "What are you doing?"

Adrienne set down the sketchbook. "Drawing. Or at least practicing." Feeling uneasy with Ginger hovering over her, she stood, stretching the kinks left from sitting in the same position so long.

Ginger looked around the room. "What do you need to practice for? That publishing company of yours would publish a grocery list if you illustrated it."

The words sounded like a compliment, but her friend's delivery seemed almost grudging, puzzling Adrienne. Wouldn't a friend be happy about her success? "Ginger?"

The redhead turned from a painting she'd been studying. "What?"

Her expression was merely curious, so Adrienne decided she must have been mistaken about her tone. "I did all those illustrations during my first bout of amnesia. I don't remember working on any of them."

Ginger shrugged. "That's too bad, but I'm sure you'll remember soon."

What that eagerness under the apathy? "I hope so."

Ginger smiled. "I know so. Now, why don't you go get changed and we'll go out to lunch."

Adrienne studied Ginger's latest outfit and wondered what she'd do if Adrienne told her *she* was the one who should change. The head-to-toe bright orange outfit was more suited to a big city like New York. Or a crossing guard at the local elementary school.

She glanced at the folksy grandfather clock that stood in the corner of the room. Two o'clock. She'd been drawing for three hours. "It's a little late for lunch, isn't it?"

"Not when you don't have breakfast till ten. You know I never get up before then," Ginger admonished.

No, I don't know, Adrienne thought, but didn't speak. It couldn't be easy to remember that your friend who had amnesia for three years finally remembered who she was. Although, Ginger didn't seem to have any trouble remembering to call her Adrienne.

"Come on, you've probably been working on this stuff for hours. Let's go out and have a little fun."

Something about her friend's voice touched a nerve. "Ginger, is something wrong?"

"No, why should there be?"

The hostility in her voice put Adrienne on alert. "Well," she said patiently, "for one thing, you just snapped at me. Did I do something to upset you?"

"Of course not," Ginger answered more calmly. "I just want to go out for lunch," Ginger said firmly. "Why would you think anything's wrong?"

Adrienne felt she couldn't just say that Ginger always acted as if she'd done something wrong. For all she knew, the woman had been a great friend to Amy, and it was Adrienne who put her off.

The front door slammed. "Adrienne, where are you?" Sam called out.

Adrienne's heart jumped. Happy to have her husband home. Especially happy that he'd interrupted this strange conversation with Ginger. "I'm in here," she called back to him.

"I guess that ruins our plans for lunch," Ginger said from behind her.

Adrienne forced a smile, trying to hide the relief she'd felt at the sound of Sam's deep voice. "I'm sorry. I just can't. Sam's been gone since early this morning. He'll be exhausted."

Sam burst into the room looking not the least little bit exhausted. His golden hair was windblown, his tan face healthily rosy. He stopped short when he saw Ginger. "Oh, hi, Ginger, I didn't expect to see you."

His tone was just short of rude, Adrienne noticed. Not at all like the Sam she knew.

"I was trying to get Adrienne to go out to lunch with me," Ginger explained, "but now you're here…"

Sam moved over to put a not-so-gentle arm around her shoulders. "What can I say? The woman can't stand being away from me," he said.

Adrienne looked up at him. A fierce light glowed from his blue eyes. He looked almost angry.

"Well," Ginger said, her glass-green eyes smoldering. "Who could blame her?"

Her sultry tone irritated Adrienne. The woman was actually flirting with her husband right in front of her! She was glad when Ginger moved to the door. "I'll leave you two lovebirds alone. Call me tomorrow."

The words sounded more like an order than a friendly invitation, but Adrienne nodded anyway.

"What is it with her, anyway?" Sam asked after the redhead left the room.

Adrienne waited until she heard the front door close before she answered. "I don't know. I don't even remember making friends with her, Sam. But I'll tell you one thing, she is the moodiest person I've ever met."

Sam had to agree. Ginger's behavior had never been what could be called normal, but lately... He shook his head. Ginger was the last thing he wanted to think about right now.

He looked at Adrienne.

She smiled. "You're home early. Is the channel cleared?"

He nodded. "The second shift should be able to clear it by this evening."

"That's great."

When he didn't answer, her smile faded. "Isn't it?"

"Yeah, it is." Unable to look her in the eye, he walked over to look out the window.

"Sam, is something wrong?"

He turned to look at the woman he'd come to love with all his heart. Twice. How could she have turned into such a stranger? Amy would never have kept such an important secret from him.

Adrienne moved over to touch his arm. "Sam?"

He mentally shook off his mood. They had a lot to discuss, but not right this minute. He had some thinking to do first. He couldn't just blurt out that he knew she and Winston had never divorced.

He looked at Adrienne, saw the concern in her eyes, and decided a distraction was in order. "Have you been drawing?"

The worried expression left her face, replaced by excitement. "Come see."

He followed her to the drawing table. On it were sketches, some he recognized from before, some new. "You *have* been drawing."

She nodded. "I finally worked up the nerve," she said, sounding proud of herself.

"That's wonderful." He knew how afraid she'd been of taking up the illustrations where "Amy" had left off. "I told you you could do it."

She smiled. "That is one 'I told you so' I don't mind hearing. Once I realized my ideas fit exactly what I'd already done, I knew you were right."

He picked up one sketch after another. She'd not only lived up to Amy's ideas, she'd improved on them. The colors were more vivid. There was movement and life in them.

He noticed one sketch seemed a jumble of images. "What's this?" He held it so she could see.

She shrugged. "Oh, that's just doodling. Just stuff I was practicing to get my mind used to drawing again."

One of the doodles caught his eyes, a circle of O's inside a triangle. Something about it struck a note of familiarity, but he couldn't quite figure why.

Adrienne looked over his shoulder. "What are you looking at so intently?"

"This." He pointed it out. "I think it means something."

"It's just a doodle. I was drawing all sorts of shapes. See? Squares, circles, there's another triangle."

Sam knew it was more than that, but since he didn't know how, there was no use worrying about it. He had more important things to think about. Restlessness gripped him. He looked at Adrienne. "What would you say to dinner out tonight?"

Her face lit up. "That sounds wonderful."

He felt guilty, knowing he'd misled her. Dinner out when you had something serious to discuss was an old trick men used. In his experience, women didn't generally cause scenes in restaurants. Not that he expected her to cause a scene. It was himself he was worried about.

"Where will we go?"

He brought his attention back to her. "Somewhere on the water, I think. After that rain, the sky's clear as a bell. The lights will be beautiful." Though not as beautiful as her, he thought. Suddenly, more than anything, he wanted to kiss her. Instead, he turned away. "I'll go call for reservations."

Needing the phone book, he went to the kitchen to make his call. It took three calls before he found a restaurant that could fit them in. The end of the rain had brought people out in droves. Their only chance to enjoy the weekend before returning to work tomorrow.

Mission accomplished, he went to the bedroom. Adrienne wasn't there, so he returned to the studio.

She hadn't moved. Standing by the drawing table, she stared down at the paper with the doodles that he'd questioned.

"Adrienne?"

She looked over at him, puzzlement in her green eyes. "I don't remember drawing this, Sam. I remember all the other sketches, but not this. Do you think it could really mean something?"

Sam looked at her concerned face, then back at the drawing. As hard as he tried to place it, he came up blank. "I don't know. Maybe it doesn't mean anything."

Concern turned to frustration. "But we both recognized it."

He reached for her, pulled her into his arms the way he hadn't allowed himself to do before. He didn't feel right about it himself. He didn't feel right about a lot of things. But he had to be strong, for both her and the baby. And he had to be practical. Going off half-cocked wouldn't do any of them any good.

"We both thought it seemed familiar," he said sooth-
ingly. "We could have seen something like it anywhere.
That doesn't necessarily mean it's important."

"I know." Her agreement was halfhearted. "But..."

He brushed his lips against her forehead, trying to ease
away the worry lines. "But we don't know. I realize that.
Unfortunately, standing here thinking about it doesn't
seem to be helping much." He smiled at her still-worried
face. "After being cooped up so long, you need a night
out. And I have a hankering for a big bowl of clam chowder. So, let's go have an early dinner and relax for a while.
Maybe it will come to us. They say fish is supposed to be
brain food."

That comment brought a smile to her face, he was glad
to see.

"You win, Sam." She backed out of his arms slowly,
a mischievous look in her eyes. "But I get the first
shower."

He grabbed her hand as she turned to leave the room.
"No way. I'm the one who's been out working all day."
It felt good to be playful. Adrienne hadn't teased him
much. That she did now showed how comfortable she'd
gotten with him.

"Tough. You're also the one who uses all the hot water!" Adrienne tugged away, but he wouldn't let her go.
That's when she came up with an idea she thought had
merit. "How about we compromise?"

She hid a smile at his suspicious expression.

"What compromise?"

"Let's take one together."

His shocked expression made her laugh. "You act like
we've never done it before," she said seductively.

Naked desire filled his eyes. He touched her cheek with
fingers not quite steady. "All the time. I just..."

"Didn't expect me to suggest it?" She smiled a little.

She didn't know what to make of this new Sam. He seemed almost nervous.

"I'm not sure it's such a good idea."

She stepped into his arms, her gaze never wavering from his. "I am."

She breathed in, reveling in the scent of pine and sea breezes that was uniquely his.

"Adrienne, I..."

She placed a finger over his lips. "I want to be with you, Sam. In your arms. In the shower. In our bed," she finished, her voice husky with desire. "I want to be with my husband."

A shutter came down over her face, and he pulled away. "We can't."

She pulled him back. "We can. I need you, Sam."

Never had she spoken truer words, Adrienne thought. She needed Sam more than she'd ever needed anyone in her life. Vaughn had never made her feel this way, even when she'd thought herself in love with him.

Sam stared down at her, desire and confusion warred in his stormy blue eyes. She put her palm to his face. "I want you to make love to me, Sam. I'm your wife."

He jerked in her arms. Now she felt confused. Just moments ago they'd been playing together, a young couple's mating ritual. What had she said to make him withdraw like this? She gazed at his face. His tight mouth. His blue eyes, usually so open, but now shadowed. "Sam?"

Then suddenly she knew. Images poured into her brain. Pictures of herself the last few days, trying to pick up missing pieces of her life. Knowing that something wasn't right. That there were secrets she had yet to uncover about the past three years. But never had she expected this.

She looked at him, saw the knowing in his eyes, the fear of discovery. "We're not married, are we?"

He shook his head.

"But why?" They lived in the same house. She was carrying his child.

Sam stood stiffly, more a stranger to her than when she'd first woken to find him at her bedside. "You know why," he said harshly.

Frustrated, she turned away from him. Moving to the window, she looked out at the forest. Sun streamed through the gnarled branches of the Monterey cypress. It was a beautiful view. One that had brought her a large measure of security during the last few days. Even while the rain had been pouring down.

With her realization, all that had been taken away. He'd claimed to love her. Why hadn't he married her?

She turned back to Sam. "If we're not married, then why am I living here? Why am I carrying your child?"

Pain crossed his face. He looked at her as if she'd just taken a knife to his heart. "You can ask that? After all we've been to each other?"

The tears she'd fought fell. "What have we been, Sam? I don't remember. I don't remember falling in love with you. I don't remember finding this house or fixing it up or cooking a meal or conceiving this child! What did we have together, Sam? Please, I need to know." She reached for him.

And he was there.

He scooped her into his arms and strode down the hall to their bedroom. Inside, he went to the bed and sat on the edge, keeping her closely gathered to him. He closed his eyes, then opened them, blue fire burning. "We have everything."

The passion in his voice sent a resounding shiver through her. Then his lips were on hers. His mouth fastened on hers with a hunger she'd never known before. Shock waves of desire pounded through her body.

And she responded with her own hunger. She wanted

this man more than she wanted anything in her life. His touch excited her, his hands on her breasts, her hips, searching and finding. Their lovemaking felt as old as the forest, yet it felt like the first time.

She delighted at his urgency as he tugged at her clothes, unfastening buttons, releasing zippers, not stopping until she lay warm and naked on the white quilt of their bed. Only then did he strip his own clothes, tossing them off with eager carelessness.

He stood before her, big and golden and magnificent, his blue eyes blazing desire. He made her feel bold and reckless. She reached out her arms. ''Come to me, Sam. Make love to me.''

He lay beside her, every inch of his body touching every inch of hers, and she turned to liquid in his arms. Her body melted against his, forming itself to him as his hands went over her back, her bottom, her thighs. They left a trail of fire whenever they touched, causing her to moan aloud.

Adrienne could hardly believe she'd been so bold. But every instinct inside her had pushed her toward this man. Somehow, she knew they were meant to be together. That Sam wanted Adrienne every bit as much as he'd wanted Amy. Lying here in his arms, feeling his hands on her body, his lips on her breasts, how could she doubt it?

Sam's tongue teased her nipple, making her gasp. His touch was gentle, showing his knowledge of the extra sensitivity caused by her pregnancy. The heightened sensation went straight through her, leaving a hot, heavy feeling in her lower body.

She reached for him, her hands feeling restless. She needed to touch him, to feel his skin, to get to know him all over again. Unlike she'd feared, this wasn't like making love to a stranger. It was much more complicated than that.

Her body knew his touch, welcomed it, responded to it with excitement and desire. Her mind wanted him as much as her body. But to her head, every touch was new. Each kiss a revelation.

Sam raised his head, gazed into her eyes. "Your skin is like velvet, it tastes like honey."

His voice, rough with desire, sent the blood racing through her veins. "You sound as if this is new to you, too," she said, not surprised that her own voice sounded husky in its breathlessness.

His teeth nibbled at her lips. "It is."

She didn't bother to question it. This was new. *They* were new. She dipped her tongue inside his mouth. Sam's response was instantaneous. A jolt went through him that found an echoing response in her. She felt electrified. A high energy buzzed through her, driving her on. "I want you, Sam," she said against his lips.

"I want you, Adrienne," Sam returned, barely a breath between them. "I always have. I always will."

"Then make love to me."

"I thought I already was."

She hardly saw Sam's smile. "Show me what I've been missing, Sam. Show me what my mind has forgotten." Tears coursed down her cheeks, she swiped them away. "I want to know how it feels to be loved by a man…one who loves me."

Sam's heart broke for the lonely woman she must have been before they'd found each other. What difference did it make that she hadn't told him the truth about her divorce? They belonged together. And it hurt so much that she had to go through this all over again. The not knowing, the needing. He'd tried so hard to erase all the pain she couldn't remember. Now that she remembered, he'd have to start all over again.

It didn't matter.

He'd never rest until she was once again as happy as she'd been the day before the accident—before the fall that had returned her memory and taken away their life together.

He kissed her. Hard.

Gentleness wouldn't work now. She had to know how much he wanted her.

The savage intensity of Sam's kisses left Adrienne breathless and weak and hot as the desert sun. His mouth seared a path down her throat, over her breast, never stopping till every inch of her body burned. The flame he had ignited with his first kiss became a raging inferno inside her.

She moved restlessly, wanting, needing. She ran her hands over his body, feeling his heat as she felt her own. When his fingers touched her womanhood, she almost jumped out of her skin.

"Do you want me to stop?" he asked against her lips.

"No! Please, no!" Determined to show him how much she didn't want him to stop, she thrust herself against his hand. His fingers found her core with ease, sending liquid warmth throughout her body. But it wasn't enough.

"Come inside me, *please*. I can't stand this anymore."

As if he'd only been waiting for her to ask, he eased her legs apart, filling her with his manhood. In a rhythm as ancient as the sea, he moved inside her. Immediately the tension began to build. Lifting her hips, she joined the erotic dance, meeting each thrust with her own.

She wound her legs around him, trying to get closer, though every inch of their bodies touched. It wasn't enough. She wanted to be inside this man, to be part of the very blood that flowed through his veins.

Tension turned to heat, heat to fire. Her blood like molten lava burned through her veins. Sam's movements became more urgent as he, too, felt the fire that demanded quenching. He cried out, exploding inside her, and Adrienne erupted into a million pieces.

As she lay panting, trying to regain her breath, she finally knew what it felt like to be truly loved by a man.

Chapter Thirteen

Adrienne looked out at the dark as Sam drove slowly along the still-damp street. A few days ago, seeing the city she had lived in for three years, yet had no recognition of, would have frustrated her. Now, after an afternoon of making love, she stared at the passing sights with affection and curiosity.

This relaxed feeling was as unfamiliar to her as the life she'd woken to. Now she knew why Amy's wardrobe had been filled with soft fabrics and misty colors. The mint-green cashmere sweater she wore felt soft and light as a cloud against her skin. Paired with leggings of a darker green, the outfit made her feel as if she wore nothing but her own skin.

Amy had had no need for deep colors and power suits. She'd had what she wanted. The sensuous clothing she'd chosen would only have enhanced her feeling of being warm and loved and contented. Adrienne smiled. Once she would have envied the woman she'd been. Now she felt only grateful that she, too, had discovered what her other self had known for three years.

Sam was the best thing ever to happen to her.

She looked over at him. His expression was preoccupied. She wondered what he was thinking. Was his mind on their afternoon together?

At a red light, he looked over at her and their eyes caught. She smiled. "Where have you been? You've hardly said a word since we got in the car."

He leaned over and kissed her. "I've got a lot on my mind."

Something about the way he said it made her stomach plunge. "Oh? Like what?"

The light turned green, and he turned his attention back to the road. "Like...the toolshed." He flipped on the turn signal. "The storm knocked over a tree down by your vegetable garden. It fell on the toolshed. If this rain holds off, I'll go cut it up tomorrow."

She stared at him. Had she heard what she thought she heard? "Did you say *my* vegetable garden?"

He nodded as he made the turn that brought them into the Fisherman's Wharf parking lot. "Yeah, it's down at the east end of our property where there's a clearing in the forest. You wanted to put one outside the kitchen door, but it didn't get enough sun."

"But I have a black thumb! Every plant I ever had wilted." She'd watered them too little or too much, given them too much food or didn't feed them at all. It never mattered. Even when she'd followed the nursery's instructions to the letter, the damn things had shriveled up and died.

He laughed. "Where did you think all the plants and flowers around the house came from?"

"You're a landscape architect. I just figured you took care of all that."

He pulled into a parking place and turned off the ignition. "I did the heavy stuff, but you gave the orders. And you're the one who did all the watering and fertilizing and such."

She shook her head, awed at the thought. "I can't believe this. I spent hundreds of dollars on plants I would eventually kill. If I'd known all it would take to bring out my green thumb was a knock on the head, I would have done it years ago.''

He reached out to touch her cheek. ''Maybe you tried too hard. Most plants tend to grow with the minimum of care, as you've told me more than once.''

''I told you that.'' My God, she had been a really different person here in California. And all it had taken was getting away from Vaughn, she thought. Maybe it was his presence that had killed the plants.

Don't kid yourself, Adrienne, she admonished herself. It was more than just Vaughn's presence that had killed his poor assistant, Barry. Vaughn was evil, and he had to be stopped.

In that moment she realized how much being connected to the right, or wrong, man could affect a woman. It was something her grandmother had tried to tell her before she'd died when Adrienne was sixteen. But losing Nana and two years later her grandfather had shoved all that wisdom out of her mind. Pain had driven her, first through college, then through her adult life.

''Adrienne? Are you all right?''

She nodded. She *was* all right, now she knew. She gazed at Sam. ''It wasn't my fault.''

He cupped her cheek. ''What wasn't your fault, sweetheart?''

''Vaughn. What he did, the way he is. I always thought I was somehow responsible for the horrible things he did. I wasn't a good enough wife, so he slept with other women. I wasn't a good enough businessperson, so he had to make all the business decisions. Why couldn't I see it?''

''See what, baby?'' Concern for her shone from his eyes.

''That he was wrong for me?'' She laughed wryly.

"Wrong for any woman. I should never have let it get that far, married him, gone into business with him."

"It sounds like you're blaming yourself again."

She shook her head. "Not really. I just wish I'd listened to my grandmother when she tried to tell me."

"Your grandmother? I didn't know you had any family. You never mentioned wanting to get in touch with anyone."

She reached over and linked her fingers with his. "I don't now. My parents died when I was a baby. My mother's parents were my only living relatives, so they raised me. Nana died when I was sixteen. Gramps, two years later."

"If she died when you were a teenager, how could she have warned you about Vaughn?"

She looked down at her hands, warmed at the connection. Her grandparents had had that. "She knew she was dying. The last couple of months we had long talks. She knew she'd never have another chance. She wanted me to know about love between a man and a woman."

Tears started to fall. "I tried to listen. I really tried to hear everything she said. But when Gramps died so suddenly when I was eighteen, I forgot it all. Success was what was important. I didn't want to care for anyone else, only to lose them, too."

Sam pulled her against him. She held on tightly. "I made it so easy for him, Sam. If only I'd listened to my heart, I would have known he was the wrong man. Because you were waiting in California all the time."

Sam's heart stopped. The look on Adrienne's face told him everything he needed to know. She hadn't said it, but it was there nonetheless. She loved him. She didn't remember much about their history together, their home, the conception of their child. She'd been with him as Adrienne for less than two weeks. And still she loved him.

He tried to speak, found his heart in his throat, cleared it, and tried again to no avail. God! Where was his voice?

She smiled. "You don't have to say anything. I'm sure I floored you with that admission. But it's true, Sam. I was meant to be with you. We were meant to be together. Whatever I went through with Vaughn was worth it if it led me to you."

He grabbed her hand, felt its fragility and eased his grip. "I hate to think of what he's done to you. The sooner he's convicted and in prison, the happier I'll be."

She leaned over and kissed him. "He will be, Sam. I know I'll remember where the evidence is soon."

"Of course you will," he soothed. The last residue of anger from his meeting with Casey left him. Adrienne hadn't been keeping from him the fact that she and Vaughn weren't divorced. She didn't remember.

Adrienne would never keep such an important secret from him. He was surer of that with each look from her beautiful green eyes.

And there was something else. She didn't seem to realize it, but every day brought Amy and Adrienne closer together. Making her the whole person she'd never been allowed to be as Amy. She could never remember, and he'd still love her forever. But he wanted her to share the memories of the last three years, as well as each new one they made. They'd been so happy. *She'd* been so happy. She deserved to know how much.

"Sam?"

He focused his gaze, saw her smile. "What?"

"I'm hungry."

He laughed. "Oddly enough, so am I." He got out of the car, walked around and opened her door. "Coming, madam? There isn't a cloud in the sky, only the stars to light your way."

She let him help her out and took a deep breath. "I love

the smell of the sea. It always makes me hungry, why is that?''

He took her hand in his and they started to walk across the parking lot. "Since you've been pregnant, everything makes you hungry."

She laughed. "I *am* eating for two, you know."

His heart squeezed at the pure joy in her voice. "I'll remember that when I order."

They waited for a car to pass, then walked to the sidewalk that edged the marina. Adrienne looked around in curiosity. Here was another spot she should remember but didn't. "So, this is the famous Fisherman's Wharf, huh?"

Sam squeezed her hand as if he knew what she was thinking. "Yes, I'm taking you to a restaurant near the end of the Wharf, called Abalonetti's."

Something in his voice said more. "Is it special to us?"

He smiled. "We've been there a few times."

She waited, knowing there was more. Typically, he didn't elaborate. "And?"

"We had our first real date there."

That confused her. "I thought I lived with you and Casey from the beginning?"

"You did. It took me months to get you to go out for dinner with me alone. As it is you only went on a dare."

She laughed. "A dare? I never take dares!"

"You did this time. I dared you to go out with me and not look at me differently the next day. You were sure you only wanted friendship. But I knew."

She smiled at his sweet arrogance. "How did you know?"

"Because you had had meals out with Casey plenty of times, but you kept finding excuses not to be alone with me."

She regarded him thoughtfully. "Why didn't you just assume I was more interested in Casey?"

He stopped at the entrance of the Wharf and put his arms around her. "Because you treated him like a brother. But with me, there was always something else in your eyes." He kissed her, sending a tingling sensation up her spine. "Besides, I knew we were meant to be together from the first moment I saw you. Why else would the angels have thrown you in the path of my truck?"

She'd always thought it was devils that had put her there. Now she looked at it differently and decided he was right. "I guess someone was really watching out for me that day," she told him.

He smiled. "And I've been watching out for you ever since. Which includes feeding you and that baby you're carrying." He turned her and started walking. "So, quit distracting me and let's go eat."

Minutes later they were seated at a table that looked out on a small part of the bay. Lights twinkled on the hill across the water that Sam told her was the Presidio of Monterey. A couple of sailboats drifted in the water. Tubs of flowers bloomed on the paved landing directly outside the window.

Adrienne looked at the brightly colored menu and smiled. This restaurant had exactly the California cuisine her acquaintances in Boston had always laughed at. Fear of having that laughter turned on her had kept her from confessing that she liked roasted red peppers and feta cheese.

Sam delighted her by ordering an appetizer of just that, along with an assortment that included Greek olives, marinated artichokes and mushrooms, roasted garlic and squid fried in a light batter.

She ate every bit of her half, along with the clam chowder and grilled salmon he'd gotten her permission to order. It wasn't until they were sitting over a shared dessert of chocolate-fudge cake and vanilla ice cream that the tingle started at the base of her neck.

She stopped, fork midway to her mouth, and looked around.

"What's wrong?"

She looked at Sam and shrugged. He frowned, indicating the uncaring gesture hadn't come off as unconcerned as she'd meant it to. "I feel like we're being watched."

Sam looked around, nonchalantly commenting on the painted tile that decorated the bar. "I don't see anyone we know."

"I guess I'm just being paranoid." Adrienne took a bite of cake and chewed it, but her appetite was gone. She set the fork on the plate.

Sam placed his hand on hers. "I don't think so. I feel it, too."

Adrienne gazed into his eyes. If they were being watched, she couldn't let that person know. "Do you think we should leave?" she whispered.

Sam smiled, as if she'd said something funny. "If there is someone here, we're better off staying."

She laughed, but kept her comment quiet. "We can't stay here all night, Sam."

He looked into her eyes. "I wasn't suggesting any such thing. I want you home in our bed."

The heat of his gaze sent her temperature up. Her pulse raced. "Sam..."

"Enjoying your dinner?" a male voice asked silkily.

They both jumped.

Sam was the first to recover. "Casey! Don't you know better than to sneak up on people?"

"What sneak up? I walked in the door and over to your table. I wasn't exactly skulking behind the palm fronds. Besides, you're the one who told me where you'd be."

Adrienne wanted to giggle with relief. The only one watching them had been a cop. "Never mind, Casey. Why don't you sit down and finish our dessert. I couldn't eat another bite." There might be nothing to fear, but that didn't bring her appetite back. Sam didn't look too hungry either.

Casey pulled out a chair across from them and reached for the plate. "Don't mind if I do. I can't remember the last time I ate anything that wasn't fast food." Three bites later, he was done. "That was great, thanks."

Adrienne smiled. The poor man must have been starved. He'd all but licked the plate clean. "You're welcome."

Sam grunted, big brother–like. "Can we order you something else?"

Casey shook his head. "No, thanks, I have to get back to work. And this isn't exactly a social call."

Adrienne looked at Sam's suspicious expression, then back at Casey. "Why are you here, Casey?"

"Did you tell Adrienne about…"

Sam shook his head.

She looked at Casey. "About what?"

"I talked to most of the banks in Monterey and Pacific Grove over the last couple of days. None of them have safe-deposit boxes rented in your name or the one on your fake ID."

She looked at Sam. "You knew this and didn't tell me."

"What good would it have done?" he asked, sounding just as frustrated as she felt. "Do you remember the name you used?"

She shook her head.

"There's something else," Casey said.

Sam shot him a warning glance.

Casey nodded slightly in response. "I got a call from my friend on the Boston police force," he continued. "It seems one of Vaughn Winston's employees died under suspicious circumstances, and they're looking to question him."

Sam leaned forward. "What do you mean 'looking to question him'? Why don't they just go pick him up?"

The same questions had formed in Adrienne's mind, but she already knew the answers. "He isn't in Boston, is he?" He was here, she thought, on the edge of panic. God, why couldn't she remember the name of that damn bank? And what name she'd used when renting it?

"Now, don't go jumping to conclusions," Casey said. "His secretary told the detectives Mr. Vaughn was attending a convention in New York until Tuesday. He's supposed to be one of the speakers."

Adrienne thought for a moment. "That must be the National Advertising Association. They always hold their conventions in January."

Sam reached over and gripped her hand. "Have they confirmed it?" he asked his brother.

"They know he was on the flight to New York City on Thursday, scheduled to return Tuesday night. His secretary gave them his itinerary. Besides the convention, he has a couple of important business meetings, along with some social stuff. His weekend should be full."

Adrienne breathed a little sigh of relief. She figured she had at least until Tuesday to remember. Vaughn would never refuse a chance to speak to the NAA. It was an honor to be asked. He'd brag about it for months.

"Adrienne?"

She had two days. She didn't know why she thought Vaughn would come after that, but it didn't matter. She would remember before he came after her. She had to.

Sam's fingers tightened around hers. "Are you all right?"

She smiled, hoping to ease Sam's worry. "Are we back to that again? I'd need fifteen hands to count how many times you've asked me that."

He laughed a little. "Sorry. You just seemed so far

away. I don't want you to worry about this. As soon as Vaughn returns from New York, the police will talk to him.''

Yes, she thought, but then they'd let him go. Like they had when they'd questioned him about Barry. He'd eliminate the witnesses, just as he did before.

Well, she wouldn't run this time. She'd built a wonderful life in California, and she'd be damned if she'd let Vaughn Winston do anything to jeopardize it.

"Adrienne." Casey's voice drew her attention. "I don't want you doing anything stupid." His gaze went to his brother. "Or you, either."

Sam put his arm around her and pulled her close. "You don't have to worry. Neither of us is going after him. We'll leave that to the cops. The only thing I'm going to do is watch out for my lady." He looked at her, his jaw clenched in determination. "And the only thing you're going to do is stay by my side."

She appreciated his concern, but he did have a business to take care of. Especially now that the rain had stopped. "Sam, you have to go to work."

He shook his head. "Not until Wednesday, I don't. For the next two days I'm yours and yours alone. And when I do go back to work, you're coming with me."

The intensity of his gaze sent a thrill through her that almost obliterated every thought of her ex-husband. Even if she hadn't been in danger, Sam would want her with him. But the danger was getting closer, she could feel it. She leaned her head against Sam's shoulder and held on.

"I think this is my exit cue," Casey said and stood up. "I'll call you as soon as I know anything."

Sam stood and gave him a hug. "Thanks, Casey."

The other man grinned. "You can count on me, big brother."

A few minutes later, check paid, Sam and Adrienne left

the restaurant. Outside, Adrienne breathed in the cool fresh air. "It's a lovely night." Too lovely to waste on fear.

Sam tugged her hand. "Come on, let's walk to the end and look at the view."

They walked to the end of the Wharf and climbed the stairs to the observation deck atop Rappa's Seafood Restaurant. Moving to the far edge, they leaned against the railing and looked out at the bay. Moonless and cloudless, the sky was clear and dark, with a million stars twinkling above. The bark of sea lions playing in the water below made Adrienne smile. The only other sound was the motor of a lone sailboat headed out to sea.

"See those lights over there?"

Adrienne looked to where Sam pointed. Across the bay, the lights of another city shone brightly.

"That's Santa Cruz. We'll take a ride over there one day. It's only on the other side of Monterey Bay, but it seems like a completely different world."

She was sure she must have known once, but that was another thing she didn't remember, so she asked why.

Sam smiled. "It's like stepping back to the sixties. Long hair, tie-dyed clothes, peace signs and beads. Until you get to the boardwalk on the beach. Then everybody looks like they should be in one of those surfer movies."

"It sounds fun." Actually, something as mundane as watching television was fun with Sam there. A chill went through her suddenly and she shivered.

Sam put his arms around her. "Are you cold?"

She nodded, though she wasn't really. She didn't know what had caused it, and she didn't want to worry him.

"Come on, let's go. We'll drive up to our favorite spot and sit in the car and watch the tide come in."

"That sounds great," she said, taking the hand he offered.

At the stairs, he went in front of her. "Hang on to the railing," he said. "I don't want you to fall."

At the bottom, he turned and looked up at her. "Maybe we'll even neck a little?" he said teasingly.

Adrienne laughed. "I think that can be arranged."

Two steps from the bottom, she stopped. That feeling was back again. She reached up and rubbed her neck where it had begun to tingle. She looked around for a reason, impatient with herself even as she did it. The last time she'd thought someone was watching them it had been Casey. Surely it would be just as innocuous this time.

Sam looked up at her. "Adrienne? Is something wrong?"

A flash of color caught her attention. It was gone a moment later, but she thought she had her answer. "No," she said, joining him at the bottom of the steps. "I just thought I saw Ginger."

Sam smiled. "As long as she doesn't see us. I intend to be alone with you tonight."

The tingle that went through her this time had nothing to do with foreboding. His intentions and hers meshed perfectly.

TWENTY MINUTES LATER, after a slow drive along the coast, they arrived at the beach where they'd had their picnic. The tide was in, the water gently lapping on the spot where they'd eaten.

And kissed.

Adrienne leaned back against the seat and sighed. Between her amnesia, the constant rain and her fear of Vaughn, this had to be the longest two weeks of her life. It hadn't been easy getting used to the fact she had a whole new life she couldn't remember. Dealing with a past that could rear up and attack her at any minute had made it that much harder.

But there had been good moments.

She glanced over at Sam who sat staring out at the water, a thoughtful expression on his face. Many good moments, thanks to Sam. When she thought how lucky she'd been to land in front of his truck, and that it was he who'd loved and taken care of her, well... She'd never been one to believe in guardian angels, but she did now.

The last time she'd married, her choice had turned out to be horrific. Vaughn had seemed to possess everything she'd dreamed of in a husband. He was handsome, intelligent, articulate, with a keen business mind and a dry sense of humor. She'd been so flattered by his interest, she hadn't even noticed that what he'd been proposing had more in common with a business partnership than a marriage. With her as the junior partner.

Dumb, so dumb.

And she would have gone on being dumb, if she hadn't been conked on the head. She was sure of it. She'd left Boston a bitter, disillusioned young woman. Determined to put past mistakes behind her, she might have gone years before letting herself love again.

But fate had stepped in. They might not be married, but she didn't intend to let another moment go by without letting Sam know how much she cared.

"Sam..." "Adrienne..."

They both laughed. Adrienne thought Sam had a wonderful laugh, deep and masculine, with true humor in it. It was only one of the reasons she'd become attracted to him so quickly.

He reached over and touched her cheek. "It's so good to hear you sound so happy. I thought Casey's information might have upset you. You've been so quiet."

"I've been thinking," she stalled. Now that she had the chance to tell him, she couldn't seem to get the words out.

"About what?"

She shrugged. "Oh, about how long these last two weeks have seemed. How scary it is not knowing what Vaughn is up to." She paused to gather her courage. "How much I love you."

Butterflies flitted around in her stomach, not at all like the ones she'd felt when the baby moved. Sam's continued silence only made them more frantic. His expression was unreadable.

She had to know. "Sam?"

He reached to turn on the inside light. His gaze went over her face searchingly. "You love me?" His stunned tone eased her nervousness.

"Yes, I love you."

"As Adrienne?"

She smiled. "As Adrienne. As Amy before that. You're the best thing that ever happened to me, Sam."

He frowned a little. "Because I saved you and protected you?"

She nodded. "That's part of it. But there's so much more. Three years ago, you didn't save and protect me because you cared about me. You did it because that's who you are.

"Our home was never in peril, yet you worked days making sure other people were safe from floodwaters. When that fence blew down, you never once yelled at those men. Instead, you worked beside them to right their mistake. And then there were the eggs..."

His eyebrow raised. "The eggs?"

"I got used to people being scared of me, Sam. My employees called me dragon lady behind my back. But you weren't nervous because I held your job in my hand. You fell apart because you wanted so much to please me. You *cared* what I thought. Not what I owned, who I'd married, or when my famous temper tantrums would surface."

Sam smiled. "I can't imagine anyone being afraid of you."

"Of course you can't. Because you never knew the woman I created to survive. The advertising world would have eaten me alive if I hadn't donned that mask. And Vaughn would have gladly buried me."

She looked out at the waves lapping against the rocks. "But being here in this beautiful place..." She returned her gaze to Sam. "And, especially, being here with you, has shown me a future I never dreamed I'd have. Now I can see only good things. Living together, working together, raising our children."

He grasped her hand. "Children, in the plural?"

She felt suddenly shy. "If you want..."

He pulled her against him, nestled his face against her neck. "I want whatever you want. It's probably not a macho thing to admit, but I've been terrified you'd never remember how we felt about each other."

Running her hands over his broad back, his shoulders, his arms, she knew he never had to worry about sounding macho. There was no doubt he was one hell of a man.

But he seemed to be under a misapprehension. "I haven't remembered, Sam."

Chapter Fourteen

Sam drew back so he could see her. "But you said you loved me as Amy."

"I said that because everything I've learned about our life together shows me that love. But I still don't remember most of it on my own. Only bits and pieces." She touched his cheek this time. "As hard as this has been on you, you've never made me feel that you wanted my 'old' self more than my 'new' self. In spite of my feelings of inadequacy, you've always treated me as the woman you love. If I'd changed some, you could live with that. You adjusted. No one ever put that much effort into caring for me before."

He laughed a little nervously. "You make me sound like some kind of saint. There've been plenty of times when I wished you had never remembered your past, especially when it was clear you didn't remember 'our' past. I wasn't even going to make love to you until you did remember."

The fact that he had anyway increased her confidence. "So, why did you?"

"Because I'm not a saint. Because I wanted you, and..."

She grinned. "Well, don't stop there."

He reached for her hand, drew it to his mouth and kissed each finger tenderly.

The tingle that resulted didn't stop until it had touched every nerve in her body. "Sam, I want..."

"What?" His breath felt warm against her hand.

"You," she whispered, then kissed him.

The feel of his hard, lush lips under hers sent the blood zinging through her veins. With a new boldness she dipped her tongue into his mouth in sweet exploration. Hearing the catch of his breath at the touch of her tongue on his, her urgency grew. Sam was hers. Hers to love. Hers to make love to.

Kneeling on the split-bench seat, she pushed against his body, longing to feel its hardness. Her hands went over his sweater. It wasn't enough. She wanted to feel his skin. She reached under his sweater, encountered his turtleneck, pulled it from his pants, and finally met her goal. The crisp hair on his chest tickled her fingers. She could feel his heart beating, its quick pace a close match with her own.

Adrienne's fingers teased his nipples, while the gentle scrape of her teeth weakened the strong cord of his neck. Sam thought he'd never experienced anything as exciting as this hot, passionate lovemaking in the front seat of his car. He felt like a teenager again, felt that same urgency to learn what everybody whispers about in the sweaty atmosphere of the boys' gym.

"Take off your sweater, sunshine. I want to see you." Not waiting for her to respond to his demand, he put his hands under her sweater, hitting his elbow on the steering wheel in the process. A blue streak of pain went through his arm, causing him to cry out.

Adrienne jumped back. "Did I hurt you?"

Cradling his sore elbow, Sam had to laugh. "No, sweetheart, I just got a lesson on why it's much more comfortable to make love in a warm, cozy bed."

Adrienne giggled. "Sorry, I guess it's my fault."

"That's all right. I know just what you can do to make it up to me."

She looped her hands behind his neck. "And what is that?"

The sweet, sexy look in her eyes made him forget his injured elbow. "Be just as demanding at home as you were a few minutes ago."

He thought she'd blush and be embarrassed, but she stared him boldly in the eyes. "Only if you'll be just as responsive, darling."

He grinned, liking this new side of her. "No problem. Now, if you'll excuse me, I have a couple of things I need to adjust."

With flattering reluctance, Adrienne moved her arms from around his neck. He opened the car door and stepped out.

While Sam tucked in his shirt and fixed his sweater, Adrienne looked out at the view. It had changed during the time they'd been "busy." A full moon had risen behind them and a wind had blown in. The result was breathtaking. The light shone on the waves that crashed against the night-blackened rocks.

Sam got back in the car, and they sat for a few moments silently admiring their favorite spot. When another car pulled up next to theirs, the spell was broken. Sam turned on the ignition to leave.

"I love living so close to the sea," Adrienne commented as they headed home. "Even as a young girl, as much as I liked my grandparents' cabin, I always wanted to live near the ocean. That's why I—" She stopped. It was there, right on the tip of her brain. If she could only retrieve it.

"That's why you what, sunshine?"

"That's why I..." She spoke slowly, thinking desperately, *Why I what?* Chose to come to California. It was true. But that wasn't it. There was something else, something important. Something about the ocean?

Sam didn't speak again. Adrienne was on the brink of remembering something, and he didn't want to ruin her concentration by asking a bunch of questions.

While he drove the last few blocks home, he thought about their evening. He'd been stunned when Adrienne had admitted she loved him. He'd known it before. But knowing it and hearing her say it had been two different things. The latter was so much more important.

Not to mention unexpected.

It had taken Amy months to finally acknowledge her feelings for him. Her lack of knowledge about her past had paralyzed her emotionally. Only months of gentle persistence on his part had convinced her the lack of a past didn't have to interfere with their happiness.

He thought he'd have to summon up the same determination to convince Adrienne that her troubled past shouldn't stop them from enjoying their life. But he hadn't. She'd come to that conclusion on her own.

She loved him.

As Adrienne. As Amy. They were meant to be together. And he'd be damned if he'd let Vaughn Winston anywhere near her.

"The bank!"

About to pull into their driveway, Sam slammed on the brakes.

"We have to get up to the house. We have to call Casey." She laughed out loud. "Sam, I've remembered the name of the bank!"

Heart pounding with exhilaration, Adrienne was on the edge of her seat the rest of the way to the house. The moment Sam stopped, she jumped out of the car.

Sam followed quickly. She ran over and threw herself into his arms. "Ocean Bank! I can't believe I've finally remembered. I took so many buses that day. I ended up in Pacific Grove. The moment I saw the name, I knew that was the place to leave my evidence. Vaughn hated the sea. Oceans were meant to be flown over.''

She knew she was babbling, but she couldn't seem to stop. To think that important evidence had been only blocks away all this time.

Sam grinned at her. ''The bank's logo. That was the doodle we both recognized. I can't believe I didn't know.''

She hugged him tightly. ''It doesn't matter, darling, I've finally remembered. That's what's important. Let's go call Casey.''

Sam's smiled faded. ''Wait!''

She looked at him.

''Have you remembered the name you used?''

''No,'' she admitted, ''but surely that won't matter, since we have the key.''

''I think you have to sign in,'' he said. ''We'll take Casey with us to smooth the way.''

Inside the house, they went directly to the kitchen phone. There were several messages on the answering machine to listen to before they made their call.

Claiming starvation, Sam got out a package of Oreos, while Adrienne poured them each a glass of milk. Then they sat at the kitchen table and played the messages.

''Sam, this is Tom Addison. Can we put off our meeting till Friday? I'm swamped till then. Give me a call.''

Sam smiled. ''Guess you got me under your feet a couple of extra days, sunshine.''

Adrienne thought she'd rather have him under another part of her body, but refused to utter such a provocative suggestion. At least, right now.

The next three calls were ''the breather.'' But this time it didn't upset her. There was no way Vaughn was going to waste his time in New York making long-distance nuisance calls.

The last message was from Ginger. "Where are you guys? My date backed out at the last minute. I thought I'd come by for a while. I'm *sooo* bored. Oh well, I guess you're out. I'll call tomorrow."

"I guess it wasn't Ginger you saw at the Wharf," Sam said with an expression that said louder than words how glad he was that they were.

Adrienne had already decided she was being paranoid earlier. Now that she had remembered where her safe-deposit box was, she felt so much more relaxed. "Let's call Casey, and go to bed, Sam."

He stood up and gathered the empty glasses in one hand and the bag with the remaining cookies in the other. "I guess you're pretty tired." He put the glasses in the sink and the package in the pantry, then walked to the phone.

She joined him there, leaning against the counter while he dialed the number. "It's been a long day. I can't remember the last time I stayed up this late," she said, ending with a yawn.

She hid her smile when Sam automatically glanced at the clock. It was only nine-fifteen.

Sam gave her a look that promised retribution. "Casey Delaney, please," he said into the phone. "He's not? Would you give him a message? Tell him to call his brother the minute he gets in. I have great news. Thanks."

He hung up and pulled her to him. "You are a tease. What am I going to do with you?"

She kissed him on the lips. "I have some suggestions, but why don't you improvise?"

Sam was very good at this improvisation thing, Adrienne thought as she lay facedown on the bed while Sam massaged her back with rose-scented lotion.

The heat and urgency that had marked their other romantic encounters had been set aside. Sam had led her to the bedroom, leaving her by the side of the bed while he lit several candles. The candlelight reflected off the uncurtained windows, bathing the room in a warm glow.

That task accomplished, he'd returned to her. Bestowing soft kisses, he'd removed each of her garments piece by piece. She'd tried to do the same for him, but he'd made it clear this was his show. And she'd felt too tantalized by his slow, deliberate movements to argue.

Once he'd finished undressing her, he'd pulled back the covers on the bed and asked her to lie on her stomach. Then he'd disappeared, leaving her to wonder what her clever husband had in mind. His delicious kisses and gentle touches had brought an exquisite sensitivity to her skin. His retreat had left her wanting more.

She didn't have long to wait. Minutes later, Sam reappeared. His clothes had been removed and he carried a pink bottle of lotion, which he now spread over her already trembling flesh.

The stroke of his fingers sent jolts of pleasure through her, triggering a sensual memory. "We've done this before," she whispered.

His hands stopped briefly. "Yes," he said, voice husky with emotion.

She could see them in her mind's eye, taking turns massaging each other, sometimes serious, sometimes reduced to giggles by tickling fingers, always happy. The memory was almost as seductive as Sam's touch. She wanted it all, him, their life together, her memories of it.

Sensing her emotional state, Sam turned her onto her back. Tears streamed from Adrienne's beautiful green eyes, wrenching at his heart.

She didn't try to hide them, didn't wipe them away. "I love you, Sam." She held out her arms to him.

Setting the lotion aside, he went to her. Side by side, he cradled her against him. "I love you, too, sunshine."

"I want you to make love to me."

He smiled against her hair. "I thought that's what I was doing."

"You were, but you stopped." She pressed tiny kisses against his chest.

"You're crying, sweetheart." He lifted her face to his and kissed the tears away.

She smiled, her green eyes shimmering with joy. "I remember making love with you like this, slowly, exquisitely, massaging, touching. I remember, Sam." She put her lips on his, caressing them until every nerve in his body had been electrified. "I want to remember more." Her hands began to move against his back, his hips, his thighs. "Make me remember, Sam."

Suddenly, the urgency was back.

His hands went over every curve, firm now instead of gentle, hot instead of warm. Adrienne's skin began to burn with a fire that matched the one deep inside her. No longer afraid of upsetting her, Sam showed his keen knowledge of every erogenous zone on her body. He touched, prodded, caressed until she writhed beneath him. "More, darling, more," she cried, never wanting to stop.

Then his fingers were inside her, playing with the moist, soft flesh, bringing more pleasure, more heat. "I want you inside, Samson, come inside."

He rose above her, entered, and began to move against her in a strong, sweet rhythm. Their bodies in exquisite harmony, they found the tempo that bound their lives together.

Shivering with love and desire, Adrienne felt herself tighten around Sam's manhood. Seconds later, he called out in pleasure while she gloried in the warmth that filled her, drove her to the peak of ecstasy, and pushed her off into a swirling vortex of light and color.

Floating down to earth, she opened her eyes to find Sam grinning at her. She put her arms around his neck. "What are you looking so smug about?"

He kissed her. "You called me Samson."

She closed her eyes and settled against him. "If the description fits. Besides, it is your name."

He nodded. "But you only use it in two circumstances."

That got her attention. She pushed him away and sat up. "Sam?"

He started to grin again. "Well?"

She caught onto the memory and held on tight. "When I'm really angry or when we make love. Oh, Sam, I remember that!" She threw herself into his arms, knocking him onto his back. "Let's make love again. Maybe I'll remember more."

Sam's answer was delayed by the ringing of the phone. When she would have answered it, he gestured her away.

"It's probably only Casey. Let the answering machine get it. We'll call him in the morning," he said, pulling her back into his arms. "Now, what was that suggestion you made a minute ago?"

HOURS LATER, Adrienne stretched luxuriously before attempting to open her eyes. There was nothing like a long night of lovemaking to make a person feel loose and relaxed. What a wonderful Monday morning. There wasn't a tense nerve in her body.

She heard Sam whistling and lifted her lids to see him stride into the room, fully dressed. She pouted in disappointment. "Where are you going?"

He leaned over and planted a kiss on her lips. "To remove the pine tree from the toolshed, remember?"

"Do you have to do it now?" she asked, thinking she

had several other things in mind to keep him occupied. "It's still early."

He sat on the edge of the bed. "Early's best. Once I finish we'll have the whole day to spend together." He ran a finger over the edge of the sheet that covered her naked breasts.

She stifled a moan. He turned her on as easily as he might flick a light switch. "If you keep touching me like that, I won't be able to let you go."

He grinned, unrepentant. "Just want to make sure you'll want me to come back."

She raised an eyebrow. "Was there any doubt after last night?"

He pulled her into his arms, causing her covers to slip off. After a brief, hot look, he claimed her lips and kissed her thoroughly. Then he stood, leaving her yearning for more. Whistling once again, he strolled to the door.

"This isn't fair, Sam."

He leaned against the doorjamb, arms folded. "I put a batch of blueberry muffins in the oven."

Something in his expression made her suspicious. "And?"

"And I'd love some coffee."

"So?"

"So, after you get dressed, maybe you could make some?"

She smiled. "Maybe I could. Then what would I do?"

"Bring it out to me and maybe hang out while I work."

She got out of bed and walked over to Sam, noting with pleasure that his gaze never left hers for a second. "That might be interesting," she said nonchalantly. She put her arms around his neck and pressed her body against his. "We'll have to see how I feel once I get dressed." She kissed him on the cheek, then turned and headed for the bathroom.

"Oh, sunshine." Sam's voice stopped her before she left the room. "Don't forget the muffins." Then he left.

Adrienne smiled after him. What a man! What a life! She couldn't have landed in a more perfect place if she'd tried. She was in the bathroom before she realized she didn't feel the least sick this morning. The knowledge made her laugh out loud with joy.

Fifteen minutes later, she entered the kitchen just as the buzzer on the stove went off. "Perfect timing," just like everything else lately. First, she'd started remembering her life with Sam. Then, she'd remembered where she'd stashed her evidence three years ago.

All they had to do now was turn the evidence over to the police, she thought while opening the oven door to take out the muffins. Reaching for the muffin tin, she realized that rather than being golden brown, the muffins were still lumpy batter.

Shaking her head, she closed the oven door. She'd have to remind Sam that muffins baked much better when the oven was turned on. She twisted the knob to the right temperature and set the timer.

Looking for a basket to put the muffins in, she found it in the first cupboard she tried. Except for the minor setback of the oven not being turned on, she decided, luck was definitely on her side.

The phone rang.

She picked up the portable phone and answered with a cheerful "Hello."

"Hey! Where were you two last night?"

Ginger's demanding tone put Adrienne off. "Hi, Ginger. We decided to have a romantic dinner out." She moved over to the counter and started to make Sam's coffee.

"Well, that explains why you didn't return my call."

Adrienne knew from Ginger's tone that her friend expected an apology, but she had no intention of giving one.

Maybe Amy had been at Ginger's beck and call, though she doubted that, but Adrienne had no intention of letting Ginger run her life.

"So, where's Sam now?" the other woman asked.

Adrienne wondered why she cared, but answered briefly. "A tree fell on the toolshed during the storm. He went to cut it up."

"Oh," Ginger said. "And what about you? How are you doing? After your little accident, I mean."

Coffee perking, Adrienne grabbed a clean dish towel and placed it in the basket. "I'm feeling a lot better. I have a doctor's appointment next week to check on my head. But it was only a little bump."

"What about your memory? Have you remembered anything else about your past?"

Adrienne wondered at the avid questioning, then wondered why she'd bothered. Ginger always questioned her as if she had a right to know. "I've remembered some," she said, not feeling it necessary to elaborate.

"That's wonderful, sweetie."

Then why didn't her voice sound as if she thought it wonderful? It sounded strained and shrill. Holding on to the portable phone, Adrienne checked the muffins.

"Did you and Sam have a late night? You sound kind of tired."

Adrienne grimaced. The only thing she was tired of was answering Ginger's questions. "Actually, I'm feeling great. I didn't even have any morning sickness this morning."

"Why would you have morning sickness?" Ginger asked flatly.

"Because I'm pregnant, of course."

A long silence followed. "You're pregnant?"

Maybe Ginger had had too much to drink on her own

last night, Adrienne thought. She'd never thought of Ginger as dense. "Yes, Ginger, didn't you know?"

"No, I didn't."

For no good reason Adrienne could think of, Ginger sounded truly alarmed. "What's wrong?"

"You're pregnant. I can't do this. Adrienne, I want you to stay just where you are. There's something I need to talk to you about."

"Ginger…"

"Please, Adrienne, it's important."

Adrienne thought it must be important to make the self-possessed Ginger plead. "I'll be here," she said.

Ginger hung up, and Adrienne stood looking at the buzzing receiver. All this because she was pregnant? Ginger acted as if she was in labor already.

Seconds later, the phone rang again.

"Hey, sis," came Casey's voice. "Feel like feeding a starving cop?"

Adrienne smiled. "Sure, Casey, what's his name?"

"I'm talking about me, smarty-pants."

"Well, come on over then," she told him. "The muffins will be ready in ten minutes, and we found…" A chill went through her and she stopped abruptly.

"Adrienne? What's wrong?"

She shook off the strange feeling. "Nothing, Casey. A ghost walked over my grave." She'd always hated that old saying of her grandmother's, but somehow it seemed appropriate to the feeling that had gone through her.

"Are you sure?"

"I'm sure," she said. "You'd better leave now or the muffins will be cold."

Casey said something, but she didn't really hear him. Hanging up the phone absentmindedly, she wondered about the feeling she'd had. Was it Vaughn getting closer? Or just Ginger's unusual behavior that had caused it?

Neither mattered, she thought. Casey was on his way over. She and Sam would tell him about her remembering the bank's name. And as soon as Sam finished cutting up the fallen tree, they would go retrieve the evidence against her ex-husband.

They didn't have a thing to worry about. Not a thing.

Chapter Fifteen

Sam turned off the chain saw, set it down and looked toward the house. Still no sign of Adrienne. He wondered what was keeping her as he wiped the sweat from his forehead. It didn't take that long to make coffee.

Hearing a stick snap, he turned. Not his wife. The noise had come from the opposite direction of the house. A movement caught his eye. A deer, probably. He picked up the saw. "Sorry to scare you, little deer."

"I don't scare that easy." The voice was cool and easy. The man who stood twenty feet away had a gun pointing his way. "Put down the saw, Sam."

Sam did, to give himself time to think. It didn't take a genius to know this was Vaughn Winston. *"Tall, dark and handsome,"* Adrienne had told him. *"And lethal,"* she'd added with fright in her eyes.

"Where's my sweet little wife?"

"She's not your wife, Winston." He had no intention of letting this man near her, in any case. But if the man killed him, he knew he'd have no choice.

"Yes, she is," the other man said coolly. "But if you want her to be yours, you'll cooperate."

Sam wanted to grab on to the hope that Winston would go away without hurting her, but he couldn't. It was possible he'd already killed two men. He'd threatened Adrienne time and time again, had her followed when she'd left town. Why go to all that trouble to let her go? The thought broke his heart. "How'd you find her?"

Vaughn smiled. "I have my little spies. For a price, most people will tell you anything."

"And you're willing to pay that price." He had to keep the man talking. He had to think. "How much did you pay for this information?"

"I didn't have to pay a thing. The cop was bargaining for his life. He gave this information easily."

Sam felt sick. The cop? Casey's friend in Boston? "Did you let him live?"

Vaughn laughed. "Interesting question." But he didn't answer it. The man played close to the vest. He knew he held all the cards.

Sam tensed as the other man moved closer.

"Don't worry, Sam, I have no reason to hurt you. As long as you help me find what I'm looking for," he ended threateningly.

"I won't let you hurt Adrienne." God, please, don't let him hurt Adrienne.

Vaughn's expression became amused. "I'm not sure you can do anything to prevent it, but as I told you before, I'm looking for something. As long as you cooperate, I won't need to kill you, or Adrienne."

ADRIENNE PUT ON an oven mitt, opened the oven door and took out the golden-brown muffins. This time they looked just like they were supposed to.

There was a sharp rap on the back door, and Casey stuck his head in. "Breakfast ready yet?"

Muffin tin in hand, she turned from the stove and smiled. "Just took these out." She walked to the counter where she'd set the basket.

Casey reached over to snag one.

Adrienne slapped his hand away. "Don't you dare!" She emptied the muffins into the basket and wrapped the towel securely over them.

Casey pouted. "Come on, sis, just one. I'm starving."

Adrienne affected a stern expression. "I know you, Casey Delaney. You'd eat the whole basket and leave none for Sam. Remember the buffalo wings?"

Casey regarded her searchingly. "You remember that?"

"I do," Adrienne said wonderingly. She'd found another missing piece to the puzzle that was her past life. "I really do."

Casey gave her a brotherly hug. "This calls for a celebration. You take the muffins. I'll carry the coffee." He picked up the thermos she'd prepared. "Let's go tell Sam the good news."

"You got it," she said. "And wait till you hear what else I've remembered."

"So, tell me," he said as they left the kitchen.

She gave him an arch look. "Nope. Sam's waiting for his breakfast."

Barely six feet down the flagstone path, Adrienne and Casey turned at the squeal of tires on the driveway. Seconds later, they heard Ginger calling, "Adrienne, where are you?" Then, more frantically, "Adrienne, answer me!"

"We're back here," Casey returned casting a curious look at Adrienne. "What's up with her?"

Adrienne shrugged. "I don't know. When I told her I was pregnant on the phone, before you called, she acted as if I told her I'd gone into labor."

Ginger ran around the side of the house, red hair flying, expression frantic. She stopped abruptly. "Casey! I'm so glad you're here. You can protect her."

Adrienne had never seen anyone react so strangely to

an announcement of pregnancy before. "Ginger, protect me from what? This isn't the Dark Ages."

Ginger drew a shaky hand through her disheveled hair. "Anytime is the Dark Ages when Vaughn Winston is around."

Adrienne's heart jumped to her throat. "Vaughn? What do you know about him?"

Ginger's eyes narrowed with hatred. "I know he's a cruel, evil man who'll hurt anyone who stands in his way. If he was here right now, I'd—"

"You'd what, Ginger darling?"

The three of them turned. First, Adrienne saw Sam. A light went on inside her, only to go out in terror as he was pushed forward by a man holding a gun. Her ex-husband.

"Vaughn." The hated name sprung from her throat.

He smirked, there was no other way to describe it. "I'm thrilled to see you, too, darling. It seems I've been waiting for ages."

He looked the same, she thought. Same arrogant good looks. Same self-important expression. Same pretentious designer suit. Same cruel mouth. Why hadn't she seen those things before she'd been stupid enough to marry him?

Her gaze went to Sam. He looked the same, too. Big and strong and handsome. The same as he'd looked that day in the hospital. Her guardian angel. "Sam? Are you okay?" He nodded briefly. That's when she noticed his eyes.

She'd never seen his eyes so angry. Or so determined. All he needed was the right moment to turn on Vaughn.

It was up to her to help him get it.

"Sam won't be saying anything, darling."

She turned her attention back to her ex-husband. "Why not?"

"I had to tell him if he did, I'd kill you." He glanced

over at Casey. "You must be Sam's little brother. Well, your being a cop isn't going to help any of you now. Put your weapon on the ground and kick it over here."

Casey did as he said. And Adrienne saw how much it cost him.

She gripped her fists, wanting more than anything to punch Vaughn. "You've known where I was all along, haven't you?"

He shook his head. "No, dear, I didn't. It wasn't until your book came out that I resumed the search I had to abandon three years ago. I recognized your grandfather's amateurish wood carvings the moment I saw them." His gaze moved to Ginger. "If I'd known you were such a good bloodhound, darling, I would have hired you to follow her."

Adrienne stared at the guilty expression on her friend's face. "You knew who I was all along? Why didn't you tell us?"

"Because she didn't give a damn about you, dear wife. Why would she?"

His smirk repeated everything he'd told her the last year of their life together. *Nobody cares about you, Adrienne. You're a worthless, untalented girl who wouldn't know how to keep a man happy if you lived a thousand years.*

Anger began to flame inside Adrienne, replacing some of the fear. "If she didn't care about me, Vaughn, who did she care about? You?" She said the single word with all the venom she could gather.

"No!" Ginger shouted. "I won't let you think that."

Vaughn raised an eyebrow. "And why shouldn't she think that, Ginger darling? We did have an affair."

Adrienne gasped.

Ginger swung her around to look at her. "It was a long time ago, Adrienne. Before I knew you. Before I knew *him.*" Hatred filled her eyes. "He killed my brother!"

"Oh, really, Ginger, you always were melodramatic," Vaughn said scornfully. "Just like my dear wife there."

Adrienne turned on him. "I'm not your wife!"

"Yes, dear, I'm afraid you are," his silky voice assured.

Adrienne saw Sam tense. Vaughn moved the handgun so it was pointed at her. "Don't even think of it, Sam old boy."

He returned his attention to her. "I know you signed the decree, but I just didn't find the time to drop the papers off at my attorney's office."

Adrienne glared at him. "Are you telling me we're still married?"

"Regrettably so, my dear."

Shock and anger ripped through her. She looked at Sam. His eyes showed pain at Vaughn's revelation, but no shock. "That's what you meant when you said we weren't married?"

He closed his eyes in acknowledgment.

"Don't worry about it, dear one," Vaughn said, all amusement wiped from his face. "You won't have to think of me again, once you turn over that money you have hidden."

"What money?" She kept her voice steady, but her hands shook.

"Don't attribute your own foolishness to me, Adrienne," he said coldly. "My friends were very punctual with their deliveries. And they weren't at all happy to find out their funds had disappeared. The only thing that saved my life was my assurance that I'd cover the loss." His expression turned frigid with loathing. "You cost me a quarter of a million dollars, dear. I want it back."

Adrienne's heart skipped a beat. He didn't know about the tape or the papers she'd copied.

"Go get it, Adrienne," he ordered.

Adrienne looked him in the eye. "It's not here. I put it

in a safe-deposit box. I'll take you to it." She had to get him away from Sam.

Vaughn laughed. "How touching, sacrificing yourself for your lover. No, my dear, that's not how we're going to handle this transaction. You are going to go get the money. You and your friend Ginger. Us boys will wait right here for you."

Adrienne gazed at Sam. His dear face was carefully expressionless, but his sea-blue eyes poured out his love for her. She hoped he saw the same emotion in her eyes.

"Where is this bank in which you've hidden my money?" Vaughn cut into their silent communication.

"Monterey," she said, "about fifteen minutes from here." She hoped the extra ten minutes she'd added would give them the time they needed to alert the authorities.

"Fine." Vaughn looked at his Rolex. "You have exactly thirty minutes to get my money and get back here. Starting now."

Grabbing Ginger's arm, Adrienne started up the path. She needed to get the key from the house.

"Oh, and Adrienne?"

She turned back at the sound of Vaughn's slimy voice. "What?"

His hard eyes stared into hers. "If you bring the police back with you, you'll regret it."

She took a last look at Sam, then at Casey. She knew what she had to do.

"Do you understand, Adrienne?"

She glared at him and nodded. "I understand."

She turned and moved up the path as fast as the uneven stones would let her, Ginger following close behind.

Neither woman said a word until they reached the back door. With her hand on the knob, Adrienne looked at the other woman. "I need to get the key. Go start the car, and I'll meet you out front."

Ginger hesitated. "Adrienne..."

Frustrated by the unnecessary delay, Adrienne turned on her. "For the last three years, you've been pretending you're my friend. Now it's time to really be one. If we're not back with that money in thirty minutes, Vaughn will kill Sam and Casey. Or is that what you want?"

"No, of course not!" Ginger protested.

Adrienne hadn't wanted to believe it, but finding out Ginger knew who she was the last three years had shattered what small trust she had. "Then get going!"

She went in the house, not waiting to see what Ginger did. The woman was either with her or against her. Adrienne would go get the money herself if she had to.

After stopping in the kitchen to grab a couple of grocery bags, she ran through the house to the bedroom. She'd resewn the key into her jacket, so she went to the closet to retrieve it.

Seconds later, she ran out the front door to find Ginger sitting in her school bus–yellow Miata, engine idling. "Move over, Ginger."

"But you can't drive, Adrienne. You don't remember the area."

She opened the driver's-side door. "Quit wasting time arguing. I'm driving."

Ginger slid out and walked around to the other side.

Adrienne got in the car and put it in gear. Barely waiting until Ginger closed her door, she threw the jacket on the other woman's lap and took off.

They traveled the next couple of minutes in silence. Adrienne was pleased with the expert handling of Ginger's sports car. She'd only driven it twice before.

"You're remembering more, aren't you?" Ginger asked.

Adrienne nodded. "I feel like I could drive these roads with my eyes closed." Maybe it was the shock of seeing

Sam held at gunpoint. All she could think about was saving him.

"Do you remember me now?" Ginger asked in the most tentative voice Adrienne had ever heard from the woman.

The nightmare she'd had that first day home flashed in her brain. The change in Ginger's hair and eye color had thrown her off, but the hostility had been familiar. "We had an argument. You wanted something from me."

Ginger nodded. "I wanted you to go to the police about Barry."

"Barry? Vaughn's assistant?"

She glanced over at Ginger, whose eyes were tormented.

"He was my brother," she explained. "I tried to get the police to investigate Vaughn, but they said he had no motive. When I showed up on your doorstep in Boston that day, you were white as a sheet. I suspected you knew something."

Stopping at a red light, Adrienne rubbed her eyes. "I did know something, but I knew the police would never believe me. Vaughn and I were divorcing. I knew he'd twist everything around until they believed his story about his vindictive estranged wife."

"You could have tried." Accusation chilled her voice. "My brother may have been spoiled and selfish and greedy, but he would never have killed himself."

"There's more to the story than you know, Ginger, but I really am sorry about Barry."

A honk came from the car behind. The light had turned green. Adrienne made her left-hand turn.

"We only have two blocks left," she said. "The key for the safe-deposit box is sewn in the lining under the right-hand pocket of that jacket. There are nail scissors in the pocket."

Without a word, Ginger got out the nail scissors and went to work.

And Adrienne began to worry. She still didn't remember the name she used to rent the box. Would having the key be enough? At the next light, Adrienne glanced over. "Not that one, Ginger, the other pocket."

"But there's something here," Ginger said, and pulled out a flannel-wrapped item.

Adrienne reached for it. The item was small and flat. Hoping against hope, she unwrapped it quickly. "Oh my God."

Ginger looked up from picking out the other seam. "What is it?"

"My other ID," Adrienne said, heart pumping. "I didn't have just one fake ID made. I had two. No wonder Casey couldn't find any boxes listed under Adrienne Winston or Amy Nichols. I rented it under this name." The light turned green. She handed the ID to Ginger.

"Annabelle Walters?"

Adrienne nodded. "My grandparents' names."

Ginger freed the key from its wrapping. "We have the key and the identification. Nothing can stop us from getting that money now."

But that didn't mean Sam and Casey were safe, Adrienne thought, not by a long shot.

At the bank, it only took five minutes for them to retrieve the contents of Adrienne's safe-deposit box. They hadn't needed the grocery bags. Adrienne had forgotten all about the backpack she'd carried the money in.

Back at the car, she placed the bag in the back seat, then opened the trunk. That's where she put the large manila envelope with the evidence Vaughn still didn't know she had.

In the car, she looked at the clock. "Good, we still have more than fifteen minutes to get back to Sam." She sent up a silent prayer that he was all right. If Vaughn touched so much as a hair on his head...

"What did you put in the trunk?" Ginger asked as Adrienne started the car.

In spite of her fear, Adrienne allowed herself a smile. "Evidence that will prove Vaughn had motive for killing your brother."

Ginger's eyes widened. "What?"

"So many things happened after you left that day. You wanted me to help you. And I wanted so much for Vaughn to get caught, but I had no evidence. Then the delivery came."

"Delivery?"

"The money, Ginger. They delivered it UPS. When I saw it, I knew I had to get out of there, threw some stuff together, then went to get my purse out of Vaughn's den. That's when I discovered my voice-activated recorder had been on. It had recorded everything. The fight with Barry. Vaughn's threats to both of us. On it, he as good as confessed to the money laundering." She spotted what she'd been looking for and pulled over.

"Why are you stopping?" Ginger asked.

"I have to make a phone call." She got out and walked to the pay phone.

Ginger followed. "Who are you calling?"

Adrienne dialed the number she used to call Casey. "The police."

"But Vaughn said…"

Adrienne waved a hand in dismissal. "We're not going back without help."

A voice came on and immediately put her on hold. She pounded the phone in frustration.

"Adrienne…"

She looked at Ginger's worried face. The fright she'd tried to hold at bay threatened. She willed it away. "We need the police, Ginger. Vaughn's gotten away with every illegal, immoral act he's committed. I'll be damned if I'll let him walk the streets anymore.''

A voice answered, and she quickly explained the situation. It helped that the sergeant she talked to was a good friend of Casey's she'd met as Amy. They made arrangements to meet in ten minutes two blocks from her house.

Adrienne and Ginger returned to the car and silently made their way to the agreed-upon destination. Unable to sit in the car, Adrienne got out and paced a little.

The quiet, wooded corner might have soothed her feelings if she hadn't been so worried about Sam. It wasn't fair for her to start remembering their life together only to lose him.

She sat on a fallen log and covered her face with her hands. Flashes of a beautiful wedding day kept creeping into her brain. Herself and Sam at the beach. That's why that spot had been so important to them.

Ginger sat beside her. ''Are you okay?''

Adrienne nodded. ''The memories are coming faster. So many of the things Sam and I did together are in my head now, and I might never be able to tell him.''

Ginger patted her hand. ''Everything will be okay. You'll see.''

Adrienne wanted to smile at the thought of flighty Ginger comforting her, but she was too grateful to make fun. Maybe in the end, she and Ginger would be able to become real friends.

That made her remember something she'd been meaning to ask. ''Ginger, how did you know Vaughn was in California?''

Ginger grimaced. ''While I've been keeping an eye on you, waiting for you to remember the past, I've had a friend at the travel agency he uses keeping me informed of whatever trips he took. After I talked to you this morning, she called and told me about his flight to California.

I didn't know if he was heading to Monterey or not." She blushed. "I'm afraid I panicked."

Adrienne shook her head in wonder. "You hung around me for three years just in case one day I might wake up and be able to provide evidence of Barry's murder?"

Ginger looked away. "Not exactly." She looked back, a guilty expression on her face. "I caused your accident, Adrienne. It was me following you that night. The noise I made frightened you, and you ran out into the street, right in front of Sam's truck. I felt I owed you something. If Vaughn had been able to find you when you had no idea who he was, I knew you'd need protection."

Adrienne stared at her, torn between gratitude and anger. "And what if he had shown up?"

Ginger shrugged. "I would have let Sam know who you were. Vaughn has hurt enough people."

Adrienne still felt a little confused. "Why didn't you just tell me who I was? Why wait?"

"What good would that have done?" Ginger asked. "You had no memory of Vaughn or his crimes. What kind of witness would you have been?"

A pretty bad one, Adrienne suspected. And she never would have met Sam. So maybe she should be thanking Ginger, instead of questioning her.

Several squad cars pulled up. Adrienne and Ginger went to greet them. Once in the car and ready to go, Adrienne looked at her watch. They had five minutes left.

Chapter Sixteen

Sam stood with his back against the trunk of a Monterey cypress. The position Winston had ordered him to nearly a half hour before. Casey stood in the same position about six feet away. Twice that distance in front of them stood Winston, looking at his Rolex for the twentieth time since he'd sent Adrienne and Ginger for the money.

"Five minutes left, Sam old boy," he said with a smirk. "Seems like the little woman doesn't care about you, after all."

Sam didn't rise to the bait. Winston was looking for a reason to shoot him. And Sam had no intention of obliging him. Besides, he wanted the jerk's statement to be true. If Adrienne didn't care about him, then she would be far away from here. And safe.

But he knew it wasn't. Adrienne loved him. He'd seen it in her eyes. And she would move heaven and earth to keep Winston from fulfilling his threat.

"Yes, sir," Winston taunted. "You sure picked a loser when you hooked up with my wife."

Sam gritted his teeth. All the insults Winston had hurled didn't bother him as much as that one. Adrienne might still be Winston's wife legally. But in every other way, she was his.

When he'd vowed his love to her on the beach two years

ago, he hadn't done it lightly. He'd known there was a possibility that she was attached to someone else. But he'd truly believed, as he did today, that she had been delivered to him by angels. She was the only woman he'd ever really loved. And he'd be damned if he'd let a creep like Vaughn Winston take her away from him.

Casey made a movement that drew his attention. When Winston wasn't looking, they'd silently communicated in an eye-blinking code they'd made up as boys. Casey had kept him patient when he'd almost snapped because of Winston's taunts.

He knew the time was near for them to make their move. All they had to do now was be patient and wait for their cue.

And then, there it was.

At the sound of Ginger's car pulling into the driveway, Winston turned his head. And Sam and Casey started shouting. Anything they could think of to drown out the sound of the other cars that were sure to follow.

Winston swung back to them, gun raised. "Shut up!"

"Go!" Casey yelled.

With teamwork perfected on their high-school football team, they went in for the tackle. Sam went high. Casey went low, bringing Winston down with a thud.

The gun went off.

REACHING IN THE BACK of the car for the backpack, Adrienne heard the shot. "No! We got here in time." Then she ran.

Barely noticing Ginger and the policemen, who yelled for her to stop and let them handle it, Adrienne headed for the back of the house. Sam was her heart. If Vaughn had killed him... She couldn't finish the thought.

Arriving in the backyard, she saw the three men struggling. Her initial relief that Sam was alive lasted momentarily. Vaughn still had the gun in his hand.

In seeming slow motion, Vaughn raised the gun.

Adrienne screamed. "Sam!" Too late.

Vaughn hit him on the head, and Sam collapsed on top of Casey.

Seeing Sam lie so still broke her heart. His head was bleeding, while Casey tried to extricate himself from his unconscious brother.

She tried to go to them, but Ginger held her arm. "Adrienne, we have to get out of here."

"Leave me alone!" She jerked free. "Sam's hurt!"

She'd barely gone two feet when she noticed Vaughn. He'd gotten to his feet and now aimed the gun at her.

"Drop the gun," a policeman ordered. They now had the area surrounded.

Vaughn smirked. "Not on your life," he said, looking directly at her.

"We don't want anyone else hurt here, sir," the sergeant said.

Adrienne knew he was trying to keep the situation calm, but it was a wasted effort. Vaughn wasn't in the least emotional.

He kept the gun aimed her way. "I didn't think you'd have the guts to go to the police."

Out of the corner of her eye, she saw Casey inching himself up behind Vaughn. She didn't dare look away from his cold gray eyes, for fear she might give Casey away. "You never knew me the way you thought you did, Vaughn."

He gave a short laugh. "I never wanted to know you," he sneered. "All I ever wanted was your money and the use of your expertise. That romantic claptrap you used to spout made me ill."

Thinking of Sam and what they'd shared, she knew

she'd never want anything but the "romantic claptrap." She shook her head. "You know, Vaughn. I hated you with everything in me when I found out what kind of man you are. But now I just feel sorry for you."

"Why, you…" He stretched out his gun arm.

"No!" someone screamed, and Adrienne felt herself pushed from behind. A shot rang out, quickly followed by others.

Then there was silence.

IN A CURTAINED-OFF SECTION of the emergency room, Adrienne watched Sam's face closely for signs of consciousness, willing him to wake up. It seemed as if he'd been out for days, though it had been barely more than an hour since Vaughn had hit him.

Though she tried, she couldn't close her mind against what had happened. Vaughn was dead. Out of her life for good. And thanks to Ginger, who lay in the other examining room with a wounded arm, she was alive.

Sam stirred. Adrienne grasped his hand. "Sam, can you hear me? Please wake up."

His lids raised slowly. After a moment, his sea-blue eyes focused on her, and he smiled. "Are you an angel?"

She leaned closer and kissed his cheek. "That's what *I* thought, you know, the first time I saw you, that you were my guardian angel."

He tried to sit up. "Winston, where is he?"

"Lie down!" She pushed him gently back to the pillow. "We don't have to worry about him anymore."

He rubbed his forehead, right under the gauze that gave him a rakish pirate look. "Did they arrest him?"

"No, big brother," said Casey, walking into the room. "The bastard's dead. How are you doing?"

"Fine," Sam answered, too quickly.

Adrienne gave him a look.

He squeezed her hand. "All right, the truth is, my head feels as if a safe fell on it."

"No wonder," Casey said, checking out the bandage. "He gave you quite a whack."

Adrienne smiled at him. "How is Ginger doing?"

"Ginger?" Sam said. "What happened to Ginger?"

"Vaughn was going to shoot me," Adrienne explained. "Ginger pushed me out of the way and got shot herself."

"In the arm," Casey added. "The bullet went through, didn't hit bone. She'll be fine." He looked at Adrienne. "She wants to see you."

Adrienne wanted to see her, to thank her for saving her life. But Sam had come too close to being killed for her to leave him yet. "I'll go in a while."

"It's all right," Sam said. "You go. Thank her for me, too."

Reluctant to leave, she hesitated. "Are you sure?"

He pulled her head down and placed a short, passionate kiss on her lips. "Hurry back."

"No problem with that," she said. The blood had begun to race through her veins at his touch. She smiled. "Five minutes, tops."

He rewarded her with a grin.

Down the corridor from Sam, Ginger occupied a twin of his room. She lay on the narrow hospital bed, her face almost as white as the sheets. Adrienne moved over to the side of the bed. Ginger opened her eyes. "You came." She half smiled. "I didn't think you would."

Adrienne touched her hand. "You were there for me when I needed you most, Ginger. I think that makes us friends."

Ginger's glass-green eyes softened. "Then you forgive me for keeping your identity from you all these years?"

Adrienne nodded. "If you hadn't, I might have gone back to Vaughn not knowing what kind of man he was.

More important, I never would have had the chance to get to know Sam. To love him. Or to be carrying his child. I don't need to forgive you, Ginger. I need to thank you.'' She gave the other woman a hug, mindful of Ginger's wounded arm, then stood back. "But what about you?"

Ginger looked puzzled. "What about me?"

"Can you forgive me for not going to the police with the tape and papers I found, for not proving that your brother didn't kill himself?"

Ginger looked thoughtful for a moment. "I'm sorry I was so accusatory about that earlier. Lying here, I've had some time to think about the day you came out to California. After we talked, I decided to wait around outside your building. When you got in a cab a couple of hours later, I followed. But I wasn't the only one."

"No," Adrienne agreed. "Vaughn had put a tail on me. The cabbie noticed. That's why I went directly to the airport, instead of dropping that tape off at the police station as I'd planned." She shuddered, remembering.

"Vaughn had a lot to answer for," Ginger said. "But as usual he took the coward's way out."

Adrienne thought about asking about their affair, then decided it didn't matter.

"About Vaughn and me," Ginger said, reading her mind. "I'm sorry. He never bothered to mention his wife until after we'd gotten involved. When Barry told me about you, I broke it off. Vaughn hated that. He always wanted to be the one in control. But I never had an inkling of his criminal activities until a few days before Barry got killed, when my brother confessed what they'd been doing."

Adrienne squeezed her hand. "Vaughn's gone now. He won't hurt anyone else. It's time to get on with our lives."

Ginger smiled. "Amen to that."

Adrienne reciprocated. "Then you won't mind helping me with something once you get out of here?"

Ginger looked suspicious, but there was a new twinkle in her eyes. "What did you have in mind?"

THE DAY DAWNED clear and bright. A typical February morning in Monterey, California. The sky was blue. The sun was shining. The weather report said to expect high seas, but that didn't bother her. The waves wouldn't touch their place.

Looking out the bedroom window at the beautiful morning, Adrienne could barely contain her excitement. It had taken a lot of sneaking around and hard work to keep her plans from Sam. He hadn't wanted to let her out of his sight. But with Casey's and Ginger's help, she'd pulled it off.

Sam didn't suspect a thing.

Sam walked into the bedroom dressed in faded jeans and a multihued sweater. She loved that sweater on him. She especially loved the way it hugged his muscled chest, making him look big and strong and solid. When he wore it, she knew he wasn't a dream or an angel. He was a man, her man. At least he would be, in exactly, she looked at her watch, one hour.

"Adrienne? Did you hear anything I said?" he asked in an amused voice.

She grinned. "Nope. I was too busy looking at you."

He shook his head. "If you like looking at me so much, why are you making me go with Casey today? I've only been home from the hospital a week. I don't think I'm ready to go out."

Laughing, she gave him a hug. "You aren't exactly an invalid. Last night proved that." In fact, the man was in very good health. "And Casey needs your help. He sounded so pitiful on the phone. How could I turn him down?''

''Then I guess I'd better put on my shoes,'' he said grudgingly and went over to sit on the cushioned bench at the end of the bed.

While he did that, Adrienne made the bed.

''By the way,'' Sam said, ''you never did tell me what exactly I'm helping Casey do.''

Fluffing up pillows, Adrienne stopped midmotion. Darn! She was hoping he wouldn't ask. That was one part of the plan they hadn't discussed. She picked up a pillow, punched it and laid it down. ''Um, I'm not sure Casey told me.''

The doorbell rang, saving her from any further explanation. The brothers left and Adrienne called Ginger. ''Sam's gone. Get over here.''

Ten minutes later, Ginger drove up in Adrienne's sedan. Having her arm in a sling made it very hard to drive her sports car, and Adrienne was enjoying the exchange.

Adrienne ran out to the car. ''Did you bring the dress?''

Ginger laughed. ''Of course I brought the dress! That was my job, wasn't it?''

''I know, I'm sorry. I'm just so nervous.'' Adrienne had dropped the dress off at Ginger's the day before so Sam wouldn't see it hanging in the closet and question her.

Ginger gave her a hug. ''You have no reason to be nervous. Everything is taken care of. Now, go get dressed.''

WHEN HIS BROTHER drove up yet another street without stopping, Sam had enough. ''Casey, will you tell me what the heck we're looking for? We've been driving around for almost an hour.''

Casey glanced over at him. ''Has it really been an hour? What time is it?''

Sam looked at his watch. "Oh, I'm sorry. It's only been fifty-five minutes," he said sarcastically. "It's five to ten."

Casey just smiled. "Then I guess it's time."

"Time for what?" Sam asked to no avail.

Casey started whistling. He drove down one street, took a left at the next, then a right on Ocean View Boulevard.

A couple minutes later, he parked on the side of the road.

Sam looked at him suspiciously. "This is *our* place. Adrienne's and mine."

Casey nodded. "I know. Come on, I have something to show you."

They got out of the car. From the short cliff, Sam could see the beach where he and Adrienne had made love many times. And on that beach was Adrienne.

And Ginger.

And the minister who had married him and Amy two years ago.

He looked at his brother. "What exactly was that paper you had me sign the other day?"

Casey grinned. "A marriage license."

Sam grinned back. "Then let's go. I'd hate to be late for my own wedding."

He knew he walked, but he felt as if he was flying as he made his way down to the beach. Adrienne ran to him. "Surprise!"

All he could do was stare. She wore a flowing dress of rainbow colors. The breeze played in the long skirt. She looked like an angel. He thanked God she was a woman.

The minister cleared his throat. "Are we ready to begin?"

Adrienne gazed up at him, a world of love in her eyes. "Will you marry me, Sam?"

He cupped her lovely face with both his hands. "Yes, I will marry you. I love you, Adrienne."

She placed a kiss on each hand and smiled. "Then let's do it."

The minister began the vows, saying the words lovers have heard for centuries, and then it was their turn.

Adrienne turned to him, her green eyes sparkling with emerald fire. She drew a deep breath and then she said, "I, Amy..."

Sam felt as if his heart stopped. He searched her gaze, and for the first time since she woke up in the hospital bed, he saw the woman he'd married two years before. He touched her face. "You remember?"

She nodded. "Everything. Every moment of my life with you, Sam. As Amy and as Adrienne. Two women who fell in love with you."

Heart full, he pulled her to him.

"Ahem," Casey interrupted. "Are you two getting married or not?"

Adrienne grinned at him. "We are."

Then Sam's blood warmed as she gazed into his eyes. "I, Amy and Adrienne, take thee, Sam, to be my lawful wedded husband. I promised to live my life with you. I promise to cherish you always. And I promise, never, *ever*, to forget the precious love that we share."

Overwhelmed by her promise, Sam closed his eyes for a moment. Then he looked at the most beautiful woman on earth. "I, Sam, take thee, Adrienne, to be my lawful wedded wife. It's not often a man gets the chance to fall in love with two very different, very wonderful women. It's even more rare that they turn out to be one and the same. And I feel very privileged to be that lucky man."

His knees were shaking, but the love that shone from his bride's eyes made him feel strong. "I give you my life and my love to hold in your heart. I cherish you with every breath I take. And I promise to take the love you offer and keep it, and you, and our child safe, always and forever."

And the minister pronounced them husband and wife.

HARLEQUIN®

I N T R I G U E®

presents

LOVERS UNDER COVER

*Dangerous opponents, explosive lovers—
these men are a criminal's worst nightmare
and a woman's fiercest protector!*

A two-book miniseries
by RITA Award-nominated author

Carly Bishop

They're bad boys with badges, who've
infiltrated a clandestine operation. But to
successfully bring down the real offenders,
they must risk their lives to defend the
women they love.

In April 2000 look for:

NO BRIDE BUT HIS (#564)
and
NO ONE BUT YOU coming soon!

Available at your favorite retail outlet.

HARLEQUIN®
Makes any time special ™

Mother's Day is Around the Corner...
Give the gift that celebrates Life and Love!

Show Mom you care by presenting her with a one-year subscription to:

HARLEQUIN®
WORLD'S BEST
Romances

For only **$4.96**—
That's **75% off the cover price.**

This easy-to-carry, compact magazine delivers 4 exciting romance stories by some of the very best romance authors in the world.

Plus each issue features personal moments with the authors, author biographies, a crossword puzzle and more...

A one-year subscription includes 6 issues full of love, romance and excitement to warm the heart.

To send a gift subscription, write the recipient's name and address on the coupon below, enclose a check for $4.96 and mail it today. In a few weeks, we will send you an acknowledgment letter and a special postcard so you can notify this lucky person that a fabulous gift is on the way!

Yes! I would like to purchase a one-year gift subscription (that's 6 issues) of WORLD'S BEST ROMANCES, for only $4.96. I save over 75% off the cover price of $21.00.   MDGIFT00

This is a special gift for:

Name _____

Address _____ Apt# _____

City _____ State _____ Zip _____

From _____

Address _____ Apt# _____

City _____ State _____ Zip _____

Mail to: HARLEQUIN WORLD'S BEST ROMANCES
P.O. Box 37254, Boone, Iowa, 50037-0254 Offer valid in the U.S. only.

COMING NEXT MONTH

#561 HER PRIVATE BODYGUARD by Gayle Wilson
More Men of Mystery

New heiress Valerie Beaufort was forced to depend on Grey Sellers for
protection. She didn't want a bodyguard, especially one with smoky silver
eyes and a secret past he refused to reveal. But with danger stalking
Valerie, neither of them could deny the attraction they shared—and
Valerie couldn't resist the lure of a man of mystery....

#562 PROTECTING HIS OWN by Molly Rice

Forced to flee with her best friend's twin children, Katelynn Adams took
on a new identity and began a new life. Until Joe Riley arrived with the
news that Katelynn and the kids were no longer safe. Life on the run led
to shared dangers and shared passions, but if Joe was the twins' father,
would Katelynn lose her children...or gain a family?

#563 THE LONE WOLF'S CHILD by Patricia Rosemoor
Sons of Silver Springs

Chance Quarrels's return to Silver Springs brought back more than old
memories for Prudence Prescott. Someone was out to silence Chance,
and when physical intimidation didn't work, Prudence and her daughter
became the villain's pawns. Chance knew he had to save the only woman
he'd ever loved. What he didn't know was that he'd also be saving *his*
child.

#564 NO BRIDE BUT HIS by Carly Bishop
Lovers Under Cover

Detective Ann Calder found undercover cop JD Thorne wounded and
without memory. Hiding out as husband and wife, Ann could only hope
that JD's instincts of friend and foe were correct. Until JD could recall
who had attacked him and the crucial evidence he had found, he and Ann
weren't safe—and unless they could put some distance between them,
neither were their hearts.

Visit us at www.romance.net